WISTERIA WITCHES

Wisteria Witches Mysteries

BOOK #1

ANGELA PEPPER

CHAPTER 1

The real estate agent didn't say anything about the house coming with a ghost. Some people would probably pay extra to get a genuine ghost, but I am not one of those people.

My name is Zara Riddle, and I am a witch. A novice witch, anyway.

I spent the first thirty-two years of my life not knowing why I always felt like such an oddball. It turns out witchcraft runs in the Riddle family. I had no idea—not until I moved across the country to a quaint little town I'd never heard of before: Wisteria.

What's that? You've never heard of Wisteria, either? There's a very good reason for that, too. You'll see.

It was a sunny spring day when my daughter and I arrived at our new home. I stood on the sidewalk in front of the property, looking around my new neighborhood and grinning like a ding-dong. Was I dreaming?

Rising up before me was pure perfection. The house—*my house*—was a three-story Victorian Gothic, painted a heart-racing shade of red all the way up to the triple lancet windows in the attic. The porch was both breezy and welcoming, with wisteria vines twisting along the eaves. The wisteria was in full bloom, dripping with fragrant pink blossoms.

Sure, the yard was a jungle, and the interior was in need of a few updates, but that was fine. After renting for years, I was eager to finally pour my love and energy into a home I'd never have to leave.

I didn't know much about the town of Wisteria, but I desperately wanted to be part of it, part of a community. I'd been affected by global events as much as anyone. With the world tilting toward conflict and chaos, it was only natural to seek refuge somewhere cozy. A town where people got involved, and looked out for each other. A town where people said hello when they passed each other on the street. A town with fewer pawn shops and more bakeries. *Way* more bakeries.

"Mom, close your mouth and stop gawking," my daughter said as she pinched my arm. "For the millionth time, you're not dreaming. Now move your butt and help me with the boxes before these moving truck pirates charge us for overtime."

"Where are the guys now?" I rubbed my arm where she'd pinched me.

"Using the washrooms," she said. "The tall guy keeps gushing about the claw-foot tub in the upstairs bathroom. What's the big deal? It's an old tub with weird chicken feet." She wrinkled her nose.

"People pay extra for old tubs with weird chicken feet."

She scowled. "He'd better not be taking a bath up there and charging us for his time."

"You let me worry about the budget. What do you think of the house?"

She shrugged. "It's a house, all right."

My daughter was usually optimistic, but not today. I wished she would show a smidge of enthusiasm and make me feel better about my decision to uproot our two-person family. She'd been willing enough, but teenagers don't share in grownups' idealized notions about small-town life. All they know is that life changes should be regarded with the three S's. Suspicion, sarcasm, and more sarcasm.

I gave her a half-hug and ruffled her hair. "At least tell me which bedroom you picked for yourself."

She ducked away with annoyance and smoothed her bright-red hair. "Let's get the boxes done first. We need to get everything inside the house before I go to school."

"Zoey, it's Saturday. Unless things are very unconventional here in Wisteria, you don't start at your new school until Monday."

She rolled her hazel eyes the way only a teenager talking to her exasperating mother can.

"Mo-o-om," she moaned, dragging it out to three syllables. "I told you. Since we don't have a car anymore, I need to walk to the school today and figure out the best route so I'm not late on Monday."

"Okay, gotcha," I said, walking around to the back of the moving truck. "I should count my blessings that I'm the proud owner of the only sixteen-year-old who actually wants to go to school."

She jumped up into the back of the moving truck and handed me a box. "I'm not sixteen until tomorrow, and you're not my *owner*." Another eye roll, but at least she was smiling.

"People who have pets are called owners, and you're like a very smart pet. You're certainly not a regular child. I swear, sixteen years ago you waltzed your way out of my womb, shook hands with the taxi driver who delivered you, and corrected my pronunciation of the name of the hospital we didn't make it to."

Zoey stopped grabbing boxes inside the moving truck, put her elbows on a stack, and rested her chin on her hands. Flatly, she said, "Gee, Mom, tell me the story about the night I was born. I'll start you off. It was eight o'clock, and the double-length prefinale episode of *Wicked Wives* had just started on TV."

3

"You've heard this story before?" I batted my eyelashes innocently.

She smirked and continued the tale. "You were on the internet, live-blogging your reactions to the episode as it aired, and adding in color commentary about your labor pains. At first you were joking, but then you started having real contractions. Your fans were arguing about whether you should go to the hospital or fill a kiddie pool with water and go for it at home with your webcams running."

"Don't stop now," I said. "This is where it gets fun. My webcam broadcast went viral as the contractions got closer together."

Zoey's grin suddenly disappeared. She stared over my head, at something or someone behind me.

A man with a rich, deep voice said, "You're Zara the Camgirl?"

I turned around slowly. "I'm just Zara now. My camgirl days are over."

"Chet Twenty-one," the man said. He had eyes. A body would have been holding everything up, probably. All I saw was eyes. The greenest of green, with glints of silver and gold.

"You have the nicest eyes," I said. "Who are you?"

He took my compliment in stride, as though he heard women gushing over his good looks all the time.

"I'm Chet Moore. I live next door to you, in the blue house with the goat on the roof. Chet Twenty-one was my internet alias back in the day. I'm sure you don't remember me. You had hundreds of regulars who'd post on your blog."

Chet Twenty-one? It sounded vaguely familiar.

I had a cardboard box in my arms, so I jabbed my chin over my shoulder in the direction of Zoey. "That charming redhead is *not* my sister," I said. "She's my daughter. She says whenever I meet a cute guy, I always pass her off as my younger sister, but it's not true. I hardly ever do that. Besides, if you followed my blog, you saw me go into labor with her, so you'd never believe me anyway."

He grinned. He had teeth. Eyes and also teeth. Just like a human being! Wow. This guy's looks were making me stupid. What was this crushing sensation I felt in my chest? Was this why people called it a *crush*? My pulse was racing. My mouth went dry. I couldn't stop staring at the tall, dark-haired man.

I'd never laid eyes on him before, and yet he was familiar. Underneath my rising temperature and tingling nerves, there was a sense of comfort. Of safety. We weren't just meeting today. We were reuniting. Together again after a painful absence.

The man who'd ensnared me so easily said, "You're staring at me. Is there something on my face?"

I forced myself to blink before my eyeballs seized up completely. *There's nothing on your face*, I joked in my head. *Unless you'd like some of my face on your face? Like my lips, for example?*

I struggled to compose myself. Chet Moore was just a regular person, not some long-lost lover. Even if we had chatted on the internet years ago, we didn't know each other. Not in real life, where it mattered.

"Nope," I said with a smile. "It's just that you're cuter than a ladybug picnic."

He smiled back. He found me charming! That made him twice as cute.

I continued. "I'd shake your hand like a normal neighbor, but I've got a box in my arms."

He looked down at the box and read the handwritten label. "A box full of XL PMS sweatpants, if the label on the front is to be believed," he said in a serious tone.

"Once a month, I balloon up to three times my size," I told him solemnly.

"At least you're prepared."

"That's a joke," I said. "I put funny labels on all the boxes to make moving more fun." I shook the box, which made a non-sweatpants-like clattering sound. "These are actually pots and pans."

"So, the box your daughter is holding is not full of Nun-Chuks and Nun Habits?"

I glanced back at Zoey, who looked embarrassed, just as I'd expected. Teenagers were so easily mortified. That was part of what made having one so much fun.

I turned back to Chet, still smiling. "No, but you could use the contents to make those things. It's craft supplies, mostly yarn and a selection of glues. Plus those googly eyes that turn any object into a Disney character."

He took the wackiness without any visible sign of surprise. "You should fit right in here on Beacon Street," he said. "Welcome to the neighborhood. We should probably shake hands now."

I jiggled the box in my arms. "I'll be done moving in about an hour."

He took my box from me, shuffled it to one strong-looking arm, and shook my hand.

"It's official," he said. "I now pronounce us neighbors."

"Neighbors," I repeated. As our hands moved up and down, his grip tight on my sweaty hand, I got a flash of us together on a beach. Wishful thinking? It felt more like a memory. For some strange reason, I added, "Til death do us part."

He abruptly jerked his hand away from mine.

From behind me, in the back of the moving truck, Zoey groaned, "Oh, Mom."

I'd gone too far. I quickly replayed what I'd said. *Neighbors. Til death do us part.* What had gotten into me?

"Sorry," I said to Chet. "That was in poor taste, considering your previous neighbor just passed away. I didn't know her, but I'm sure she was a lovely woman."

6

"It's fine," he said with a casual shrug. "Let me give you a hand with these last boxes."

"We Riddle women can do it ourselves. We're tougher than we look, and we've done everything for ourselves for sixteen years. Plus there are two burly guys around here somewhere, and they're supposed to be helping. I'm not paying them the big bucks to defile my new bathrooms."

"I insist," Chet said. "Many hands lighten the load. You'll be saving me time because I won't need to hit the gym today." He set the box on the edge of the moving truck and reached up to offer his hand to Zoey.

"Chet Moore," he said. "Let me wish you an early happy birthday, Zoey. It seems like only yesterday I saw you smashing your very first chocolate cake with your baby fists."

"That was on the internet," she said coolly. "You don't know me." She didn't shake his hand. Apparently, the man's knee-melting, heart-crushing, stupidity-inducing charms only worked on adult women.

"Fair enough," he said with a good-natured smile. "Stack a couple more boxes on here, would you?"

She did, and he left for the front door without another word.

I turned and gave my daughter The Look. Could she try a little harder to make a good first impression in our new town? Could she extend to her mother the tiniest bit of credit that she was a good decision maker? Didn't she see how hard I was trying to improve both of our lives? Couldn't she say just one nice thing about our new house? I squinted hard, putting all of these things into The Look.

She responded by rolling her eyes while sighing.

The Look could be magical at times, but it could only do so much. We would have to talk this through, the way we usually did.

I gave up, relaxing The Look off my face, and nodded for her to keep handing me boxes from the moving truck.

That sunny Saturday, I decided to be patient with my daughter and enjoy our day of moving as much as it's humanly possible to enjoy a day of moving. Zoey was a great kid, and she'd come around eventually. Change is hard for people, even when it's a positive change.

I carried my armload of boxes into the house and got busy supervising the movers. Zoey took care of the upstairs stuff while I started unpacking the kitchen.

Hours later, I was finally able to take a break. I brought a bottle of water with me to the back yard, which had become even more of a jungle since the day I'd decided to buy the house. I was dazedly staring at the tangled shrubs when a shrill voice broke the silence.

"Zara, be careful."

Who said that? I was alone in the yard. I looked up at the house, to see if it had been my daughter. The windows were all closed, and besides, she called me Mom.

Cautiously, I said, "Hello?"

There was no response from the jungle of my back yard.

After a minute, some of the greenery shifted, and a blue jay flew out from the leaves and across the yard. It landed on the fence and gave me a cocky look, its feathered crest ruffling in the breeze.

"Was that you?" I asked the bird. Blue jays, like other members of the corvid family, are capable of mimicry, including human speech. It responded with a sassy head tilt.

"Listen," I said to the bird. "It's not crazy for me to think that was you talking to me." I paused and took a breath. "But it is a wee bit crazy for me to expect a conversation."

The bird let out a scolding cry, spreading its wings as though about to take off, but stayed there. It seemed to be interested in my daughter, who was coming out through the back door.

Zoey glanced around before asking, "Who are you talking to?"

"That blue jay." I pointed to the bird on the fence. It began performing for us, puffing out its feathers to look rounder before smoothing them down again.

"That can't be," Zoey said. "Blue jays don't live this far west. Only Steller's jays, which are black and blue. This is like the birds we have at home. I mean, back at our old home."

"Do you think it stowed away in the moving truck?"

The bird opened its beak as though silently laughing at us. It seemed genuinely fascinated by our conversation.

"Maybe," Zoey said.

"Or maybe it's someone's pet," I said. "That would explain it being able to talk."

"What did it say?" There was concern in her hazel eyes.

"The usual stuff," I said lightly. "Hello. Goodbye."

She raised her eyebrows, calling my bluff.

"Fine," I said. "The blue jay told me to be careful. And I swear it said my name, too. 'Zara, be careful.' Just like that."

"Ominous."

"I know." I tipped up my plastic bottle and finished drinking the water. "Dehydration can make you hear things. That's probably all it was."

"Sure, but dehydration doesn't cause a hallucination that two people can see, and that bird is not native to this area."

I turned to face her. "Never mind about the silly bird. Did you pick a bedroom?"

She gave me a shy smile. "Yes. I decided you should have the big one."

"That's sweet of you. So, which one do you want?"

She pulled her head back. "Mom, there are only two bedrooms upstairs. If you take the big one, that means I'll be in the small one."

9

I snorted. "Very funny. Let's go up there right now and decide."

She turned to the blue jay, which was still on the fence watching us, and said, "My mother is crazy."

The bird nodded twice before taking to the air in a flash of blue feathers.

Zoey and I went inside and up the old wooden stairs, teasing each other the whole way about who was wrong about the number of bedrooms.

"One, two, three," I said triumphantly, pointing at each of the doors once we'd reached the hallway.

Zoey sighed and opened the first door. "Bedroom number one," she said. She walked past the hallway's second door and opened the third. "Bedroom number two." She returned to the middle door and pulled it open with a flourish.

"Hey, that door opens in the wrong direction," I said.

"It has to, Mom. It's a linen closet." She patted the empty shelves of what appeared to be... a linen closet.

I approached slowly. Timidly, I knocked on the back wall. It seemed solid enough, as though it had always been a linen closet, ever since the day the house was built.

My daughter patted me on the shoulder. "It's okay," she said gently. "Two bedrooms is more than enough for us."

I put my hand over my face. "What have I done?"

"You've done what you always do."

I laughed hollowly. "You mean I've made a terrible, impulsive mistake, yet again."

"No." She sounded hurt by my self-deprecating remark. "You've done what you think is best for me. So what if you got confused about the number of bedrooms? There's enough stand-up space in the attic that it could be a third bedroom if we ever need one."

I dropped my hand from my face and turned to look at my daughter. She could be sarcastic at times, but she was also wise beyond her years, and sensitive, and kind, and my favorite person in the whole world.

She must have known I was about to get mushy and hug her, because she took a step back and put her hands in her pockets.

"It's super old," she said. "But this house has good bones. Or good *feng shui*. Or whatever. It's a good house."

"You love it! Admit it. You *love* your new house."

She smirked. "I *like* it. Don't get carried away."

Smiling happily, I slowly closed the door to the linen closet. "You know, we'll probably get way more use out of a linen closet than we would from another bedroom. After all, there are only two of us." I knocked on the door two times.

"Actually, there are three of us." She knocked on the door three times. "You, me, and the ghost."

CHAPTER 2

"I heard our ghost walking around in the attic," Zoey said as she entered the kitchen.

It was after six o'clock, time for relaxing after a long day of moving, but she'd been driving me nuts with the ghost talk. Apparently, one of the movers was the superstitious type. He'd told Zoey a tall tale about seeing a ghost in our upstairs bathroom. Being the rational type, she didn't believe him for a second, but she seemed to find it amusing to *pretend* there was a ghost. She'd never had an imaginary friend as a child, so now she was making up for lost time.

"The ghost was rattling something," she said. "It sounded exactly like ice in a martini shaker."

"Very funny," I said.

"The opposite of funny," she said gravely. "Mom, there's a ghost in this otherwise-perfect house."

"So, you admit that this house is perfect?" I set down the head of lettuce I'd been holding and stuck my finger in the air. "You can't take it back. You admitted the house is perfect."

"I said the house *would* be perfect, except for the ghost. But it really is haunted by a martini-shaking ghost." She sighed. "I guess we'll have to move back home and return to our old life."

"Already? But we just said goodbye to everyone and went to all the going-away parties. Mrs. Hutchins made us her famous tuna-noodle casserole, and then she prayed for us. The woman *prayed.* She wished us a bountiful new life full of blessings. We can't go back and tell Mrs. Hutchins her prayers didn't work. We'll just have to stay here in Wisteria to avoid breaking the sweet old woman's heart."

Zoey sighed and rested her elbows on the kitchen island. "I did hear something, but maybe it was just this house getting used to us. Why are old buildings so creaky?"

"Because the metal parts contract more than the wood, so the nails, pipes, and air ducts rub against the wood."

She squinted her hazel eyes at me. "You're such a librarian."

"I've been called worse." I winked at her.

She gazed up at the ceiling of the kitchen. "Wouldn't it be cool if there was a ghost? I've always wanted something special to happen to me, to make me less boring."

I stopped my food preparation and circled around the kitchen island to give her a hug. She grunted and tried to escape, but I wrestled her into my embrace using my motherly brute strength.

Once she'd calmed down, I kissed the top of her bright-red head. "You're not boring, Zoey. You excel at everything you try. You're brilliant, and you're the best daughter in the whole universe."

She pretended to gag. "You're only saying that to boost my confidence and make me feel secure and happy."

"Stop decoding my motherhood skills and just enjoy them."

She snuggled in and hugged me back.

I inhaled deeply. Was this the moment I'd been waiting for? Two days earlier, when the movers had loaded everything but our toothbrushes into a big white truck, I'd been hit with a blast of anxiety unlike anything I'd experienced before. The feeling was sharp, like the point of a pin, threatening to burst my protective bubble of optimism and hope. In the days since, I'd felt as if I'd been holding my breath, waiting to exhale once I felt safe.

Was this it? The moment I could relax?

Nope. I felt my muscles tightening, squeezing me with a fresh, new wave of anxiety. I hugged my daughter even tighter. She made a strangled noise and then squeaked, "Can't breathe."

I threw open my arms and spun her out of my embrace like a ballerina. She twirled and giggled.

I waved my arms around and did a silly dance to keep her laughing. My daughter was nearly sixteen, but when I made her laugh, I saw the sweet little kid who'd started a plant-watering business at our old apartment building so she could spy in other people's apartments and report back about what "normal" people did. Normal people did things like bake tuna-noodle casserole and host dinner parties.

That was it! I could alleviate my moving-related anxiety by hosting a celebration.

I stopped dancing and made the announcement. "Let's throw a housewarming party!"

She twisted her lips to the side and gave me a dubious look. "For all of the *many* people we know in this town?"

"Good point. We need more prospects."

"I might make a new friend or two at school next week, but I won't bring them over unless you promise not to embarrass me."

"I *never* make promises I have no intention of keeping."

She groaned.

I rolled a ripe tomato across the kitchen island at her. "Chop that," I said. "Don't slice it or wedge it. We're making chopped salad for dinner, and everything has to be chopped."

"Since when do we eat salad?" She squinted at me. "This house might not be haunted, but I think it does have magical powers. We've only been living here a few hours, and you're like a whole different person. A person who makes salad."

"We're getting a fresh start," I said. "We can reinvent ourselves. I'll be the mom who goes to pottery lessons, or learns how to scuba dive. I'll be the mom who makes salads instead of licking the icing off ten-day-old cupcakes. Why don't you try something new, too? Dye your hair cobalt blue and be the new freaky kid at your school. What's the dress code there? You can borrow my leather bustier and those sexy boots you won't let me wear in public."

"Gross," she said.

"Live a little," I said.

She wrinkled her nose and chopped the tomato in the Riddle family tradition—two hands on the knife handle, safely away from the blade. Both of us suffered from a vegetable-slicing phobia. She caught it from me, and I got it from TV and movies. Outside of cooking shows, every time someone on screen is shown chopping vegetables, they cut themselves. Okay, not every time, but often enough that whenever you see the knife and carrots, you tense up because you know something's coming, right?

Zoey finished chop-smashing the tomato. "I think I'll borrow your boots," she said. "But everything else is going to be normal."

There was that word again. *Normal.* Why couldn't my daughter give up on being normal the way I had and learn to embrace being weird?

"Make a bunch of new friends so they can come to the housewarming party," I said. "Speaking of new friends, I wonder what our Realtor, Dorothy Tibbits, is up to?"

"Something nutty, I'm sure. She's... what's the word? Cuckoo."

"You're so judgmental. Sure, the woman dresses up like Dorothy from *The Wizard of Oz*, but does wearing a blue pinafore make one cuckoo?"

"Not on its own, but carrying business paperwork in a wicker basket is not something a normal person does. Especially not a woman who's over sixty."

"She might be sixty, but her face is barely forty," I said. Dorothy Tibbits had the confusing appearance of someone attempting to look decades younger.

I'd bought the house on a solo trip to Wisteria, so Zoey had only met the real estate agent in person earlier that day on the front porch. When Dorothy Tibbits pulled the house keys out of her wicker basket, Zoey had taken a cautious step away from the blue-pinafore-wearing woman and refused to say more than two words to her.

If Zoey was going to reject people who were unusual, how long would it take before she abandoned me? I had to hope it was just a phase she was going through.

"We should give Dorothy Tibbits a chance," I said. "Sure, she smells like incense and camping gear, and she talks to your eyebrows rather than looking you in the eyes, and she's just *terrible* at selling houses, but she seems nice enough."

"Super," Zoey said with the exact opposite of enthusiasm. "Dorothy and her Botox face can be your new best friend."

Lightly, I added, "Or maybe Chet Moore, from next door. He's not horrible."

She narrowed her eyes at me. "Turbo-flirter."

I pretended to be hurt by the label of Turbo-flirter. Can I help it if I don't like small talk? What's the point in talking about nothing when you can dig into something juicy? You can learn a lot about someone if you throw out a good question or two.

Zoey said, "I can see the appeal of Mr. Tall Dark and Green Eyes, but isn't he too *normal* for you? He was wearing chinos. He looked like a catalog model."

I hadn't actually noticed his clothes. "The man's got a goat on his roof."

"But not a real goat. It's just a decoration on a weather vane. Besides, the inside of his house is colossally normal. I can see right in through his windows."

"Have you been spying on our new neighbors?"

"They started it," she protested. "There's a little boy with dark hair and big eyes. He was watching me from his window the whole time I was unpacking my bedroom. The way the houses are lined up, he can see right in. I felt like a monkey in the zoo."

"Do you want to switch rooms with me? I want you to be happy. We moved here as much for you as for me."

"Mom, stop being such a mom." She turned her head. "Shh."

Something thumped somewhere inside the house. It sounded a lot bigger than expanding nails or air ducts rubbing against wood. It sounded like trouble.

Zoey's hazel eyes widened. "The ghost," she breathed. "That wacky mover guy was right. We're being haunted."

"Let's hope it's a friendly ghost," I said with a shrug.

She shook her head and pulled out her phone. She tapped away, frowning at the screen for a few minutes before announcing, "This website says we can get rid of the ghost."

"Is it expensive? Can we use that white chalky stuff that keeps out slugs and silverfish?"

She ignored my questions and kept reading. "We need to go into every room, and clap and sing really loud to scare the ghost away. The key is making lots of living-person noises." She glanced up at the ceiling. "It's probably the ghost of the old lady who used to live here. Do you think she died inside the house?"

"I hadn't thought that. Not until now."

"What if the ghost doesn't know she's dead? What if she climbs into bed with me tonight, and screams because she thinks *I'm* the ghost?"

I'd been getting the creeps from the conversation, but imagining a ghost screaming at my daughter gave me a shiver down my spine. What if there was a ghost? I quickly pushed away the idea. I'd never believed in such nonsense, and I wasn't going to start now. No, I'd stick to my usual strategy for dealing with nonsense. Hitting right back with even more nonsense of my own.

"Zoey, did you say we should sing?" I gave her a playful look. "That won't work. People *adore* my singing, so that wouldn't drive anyone away, ghost or otherwise. But you could play some of your favorite music."

My daughter gave me a blank look.

Something inside the house thumped again. I thought of the blue jay, then quickly dismissed the notion. Even the biggest blue jay weighed less than a pound. Whatever made the noise must have been big, like a person.

It thumped again.

Zoey shrieked and threw herself into my arms.

Another thump.

My spine became entirely made of chills. Again, I wondered, what if ghosts were real?

My anxiety escalated into a whirling panic.

Dread set in. We were being haunted, and it was all my fault. My bad decisions were catching up with me. I'd been impulsive, taking a job in a new town and buying a house immediately rather than renting and taking things slow. I had been so sure of myself. I'd felt there was a larger entity guiding me toward some great destiny.

I'd trusted that everything would turn out for the best, but now I had a ghost.

What next?

I was as broke as any first-time homeowner, but I'd held some money back from the deposit to cover maintenance surprises. If the old pipes broke, I'd call a plumber. If a tree got diseased, I'd call an arborist. And if ghosts were real, then by the same logic, there'd have to be a whole industry of people around to deal with them.

I'd simply consult the internet and call in a spiritual medium. Or a priest. Or Beetlejuice.

There was yet another thump, followed by a crash. It sounded like dishes breaking.

"My fine china," I joked, my hand over my heart.

"The ghost is in the den now," Zoey said.

"Uh, which room is the den?"

"The one with the smaller of the two fireplaces," she said.

"We have two fireplaces?"

The crash was followed by rustling noises. Zoey buried her head in my shoulder and whimpered.

"Maybe a cat or a wild animal climbed in through an open window," I said. "It's not a ghost, because ghosts aren't real."

"It could be a zombie," she said.

"Now you're just going through monsters willy nilly. Next you'll say Frankenstein's creation is in the den."

"Don't let it eat our brains," she said with a manic giggle.

With my daughter clinging to me, I grabbed a broom and walked us both out of the kitchen and toward the den, which was a cozy room on the main floor that I planned to turn into a home library.

The den was empty. No zombies or stray cats.

But there was a mess. The welcome gifts we'd been given by the real estate agent had fallen off the fireplace mantel. The leafy fern, which hadn't stood much chance of survival even in the best of circumstances, was now a pile of smashed fronds mixed in with dirt and shattered pottery. Next to the plant lay the shredded remains of a wicker basket and scented bath products.

Zoey crouched over the mess and sniffed. "Smells like vetiver oil."

I raised an eyebrow.

She explained, "Vetiver is a grass from India. The scent is supposed to be grounding."

I inhaled deeply. "Your nose must be better than mine, because all I smell is dirt."

"You don't smell something like a hippie dipped in lemonade?"

"No, but that does sound interesting."

Zoey gathered the bath products, examining them closely. "None of these are open," she said. "Where's that smell coming from?"

"The ghost."

She opened a bottle of bath oil and sniffed it. "There's no vetiver in here. Where's it coming from?"

"Your butt," I said. *Your butt* was one of our favorite answers to dumb questions. *Where are my keys?* Check your butt. *Am I forgetting anything?* You forgot your butt. *What time are you coming home?* Ask your butt.

In a serious tone, Zoey said, "The ghost smashed our welcome gifts."

"There's no such thing as ghosts." I examined the wooden ledge where I'd left the gifts. "Look at the slope on this mantel." I patted the wood. "Every time those big mover guys went up and down the stairs, they sent vibrations through the house. Eventually, the stuff on here slid off."

She made a hmm noise, unconvinced but considering.

Since I had a broom in my hands anyway, I began sweeping the dirt into a pile.

"But we were both in the kitchen, not anywhere near the stairs," she said. "Someone pushed these things off the ledge."

"Why would someone do that?"

She blinked at me, her hazel eyes looking exhausted. "These were *welcome* gifts, and someone literally destroyed them. The message is pretty clear. We are not welcome here. We are *unwanted* and *unwelcome*."

"This isn't about a ghost," I said, still sweeping the dirt toward a corner. "You're projecting your fears about moving here onto some imaginary ghost because you'd rather repress your fear than admit you're scared."

She finished gathering the bath products and stood to face me. She'd grown recently, and we were practically the same height, nearly eye to eye.

I asked, "What's really bothering you?"

"Someone doesn't want us here." She turned and went to the den's small window. She pressed her forehead against the glass and said, "Look!" She pointed to our yard.

I joined her at the window and looked.

At the edge of our back yard was a small, slim figure clad in black. The figure climbed over the fence separating our yard from the neighbor's.

"It's that stupid boy," Zoey said angrily. "The one who was peeping at me in my room. He must have gotten inside the house and smashed our things. The nerve!"

I grumbled under my breath. I was having a hard enough time getting my daughter settled in without having to deal with a *saboteur*. I grumbled some more, this time muttering about torture devices.

Zoey said, "Mom, calm down. Don't get all lightning-bolts-and-brimstone. He's just a bratty kid."

Too late. The day had been long, and full of cardboard boxes and whining—some of it mine—but we'd survived. Our new life awaited. Nobody, and I mean *nobody*, was going to stand in our way, especially not an ill-behaved child.

I muttered a few more choice words, turned on my heel, and marched straight out the front door into the twilight of the spring evening. The sweet scent of the wisteria blossoms on the porch hit me like a potion. I fantasized about grabbing the kid and holding him upside down over a bubbling cauldron. The air seemed to crackle with blue sparks around me.

I marched over to the door of the Moore residence. My daughter ran along right behind me. My hair was a mess, I was wearing the only other clothes I'd unpacked so far—a weird black dress I used as a nightshirt—and I clutched in one hand the straw-bristled broom I'd been using to clean up the mess. As I banged on the door of Chet's house, I couldn't have looked more like a mad witch if I'd tried.

CHAPTER 3

With the broom in one hand, I used the other to bang on the neighbor's door.

To make it wildly clear I meant business, I yelled, "Open this door right now! I know you're in there!"

Zoey tugged on my arm. "Mom, it was just smelly soap and a potted plant."

Through clenched teeth, I replied tersely, "That lovely fern was a symbol. A gesture of welcoming."

"We should get some food into you," she said sagely. "What's gotten into you today? Are you so hungry it's turned into *hangry*?"

With effort, I unclenched my teeth. Something had gotten into me. I felt a bit like something huge and terrifying, with big, scary tentacles, was trying to jump out of me and swallow everything into a gaping chasm of a hellmouth. If that was *hangry*, then maybe I was.

She glanced at the door. "We can deal with him another time."

"Don't be so sure of that. If we don't nip this problem in the bud, one day we'll be the ones smashed to pieces at the hands of that sociopath."

She smirked. "He's just a little boy."

My daughter was right, but my pulse was still racing. "Sure, he's just a little boy now. But before they grew up, so were all of history's worst dictators."

The door creaked open. A man said, "Are you comparing my sweet boy to Hitler and Stalin?"

"Yes, I am. Your *sweet boy* broke into my new house and smashed..." I trailed off and blinked at the man standing in the doorway. I'd been expecting someone handsome with green eyes, and while this guy fit the description, he was also well into his grandfather years.

"You're not Chet," I said.

The older man pinched the wrinkle of skin on the bridge of his nose. "What's Chet done now?"

"Not Chet. It was a little boy." I held my hand four feet above the porch's floor. "About this high. Dressed in black, like a ninja, with dark hair falling over his forehead. He was inside my house less than five minutes ago, smashing things and making both of us feel generally unwelcome."

The man dropped his hand from his face and gave me a curious look. "Are you two the chumps who bought the old Vander Zalm house?"

Zoey chose this moment to speak up. "Hey! Who are you calling chumps?"

"That's us," I said with a forced smile. "But this one is a minor dependent. I'm the one who's on the hook for the mortgage, so that makes me the chump."

The man said, "Whatever you paid, it was too much."

And then he slammed the door shut between us.

Zoey gave me her told-you-so look.

I gave her my don't-make-things-worse-for-your-mother look.

I knocked on the door again. This time nobody answered, which was probably for the best, since I was still clutching the broom and thinking about hitting people with it.

The curtains on the window next to the door twitched, and a pale, round face appeared. The little boy had his eyes crossed and his tongue sticking out.

Zoey clenched her hands into fists and shook one at him. "You creepy little brat. You don't scare us."

The boy responded by jamming a finger up one nostril and using his other hand to make a rude gesture.

I smacked the glass with the broom and made a scary face right back at him. His eyes widened, and he ran away from the window.

Zoey said, "Good job, Mom. Now, let's dial your crazy down and go home to our delicious... chopped salad."

As we stepped off the porch, I said, "Forget the salad. I'm having fantasies about turning day to eternal night and consuming entire cities. Is that normal, or am I so far beyond *hangry* that I'm in some new, universe-destroying state of mind?"

"We wouldn't want to cause an apocalypse," she said wisely. "To be safe, we should order pizza."

"But we don't know which place in Wisteria has the best pizza. We know nothing about this town, except that they have a ridiculously well-stocked zoo for a population of this size."

We climbed the steps to our own porch and both stopped to admire the dangling wisteria blossoms. Zoey stood up on her tiptoes and gave them a sniff.

She asked, "What's up with the zoo, anyway? I mean, it's not big enough to be world famous, but it does seem awfully large. And parts of it are blurred out on the aerial view maps on the internet. Actually, entire sections of the town are blurred out."

I put my free hand on my hip and stared into the round face and hazel eyes that were a mirror of mine. "You got me," I said with a smile. "This town is part of a huge conspiracy, and there are top-secret organizations here, running underground research facilities, doing science experiments, and manipulating the space-time continuum."

"Figures," she said. "But with all that going on, there should be plenty of amazing takeout options." She quirked an eyebrow. "Mad scientists don't have time to cook dinner."

"You're pretty wise for someone who's only sixteen minus a day. That must be why people are always telling me you have an old soul."

She wrinkled her nose. "I don't like people talking about the age of my soul."

My stomach made a very loud growl. "That's ominous," I said.

She gave the pink wisteria blossoms strung across the front of the porch one more sniff before turning and opening our front door.

"Come on," she said. "Let's order pizza before your stomach brings on the End of Days."

"Don't worry about my stomach," I joked. "It's the sanity-shredding tentacles you have to look out for." I paused at the threshold. "Speaking of losing all grip on reality and succumbing to despair, I don't know which box we packed the TV remote in, so we'll have to unpack all of them."

"That was a dirty trick," she said.

"The dirtiest of all, because I unwittingly played it on myself."

We went inside, where we rejoiced in the miracle of finding an unsecured wireless network somewhere along the street. Our own internet would be hooked up on Monday, but in the meantime, we were in business.

We each took one side of our comfy sofa and ordered the pizza.

After a few minutes, I said, "If you're going to the kitchen anyway, I could use a cup of tea."

She gave me a playful scowl, but she did get up and make us two mugs of tea with honey to keep my stomach grumblings from deafening us before the pizza arrived.

As I was reaching for my tea, I bumped the spoon, which clattered to the floor.

Without looking up, Zoey said, "Company's coming for dinner."

"You think? Are you psychic now?"

"You dropped a spoon. That's an omen. I was reading all about these things on that website about witchcraft. Dropping a spoon means we'll get a visitor." She rubbed her temples and closed her eyes. "A dark, mysterious visitor who brings foreboding."

"You mean the pizza delivery guy? He'd better not bring any foreboding. I specifically asked for pizza only."

CHAPTER 4

The doorbell chimed.

"Doorbell," I said.

My daughter raised her eyebrow at me. "And?"

"We talked about this. Now that we have the pleasure of owning a doorbell and a front door, it's your job to answer it."

"Okay," she said amiably. She jumped up from the couch, raced to the door, and flung it open. I followed behind her, opening my wallet.

We found a skinny twenty-something girl holding our pizza. Standing behind her was our new neighbor, Chet Moore, gripping a small, dark-haired boy by the collar.

Zoey leaned to the side to look around the delivery girl and glared at the big-eyed boy. She spoke with an accusatory hiss. "You dare darken our doorway, pestilence?"

The boy stuck out his tongue.

Zoey jerked forward, reaching for his tongue, but he recoiled quickly.

"Too slow," he taunted. "And I'm not *pestilence*. That's what you are. I was here first."

I grabbed Zoey by the shoulder and hauled her back.

"Kids," I said to Chet. "Every day is like a trip to the zoo with no admission fee."

Chet nodded and gave the boy, who looked about ten years old, a stern look.

The pizza delivery girl cleared her throat. I paid her for the pizza plus a tip. As she left, I realized I'd never had a meal delivered by a female before. Things were different here in Wisteria. Safer, it seemed.

The neighbors were still standing on the porch. I waved for them to join us inside. "Come in and partake of pizza delights. The internet says this is the best kind in town, but we need an expert's opinion."

"We don't want to impose," Chet said. "Grampa Don told me what happened today. I only brought Corvin by to apologize."

The boy—Corvin—squirmed like a fish on a hook. "Sorry," he croaked.

"Corvin's *very* sorry," Chet said. "I'll pay for the damage to whatever he broke. How much?"

"Don't worry about the money," I said. "But I do love a good heartfelt apology. I'll accept your apology if you come inside and join us. It's just pizza, plus we're having lime cordial in martini glasses because that's all the glassware we've unpacked so far."

The little boy jerked away from Chet's grip on his collar. He flew into the house like an opportunistic housefly on the first day of spring, followed by Zoey with the pizza.

As they neared the dining room, I heard Zoey say, "Corvin? That's such an interesting name. It means raven."

"I know that," spat the boy. "I'm not a dummy. I'm a genius. I'm smarter than you. I'm smarter than everyone."

"You think you're smarter than me?" Zoey grew more animated as she quizzed him. "How big is the moon in relation to the earth?"

"Twenty-seven percent."

"That's a bit high, Corvin."

"Dummy! You didn't specify," he said. "By *diameter*, the moon is twenty-seven percent compared to Earth, but by *volume* it's two percent."

"Very good. Here, have some pizza." A few seconds passed. "Hey! Leave some for the rest of us."

While the two kids quizzed each other and fought over the pizza in the dining room, I smiled sweetly at Chet. We stood near the front door, where he was examining the carved wood table we'd positioned in the hallway to receive keys and mail. He nodded appreciatively at the dovetail joints visible inside the drawers. He had an eye for detail and craftsmanship.

"Your son is a clever boy," I said.

"Corvin? He doesn't get it from me."

"What does your wife do?"

"Nothing," he said.

"Lucky lady," I said.

"She's dead." He quickly added, "It was many years ago, before I moved in next door with my father. My father was supposed to help me raise Corvin to be a well-adjusted and perfectly normal boy. As you can see, that didn't work out as planned."

"Boys are tough," I said. "So are girls, but I got lucky. People say Zoey has an old soul."

Chet finished examining the entry table and glanced down the hall toward the den. "May I? It's been a while since I've been inside this house."

"Be my guest."

He led the way to the den, where he frowned at the dirt and mess on the floor. I apologized for the disaster and used the broom and dustpan to clean it up.

"Don't apologize." He knelt near my feet and gathered stray pottery from the corners of the room. "You're not the one who did this."

"To be fair, we didn't see your son break these things. We only saw him running away from the house."

"Corvin's supposed to be out of his destructive phase," Chet said. "He's relapsed. Dr. Bo—uh, the therapist says I need to be firm but not overreact. How's a parent supposed to do that? We've been trying to come up with a fair punishment, but he keeps lying. He says it wasn't him. He says a ghost knocked over your welcome gifts."

"Ask him how he'd know about this so-called ghost if he wasn't inside the house. You can't see into this room from your place."

Chet went to the window and sighed as he leaned on the windowsill.

"Corvin isn't like other kids," he said.

"What's wrong with him?"

"Wrong?" He turned to face me, his green eyes blazing under thick, dark eyebrows. "I try to focus on what's *right* with him. He's still a person."

"I've offended you," I said. "I'm very sorry."

His expression softened. "No. Don't be. We came here to apologize to you, and you're not wrong about Corvin. He's not normal."

I grabbed his arm playfully. "Honey, there's something wrong with all of us, and thank the stars, because it'd be a dull world if we weren't all a bit bent."

He looked down at my hand on his arm as though he'd never seen a hand before. Was he one of those people with an aversion to being touched? Earlier in the day, when we'd been shaking hands, he had yanked his away suddenly. What would happen if I kept holding his arm? I got the funniest image in my head of him turning to stone.

I studied his face while he stared at my hand. He had long, thick, dark eyelashes. His cheeks were smooth, shaved that day, even though it was the weekend. His internet handle had been Chet Twenty-one. Did I remember anything at all about him from my days of internet fame? Nothing came to me, yet I couldn't shake the sensation we knew each other really well. We had

34

history, whether I understood it or not. He cleared his throat and gently pulled his arm from my grasp.

"We should check on our kids," he said, his voice thick and gravelly.

I cocked my head. "I hear laughter. That's a good sign. You only have to worry when they're quiet."

"Corvin is very quiet sometimes."

"Maybe they'll become friends. Zoey always wanted a little brother, but as time went on and I got used to being on my own, that became unlikely. Not impossible, because everything works fine down there—better than fine—but you know what it's like being a busy single parent."

He seemed amused by my over-sharing. He licked his lips and said, "Zara Riddle, formerly Zara the Camgirl, I'd be shocked by you discussing your plumbing with a man you just met, but I feel like I know you. It's the strangest feeling. Do you know what I mean?"

"It's not really that strange," I said. "I was famous on the internet for about fifteen minutes, plus you watched me on my webcams and read my journal entries."

He shook his head. "Life is funny. I can't believe I live next door to Zara the Camgirl. You were all the way across the country then. You're a long way from home."

"I got a great job offer out of the blue and decided to make a leap of faith."

"To Wisteria," he said, chuckling. "That's a big leap of faith."

I grinned at him. "Too late! You guys are stuck with me now. For better or for worse."

He finished, "Til death do us part."

"Speaking of which, while we were waiting for our pizza to arrive, I dug up a little information about the previous owner of this house. It's probably stuff you already know."

"Try me." He flashed a flirty smile. Who was the Turbo-flirter now? Chet Moore. That's who.

"Winona Vander Zalm was a wacky diva socialite who showed up at parties for just about anything. You could open a sandwich shop and she'd be there helping to cut the ribbon. I found photos of her at every event in Wisteria since people started posting on the internet. She was stunning for her age."

"Ms. Vander Zalm was a very dynamic woman."

"How did she die?" I waited with breathless anticipation. *Was it right here in this house?*

The den filled with a buzzing sound. The lighting brightened. The room got icy cold.

From out of nowhere, I remembered a line I'd memorized for a high school production of *Macbeth. By the pricking of my thumbs, something wicked this way comes.*

The den got brighter and colder.

Chet looked into my eyes. "Are you doing this?"

And then, with a sizzling pop, the two sconce lamps on either side of the fireplace flashed and burned out.

CHAPTER 5

Chet quickly decided the burned-out bulbs came courtesy of a problem with the electrical circuits, and left to check on the panel.

A few minutes after leaving me in the dark den, he returned to find me sweeping the broken plant and dirt into a garbage bag. It wasn't the easiest task to do one handed while holding a flashlight.

"Your electrical looks safe enough," he reported back.

"No ghosts?

He snorted. "You should have a certified electrician come in and upgrade the whole panel, but I don't think there's any rush." He stood in the doorway to the den, his face in shadow.

I finished sweeping up and stood with the flashlight under my chin, pointing up.

"Chet, you were going to tell me how Ms. Vander Zalm passed. Specifically, whether or not it was inside this house."

He crossed his arms and leaned casually against the door frame as he chuckled. "Is it that time of the night already?"

"Do you mean the time of night where we tell spooky stories?"

He kept chuckling.

"I do know quite a few spooky tales," I said. "It's one of the hazards of my career."

"Hmm." He rubbed his chin. "Let me guess. You're a camp counselor?"

"Close but no prize." I pulled the flashlight away and blinked at the blurry splotches in my field of view.

Through the haze, I could see his shadowy outline nodding. "Let's leave the ghost stories to our kids," he said. "As for Ms. Vander Zalm, she passed away peacefully in her sleep."

"Here? In the house?"

"I did say peacefully. Can you imagine anything more peaceful than passing into the next world from the comfort of your own home?"

I crossed my arms and sighed. "Chet, I like how you don't give straight answers. I'm sure it drives *some* people crazy, but I dig it. You're interesting."

"Are you being sarcastic?"

"Let's leave that open to your interpretation."

"Zara Riddle, you are so much more than Zara the Camgirl."

"I'm also a librarian."

"Not a camp counselor?"

"Nope. I'm one of Wisteria's librarians. Starting Monday."

"Tell me more about this librarian job of yours," he said.

"Oh, I will," I said. "Let's get some of that pizza before I faint, though."

* * *

We found the pizza in the dining room and put a few slices onto plates, which we took to the half-unpacked living room. I resisted the urge to mash the food into my face double handed. I didn't want Chet to see my monster side just yet.

Chet took a seat on an upholstered chair and spread two squares of paper towel across his lap. He had another two squares he was using as napkins, and he took careful bites of his pizza slice, holding the plate up under it to catch crumbs.

He held himself up with excellent posture. I became self-conscious about my slouched position on the sofa. I got the feeling the Moore house next door had a lot of rules about where eating happened, and it didn't happen in the living room.

The two kids darted in and out while they explored the house together, chatting away about science facts, oscillating between becoming sworn nemeses and the best of friends.

Corvin seemed very comfortable inside my house—the opposite of his father. Chet had been warm and polite about checking the electrical panel and answering my nosy questions about his former neighbor, but from the minute he'd taken a seat, he'd looked uncomfortable.

A peal of laughter floated down from the upper floor.

"I'm glad they're getting along," Chet said.

"How old is Corvin?"

Chet winced, looking even more uncomfortable. I wondered if there was something wrong with the chair, or with his back. He adjusted the tiny throw pillow on the chair behind him. "Ten."

"Those two may be six years apart, but Zoey has the same sense of humor as a ten-year-old boy, so they're not as different as they appear." I didn't add that I also laughed at puerile humor and butt jokes. As my neighbor, Chet would figure that out soon enough.

Chet took a sip of lime cordial from his martini glass and asked, "What does it take to be a librarian?"

I listed the requirements on my fingers. "A corkscrew for all the wine, a closet full of cardigans, the optimism to assume that all brown mystery stains found in books are chocolate, a desk calendar featuring cats in hilarious costumes, and, um, did I mention the cardigans? Sometimes you need to wear a cardigan over top of your other cardigan if the library is really cold or you spilled wine on yourself."

He smiled, and it was a smile that radiated beams of light into the darkest reaches of my heart. My joke seemed to have relaxed him a little. I looked away quickly, before I blushed. Too late. My cheeks were hot.

I took a bite of pizza and then answered his question more seriously, telling him about the education I'd taken to qualify for a librarian job.

"That's a lot of schooling," he said. I expected him to finish the thought with, *to do what the internet does for free*. Bless his heart, he didn't say it. Could he be any more charming?

"I did put in a lot of long hours," I said. "During the times I was tempted to give up, I pushed on so I could set a good example for Zoey."

He raised his eyebrows in a look of admiration. "And you did it all while raising your daughter as a single parent." He jerked his head back, frowned, and quickly added, "Oops. I didn't mean to say that. I hate it when people call me a single parent. Labels are so stigmatizing."

"Labels really are the worst," I agreed. "I wasn't thinking ahead about the label when I got pregnant." I stood up and refilled our glasses with green cordial. "I wasn't thinking at all," I said.

Chet gave me a sly look. "Thinking is overrated. Life is for living."

"Yes," I agreed. "And even if I could go back in time and confiscate those Barberrian wine coolers from the younger version of myself before I got in trouble, I wouldn't change a thing."

Chet picked up his martini glass and raised it in a toast. "To not changing a thing."

I raised mine as well and clinked it against his glass.

"I wish I could still get those wine coolers, but the company went out of business."

"What a shame," he said, his eyes twinkling.

* * *

While the kids ran around the house, exploring the attic and all the crawlspace storage cubbies, Chet and I continued our chat in the living room.

His posture remained rigid, and he continued to give off the aura of waiting to escape, but I found him to be a wonderful conversationalist. When I talked, he really listened, and the words flowed. It probably helped that I was so complimentary of his hometown.

I told him how excited I was to be working my dream job in a town that felt like an undiscovered gem. How did Wisteria even exist? The town had just enough of everything, was as pretty as a postcard, and my dream house was totally affordable. How had the rest of the world not packed up their bags and moved there ahead of me?

Chet didn't have any answers but agreed that Wisteria had to be paradise because people kept telling him that. He'd grown up here, so he knew little else.

I tried to find out more about him, but he kept skillfully redirecting the conversation back to me, and heaven knows I do love a captive audience.

We joked around about ghosts and werewolves and things that go bump in the night.

After we'd finished all the pizza, Corvin and Zoey ran next door and returned with fresh brownies and vanilla ice cream. We invited Grampa Don, but he declined, as he was watching something on TV.

I was so cozy. My body felt like an *al dente* noodle. I relaxed into the corner of the sofa and reached for my favorite patchwork quilt to draw across my lap.

Chet was talking to Zoey about her aspirations beyond high school and then...

A clock began striking midnight with loud gongs.

I said, "What was that?" We didn't own a clock that made gong sounds.

The gonging continued, ringing in my head.

Chet and Zoey continued to talk about careers, as though they couldn't hear the thunderous clangs of the clock striking the time.

I tried to speak again, but I was frozen, as if in a dream.

The room shimmered and wavered around me.

Was I dreaming? Was any of this real? It did feel too good to be true.

My eyes felt like they were burning.

I was falling down a tunnel that was both dark and bright at the same time, a swirling rainbow of starbursts. The gongs of the clock turned to thunder, cracking around me. The world tipped sideways, and I lurched to a stop.

Everything was dark.

CHAPTER 6

Where am I?

I opened my eyes. My environment was still dark, but things started taking shape, looking more familiar.

What happened?

I'd been sitting on the couch, across from Chet, thinking about taking the last brownie in the pan. Then a clock had gonged at midnight.

Midnight?

Something had changed. Today was Zoey's birthday. My daughter was sixteen.

But something else had happened, and now I wasn't in the living room anymore.

I was alone, in a kitchen. My kitchen.

The room's lights were off, but enough ambient light came in from the street lamps that I could dimly make out my surroundings. How did I get to the kitchen? And why was I wearing my black sleeping dress again? I must have fallen asleep in the living room. *How embarrassing.* My daughter must have helped me get undressed and changed into the nightgown.

And now I was in the kitchen. Was I sleepwalking? That was a new one for me.

A burning smell made my sinuses ache and my eyes water.

Something in front of me was glowing red. Two rectangular lines. The toaster.

KERCLUNK.

The toaster's handle popped up, along with two pieces of blackened toast. The toast was beyond edible, practically ashes.

I yanked the charred toast from the still-glowing appliance and tossed both pieces in the nearby sink. The blackened squares continued to smolder. I quickly doused them with water to stop tendrils of smoke from reaching the room's smoke detector.

Think, Zara. What's the last thing you remember? Feeling drowsy on the sofa. Chet's green eyes watching me as he sat straight-backed in the chair. The familiar comfort of being near him. Being completely relaxed.

And then I must have fallen asleep right in front of the poor guy. How rude. But he'd probably be understanding. I had spent the day moving.

When I'd heard the gonging on the clock at midnight, it could have been an auditory hallucination brought on by exhaustion or even the beginning of a dream.

My tiredness explained my patchy memory but not sleepwalking, let alone this new phenomenon of *sleep-toasting*.

I chuckled to myself as I wrung the water out of the black toast, tossed the soppy remains into the food compost bucket under the sink, and poured myself a glass of water. Dehydration makes people do funny things.

I checked the time on the stove. It was three o'clock in the morning.

Today was Sunday, Zoey's birthday. I yawned. I had to get some more sleep before taking her shopping to get new bedroom stuff for her sixteenth birthday.

She'd laugh her butt off when she heard about my sleep-toasting.

Actually, I'd never hear the end of it. Maybe I wouldn't tell her about this incident.

It was probably just a one-time event, nothing to be concerned about.

I turned to leave the kitchen and accidentally dropped the water glass I'd forgotten I was holding. The glass headed straight for the floor, right between my bare toes. My breath caught in my throat, and time stood still.

No, really.

Time stood still.

Not like a car accident, when something scary is happening quickly and your mind speeds up to make it *seem* like everything's moving in slow motion.

Time truly stood still, and the glass paused in its descent, floating about three inches from the floor.

I leaned forward to see what the glass had caught on. Was it a trick of the light, a bump in the flooring? I blinked, and time seemed to flow again. The glass dropped the rest of the way and landed on the floor with a soft ringing sound.

I picked up the glass and examined it. There was nothing unusual about the glass except that it had hung in midair for a second.

As if by magic.

I snorted at my wild imagination, put the glass back on the counter, and went back upstairs to bed.

* * *

In the morning, I chuckled to myself over the previous night's sleep-toasting. I knew I hadn't dreamed the incident, because the charred toast remains were still sitting in the compost bucket under the sink.

I made a pot of coffee and fresh, noncharred toast for breakfast.

At ten o'clock, I went upstairs to get Zoey up and found her bed empty and neatly made. I raced around the house, checking all the rooms and calling her name. She was sixteen and able to take care of herself, but we were in a new town, and I couldn't help but get those motherly worries.

I eventually found her in the back yard, reclining on a weathered lawn chair, soaking up some morning sunshine with her eyes closed and an open paperback resting on her chest. Like me, she had pale skin to go with her red hair, and so sunbathing was limited to the spring and fall months only.

"Happy birthday, Sleeping Beauty," I said.

Her eyelids fluttered open, and she sat up. Except for the rusty lawn chair that squeaked with her movement, she could have been a slumbering princess from a fairy tale. My chest ached with love, as it always did whenever I saw my daughter immediately following a bout of motherly worrying.

I took a seat on a wooden stump next to her chair. "Do you feel any older?"

"I think I feel different," she said as she rubbed her eyes. "But I can't tell if it's from turning sixteen or if it's from waking up in a new place. I was so disoriented this morning. I thought I was going into the bathroom, but I opened the door and it was a linen closet. I spent a whole minute being mad at you, because I thought you switched things around to play a joke on me. But then I found the actual bathroom, so you're forgiven."

"As much as I love pranks, I have neither the magical powers nor the team of construction workers required to swap rooms around willy nilly."

She reached for the mug of coffee in my hands. "For me?"

"Sure." I handed it over. "Happy birthday. I'll just go get another one for myself."

I went back into the house and poured myself a cup. My daughter had been drinking coffee for the last year. Sometimes other mothers would give me disapproving looks while ordering sugary cocoa for their children. I allowed Zoey to drink coffee as long as she avoided the heavy syrups and kept it to a reasonable quantity. As far as vices went, her caffeine habit was mild. I hoped she would continue to be such a smart, thoughtful teenager now that she was another year older. I knew the risks of small-town life for teens. On one hand, it could be safer, because people knew each other and were more community oriented. But on the other hand, some small towns were lacking in activities for teens, which left kids with little choice but to find their own amusement.

Only time would tell what kind of life Zoey would build for herself in Wisteria. She had been a well-liked student at her former high school, but it hadn't happened overnight. She'd grown up with most of the girls in her small circle. I did worry about her sometimes, because she was content to spend her weekends with her nose in a book. It could take months for her to come out of her introvert shell and make friends. I smiled at the memory of her chasing Corvin around the house the night before. At least she had one new buddy, a pseudo-brother.

Mug in hand, I stepped out into the back yard once more.

"This is amazing," I said to Zoey. "Am I dreaming? We have an entire back yard that belongs to us. This is so much better than a tiny, rusted fire escape looking out over an alley, don't you think?"

She'd gotten up from the old lawn chair and was digging around under the stalks of some overgrown vines. "It's like a jungle back here," she said.

"But a real jungle. Not a concrete jungle." I looked around at the shrubbery and trees and flowers that were all mine, mine, mine. I'd dreamed for so long of having a yard of my own that I relished the idea of toiling away back there, planting and pruning things.

"That's weird," Zoey said.

"Is the talking blue jay back?"

"I don't know, but..." She was still crouching with her back to me, pulling something from the dirt. "These little rocks aren't rocks at all."

"Are they smooth and white? They could be bulbs for daffodils or tulips that finished blooming already."

"No. Bulbs look like tiny onions, and these are gray rocks that look exactly like... Well, you tell me."

She plopped three gray stones into my palm. They looked like concrete hornets, right down to the detail of wings folded against their backs.

"These are weird," I agreed. "Mrs. Vander Zalm must have had eclectic taste when it came to garden ornaments." I handed back the three pebble-sized ornaments as I glanced around at the shadows between the fence and the overgrown shrubs. "Keep an eye out for garden gnomes. They sneak up on you when you're not looking."

"Very funny." Zoey scooped a handful of water from a concrete bird bath and rinsed off the concrete hornets. "These are incredibly detailed," she said.

"You look like you're enjoying yourself. Do you want to spend the day poking around in the garden, or do you want to hit the shops?"

"Shopping," she said. "I don't really need anything, but we should explore our new town."

She set the curious little hornets back on the ground where she'd found them.

CHAPTER 7

We were walking along one of the quaint shopping streets of Wisteria when Zoey said to me, "What's the name of that show where some of the people are robots?"

"Do you mean *Westworld*?"

"Not that one."

"*Robocop*? *The Terminator*? *Blade Runner*? *Aliens*?"

"The one with the pretty robots," she said.

"Like the fembots in *Austin Powers*? Or do you mean pretty like Jude Law in *A.I.*?"

She stopped walking and raised her red eyebrows at me. "Wow. You're really good at the whole librarian thing."

"So good, it never shuts off. Just call me Walking Wikipedia." I gestured for her to step over to the side, so we weren't blocking the sidewalk. "Now tell me more about this show you're thinking of."

She rubbed her chin thoughtfully. "The remake has Ferris Bueller in it."

I snapped my fingers. "You mean Matthew Broderick, and the movie is *Stepford Wives*." I fist pumped the air in a most un-librarian-like gesture. "Nailed it!"

She gave me a patronizing pat on the shoulder. "Very good." She gestured for us to start walking again. "I was trying to think of the name of that movie, because there's something wrong with the people in this town."

I looked around, trying to see what she did. All I saw were regular people up and down the sidewalks, carrying shopping bags or walking dogs and stopping to say hello to each other.

"Zoey, I don't see anything wrong with these folks."

"Exactly." She glanced over to give me a knowing smile. "They're all perfect. Like extras in a movie about a quaint small town with a dark secret."

"Like *Wayward Pines*," I said. "Or any number of Stephen King adaptations."

"Exactly. Do you think it's the town, or do you think it's just me? Did growing up in a big city warp my mind somehow?" We'd both slowed our walking again, and she stopped to gaze at our reflections in a store window.

Now it was my turn to pat her on the shoulder. "Oh, sweetie. You are warped, but not from—"

We were interrupted by a person approaching and lightly touching my elbow. I turned quickly to find a very small man with a big, round nose staring up at me with tiny dark eyes. He had a pair of wire-rimmed eyeglasses in one hand.

"And a very good morning to you, Ms. Riddle," the gnome-like man said.

"Same to you," I said politely, even though I had no idea who the small fellow was. If I'd ever met someone who looked exactly like an adorable garden gnome, I would have remembered the face.

He kept squinting up at me, waving the glasses in his hand as he spoke. "And who's this lovely redhead accompanying you this fine morning? Is this your niece?"

"My daughter," I said. "Zoey, this is..." I turned to the man, expecting him to give his name.

The small man laughed. "Such a joker, you are!" He passed his glasses to his other hand and extended his right hand to Zoey. "Lovely to meet you, miss. I'm Griebel Gorman. Call me Griebel."

"Griebel," Zoey repeated, giving me a raised eyebrow as she leaned down and shook his hand. "And how do you two know each other?"

The big-nosed man let out a merry laugh. "Oh, this one"—he nodded in my direction—"and I go way back." Griebel pulled a crisp handkerchief from his pocket and turned to walk away, cleaning his glasses as he went. "Toodles," he called over his shoulder.

Once he was out of hearing range, I whispered to Zoey, "I have no idea who that was."

"He must really need those glasses if he thought you were someone else."

"Someone who's also called Ms. Riddle?" I shook my head. "Weirdly enough, the little guy did seem familiar. I must have met him before and forgotten."

"Does he work at the library? Maybe he was there at your interview."

"No, but weirdly enough, I do have a faint recollection of giving him an autographed book of recipes."

"A book? Well, that explains it," Zoey said. "You must have met him at a librarian function or a book signing."

"Sure," I said. "That seems a lot more logical than your theory that this town is populated by humanoid robots."

"Or that there's a giant conspiracy and everyone here is a paid actor, like in *The Truman Show*."

"Ooh." I looked around at the colorful storefronts, clean streets, and orderly flow of smiling townspeople. "This town does have a *Truman Show* vibe. Maybe we should move back to the city right away? It will be so much fun to put all the things we just unpacked back into cardboard boxes again."

"Hmm," Zoey said. "Let's not be hasty."

"Admit it. You love Wisteria."

She frowned. "Undecided. Let's go across the street to that appliance repair shop and see if they have a nice lamp for my bedroom."

We went to the crosswalk, and the cars in both directions immediately stopped and waved us across, both drivers smiling.

Zoey was right about one thing. There was definitely something unusual about the whole town.

At least I'd be starting at my new job the next morning. My fellow librarians would be able to let me in on the many secrets of Wisteria.

CHAPTER 8

An Old English word for library is bochord, which literally means "book hoard."

Given the size of the town, the Wisteria Public Library was a very well-stocked *bochard*. The library crouched on a downtown corner, low and squat, like a slumbering dragon made of concrete. It had been built in the brutalist style, during an era when municipal buildings seemingly erupted from the ground, raw in material and devoid of frivolity. The only color was the slate blue of the doors. There were windows on the lower floor only, and they were deep set within the folds of the concrete walls.

I'd had low expectations from the exterior but was dazzled to find the interior of the library surprisingly bright, thanks to a grid of skylights and a lofted central area.

When I'd visited the month before for my interview, I'd taken one look around and instantly known it was the place for me. A book hoard inside a bunker. From the sensible layout to the gorgeous, double-height shelves with rolling ladders for staff to access the closed stacks, this was the library I'd been longing to call home.

Call it love at first sight. And I was pretty sure the Wisteria library loved me back.

My new boss, however, wasn't too sure about me.

I was nervous on my first day at my job, and the head librarian, Kathy Carmichael, wasn't giving me much feedback.

Two hours into my Monday shift, we walked together into the staff lounge in the northwest corner of the library. We were supposed to be taking a coffee break, but the head librarian kept remembering more important things she needed to tell me.

"Oh, you'll need to get on rotation for FPF," Kathy said.

"That sounds serious." It was also, surprisingly, a term I didn't know.

Kathy had spent the morning drilling me on the library's computer system and more three-letter acronyms than a person typically hears in a single day. The Wisteria Public Library (WPL) used an open-source, web-based integrated library system (ILS) to manage acquisitions, and a geographic information system (GIS) to map the physical layout of everything.

Kathy looked at me with pinched lips, as though she wasn't sure if I could handle the shocking revelation of whatever FPF was and what it meant to be on rotation for it.

"Whooo am I kidding," she said, drawing out the word *who* so it sounded like she was hooting. "This is a lot of acronyms I'm hitting you with. We should take a break." Her small eyes darted toward the box of leftover birthday cake near the staff lounge's sink.

I nodded and gave Kathy my serious face. "There are a lot of acronyms, boss, but I've worked at libraries before, as a page and also an assistant. I can handle it." Plus I really wanted to know what FPF meant. The P could easily stand for patron, which is what libraries call the people who patronize the institution, rather than *customer* or *client* or *muggle*.

She didn't hear me, though. I'd lost the head librarian to the box of birthday cake. She loaded a sturdy square onto a plate and took a bite.

"Stale," she commented. She kept eating anyway.

I wasn't too eager for stale cake, but I wanted my new boss to like me, so I took a square and joined her. "Not bad," I said.

"It's from the Gingerbread House of Baking," she said. "Have you been there yet? Oh, you *have* to go. Their recipes are simply *magical*."

"There are so many bakeries in Wisteria, it'll take me ages to visit them all."

"You have to go to this one," she said solemnly. "Promise."

"I promise to go," I said.

With each bite of cake, the color returned to Kathy's pale cheeks. The woman was in her forties, with medium-brown hair falling in curls, light-brown eyes that glowed golden orange under the bright lights, and an oval face with high cheeks that nudged her glasses whenever she got animated and talked faster. The lenses of her glasses were perfect circles, framed in gold with delicate filigree around the hinge connecting the arms. The round glasses gave her an owl-like appearance, and I noticed she drew out the word *who*, so it sounded like she was hooting. And she loved rhetorical questions. Already that morning, she'd said, "Whooo can resist a book with a dog on the cover?" as well as, "Whooo doesn't love a trashy beach read on vacation?"

We ate our cake in silence.

She kept looking at me as though she expected something shocking to happen, like for me to reach into my purse and reveal the cat I'd brought with me to work. Then again, given what I knew about my fellow librarians back home, a cat in the purse wouldn't exactly be shocking. Two cats would raise an eyebrow.

The cake didn't have any flavor in my mouth, but I chalked it up to nerves. I hoped Kathy Carmichael liked me, but she seemed guarded, unsure about something.

She gave me a tight smile as she carved off another slice of cake.

"Zara, do you have any hobbies? Are you into crafting?"

"Not really," I answered honestly, and as soon as the words were out, I knew I'd made a mistake. She'd asked me because she liked crafting. Now what could I do? "I like costumes," I said.

"You sew?"

As much as it could potentially help my career, I couldn't lie. "No. I just buy costumes when theater companies sell off their excess."

"Hmm," she said.

"Are you a crafter?"

Her orange-brown eyes brightened, but she'd just taken a huge bite of cake and couldn't speak.

I decided to go out on a limb and regale her with something personal.

"The strangest thing happened to me last night," I said, and I recounted my unusual nighttime activity.

When I finished the anecdote, Kathy stared at me like I was a talking raccoon. As the head librarian as well as the director, she was the one who'd interviewed me and hired me the previous month. Now she looked like she was having some regrets.

"Sleep-toasting?" Kathy pushed her round glasses up her pointed nose and scrutinized me with owlish blinks.

"Never mind," I said with a hand wave. "I'm sure last night's sleep-toasting was just a one-time thing, like making a soufflé. Everyone has to try it once to figure out it's not for them. After all, a soufflé is just a weirdly eggy cake with a bunch of hot air inside."

"Soufflé is overrated," Kathy agreed, smiling. An image came to my head of Kathy in a kitchen, proudly offering someone a wedge of her prized quiche.

I didn't know where the idea had come from, but I ran with it. "But you know what's not overrated? *Quiche*."

Her orange-brown eyes widened behind her round glasses, and she hooted, "Whooo doesn't love quiche?"

I got a mental image of a box of recipes. "I'm on the hunt for a great quiche recipe," I said, which was a string of words I'd never expected to hear coming from my mouth. I've never been a fan of cooking by the rules, or cooking at all. Recipes, I've often joked, were for the olden days, before the invention of takeout menus.

Kathy grabbed a pen and note card from a nearby stack and began hastily writing something out. Her handwriting matched her appearance. Her Vs were small and pointy like her nose, and her Os were perfectly round like her glasses.

"You'll love my recipe for asparagus and crispy bacon quiche," she said.

I took the note card and held it to my chest. "Thank you so much," I said. "Now, are you going to tell me what FPF stands for?"

She glanced over at the remaining cake. "Fresh Pastry Friday," she said with a sigh. "It's also the day we clean out the fridge."

"Put me on the rotation for this week," I said.

She gave me a blank look. "So, you're staying?"

"Of course," I said. "Why wouldn't I be staying? Don't tell me you guys have a trap door here, leading to a dungeon where you dispose of new librarians who don't fit in."

Her blank look became one of puzzlement. "Trap door?"

"Never mind." I gave her a big smile. "Break time's over. Back to acronyms. Tell me more about your WSC and ILL."

* * *

Kathy continued to train me throughout the morning.

The library's procedures were not atypical, but the place did have some interesting quirks.

One unusual thing in particular was the Grumpy Corner. This was a darkened corner of the staff lounge that was outfitted with beanbag chairs, big pillows, and two space heaters for winter use. Any member of staff could go there to chill at any time, even outside of official breaks, without judgment.

"That's a really good idea," I said when Kathy showed me the Grumpy Corner.

"Isn't it, though? I love being a librarian, but, well, you know."

I agreed completely. Being a librarian is a wonderful job, but like all careers, it comes with specific stresses. Patrons expect you to have all the answers, and sometimes you don't. When one thing goes wrong, it can become a cascade. A patron complaining about the homeless gentleman snoring in the science fiction section can lead to tension that aggravates the RSI earned from hours of repetitive book shelving. And then there's the local Conspiracy Guy, and the students who expect you to do their homework for them, and the people who hand you their phone because they can't understand the accent of the person they've reached at customer service for their online banking.

At lunchtime, Kathy forced me to go on my break. I wanted to keep learning more, but she insisted I take my mandatory meal break.

Alone in the staff lounge, I nibbled through my lunch while jotting down a to-do list for home. I wrote *finish unpacking*. That didn't feel very inspiring, so I wrote underneath it, *buy new boots to celebrate being unpacked*. Then, upon further consideration, I crossed out everything except *buy new boots*.

I finished my list and still had a few minutes left, so I looked around for a way to make myself useful. Kathy had mentioned that a fridge clean-out happened on Fridays, so I got a head start on things. I opened the staff fridge and removed all the plastic containers holding moldy leftovers and mystery mush, chucked the food into the compost bin, and gave all the containers a good scrub with hot, soapy water.

I dried my hands and ran out to the circ desk to relieve Kathy for her own break.

She returned a few minutes later, clutched my arm with her cold hand, and whispered, "Who threw out my lunch? Whooo?" Her golden-orange, owl-like eyes blinked behind her round glasses.

"Who?" I winced and thumbed my chest. "That would be me. But I swear I only tossed out the old stuff that looked gross."

"You threw out my acorn jelly?" Her voice cracked like she was on the verge of crying.

"Was it a brown, gelatinous sludge?"

Kathy nodded and sniffed. "It's called *dotori muk*. My Korean neighbor made it for me."

"Does your neighbor not like you very much?" I grinned, waiting for her laugh, but it never came.

"Who would throw out someone's lunch? And then joke about it? Did Vinnie put you up to this? I should have known better."

I didn't know who Vinnie was, but didn't ask her to clarify. I hung my head. "It was all my idea. Just me. I'm so sorry, boss. I'll run out now and buy you a whole new lunch. What do you want? Sushi? Pizza? Let me make it up to you." I gazed at her with my most repentant expression.

"Never mind," she said softly, turning away. "You have a patron waiting at circ."

She was right. A woman stood at the counter, impatiently tapping her library card on the top of a stack of books. Card tapping was the height of passive aggressiveness in a library, but maybe I deserved it.

I checked out the patron's books, and when I was done with her, I popped my head into the staff lounge.

Kathy was sitting in the Grumpy Corner with a blanket over her face.

My heart sank.

So much for my first day.

My Monday had started off so well. The patrons I'd met so far were wonderful.

I'd introduced some juvenile readers to the perfect new series.

And I'd experienced the profound joy of reuniting an older gentleman with a beloved story he'd feared he'd never see again, its title forgotten long before the emotional resonance. With the book in hand, he'd practically skipped out the front door.

But all of that felt hollow now that I'd failed to win over my new boss.

I wanted to throw myself at her feet and beg forgiveness. If she were my daughter, I'd know exactly what to do. I'd tickle her and wrestle her for the best beanbag chair. But Kathy Carmichael was an adult, a grown woman with somewhere between two and five full-grown sons—she'd kept mentioning various sons in passing but hadn't gone into detail.

I left the head librarian alone and decided to try harder on Tuesday.

I kept my head down for the rest of the day and focused on doing my job.

At the end of my shift, I used the library's old-fashioned punch-card system to punch out my time card with a loud KERCLUNK.

The loud punch-card system was another of the institution's strange little quirks. It was an awfully noisy choice for a place of quiet.

As I exited through the front door, I pulled out my phone and checked my daughter's recent messages. According to the last grouping of texts, she'd had a smooth first day at her new school. She was staying late to get some extra homework. The teachers didn't want to overload her, but she insisted.

I smiled.

That was my Zoey.

Since I had some free time, I took out my to-do list to figure out what to do next.

There was only one item: *buy new boots.*

CHAPTER 9

After the dry air of the library, the outside world felt moist and breezy. The clean, floral scent of spring invigorated me. I had a spring in my step as I walked down the street. The pretty town of Wisteria was all around me, so charming with its old stone buildings and many downtown churches. I'd never seen so many churches in such a relatively small area.

Something dark in the sky caught my eye. I looked up at the biggest bird I'd ever seen. Was it a bald eagle? They did nest in this area. But no, the huge bird's head wasn't white. And if anything, this winged beast was larger. What was bigger than a bald eagle? My librarian brain kicked into research mode. *By biggest, are we looking for heaviest by weight or longest wingspan?* I'd looked up this exact question earlier today for a patron. The Andean condor of South America is the largest flying bird in the world by combined measurement of weight and wingspan. It has a wingspan of twelve feet. You might wonder, what does the Andean condor eat? Anything it wants!

The giant bird, which couldn't have been the Andean condor given I wasn't currently in the Andes Mountains, flapped away out of my sight.

My fingers twitched. I rubbed my hands together while I kept my eyes on the sky. My hands felt funny, like they were crackling.

The strange tingling sensation was probably my skin getting used to the particular brand of hand sanitizer used at the WPL. There's nothing quite like an alcohol-based lotion to let you know how many fresh paper cuts you've acquired during a day at the library.

The bird didn't reappear, so I continued my walk.

I reached a corner and turned left without thinking, as though I'd lived in the town far longer than three days plus two nights.

Strangely, there seemed to be something pulling me from the inside, guiding me somewhere. I kept walking, following the pull, curious to see what would happen next.

I'd never felt anything quite like this. It was like hunger, but not hunger. I did have a powerful craving for something. Fried chicken? Carrot cake? That Malaysian durian fruit that smells like rotten onions and pungent gym socks? No, this craving was more complex.

The feeling, which was near my stomach but not in my stomach, tugged me down the street. An image of leather boots came to mind.

Wow, I thought. *I must really need to buy new boots.*

As I passed a store window and glanced at my reflection, I noticed a familiar figure behind me, across the street. Had Zoey finished at school already and come to meet up with me? When I turned to wave at my daughter, though, she wasn't there. Just happy-looking people walking to and fro. I caught a glimpse of the back of a woman who had long red hair. But she wasn't my daughter. Zoey would never wear a big skirt with giant flowers all over it, let alone paired with a floral blouse.

A door opened next to me, and the scent of leather hit my nostrils.

My brain practically screamed. *New boots!*

I wasn't normally such a shopaholic. I was a little concerned about these new compulsions I was feeling. I had half a mind to go straight home and put my feet up until it passed, but the other half of my mind was already propelling me through the shoe store's entrance.

I decided to roll with it. Even if there was some mystical force compelling me to visit that particular store on that particular street, what was the worst thing that could happen?

I paused just long enough to read the name of the store. Open Toad Shoes. I chortled to myself. You move to an adorable small town, you get stores with pun names. I went inside Open Toad Shoes with a smile on my face.

Like most of the stores in Wisteria, this was an independent seller, not part of a chain. The decor was old fashioned, but the store had wonderful boots, in every heel height and color imaginable.

A friendly-looking man with a white mustache gave me a cheerful sales pitch. "We're having a special today, since it's Monday. You can try on every boot in the store for free." He grinned to show me he was joking. "That's the special deal we run on days that end in Y. Left foot and right foot. All test walks inside the store are free."

I smiled back. "Is everyone in this town so delightful?"

"Yes," he said with a serious nod. "It's the law, ma'am. See any shoes you like?"

I pointed to some cute saddle shoes with dark laces. "I'd love to start with those if you have them in my size, which is—"

He held up one hand and cut me off. "Don't tell me! Most people don't know their true size anyway, so we'd better get you measured up." He waved me over to a bench. "Have a seat, please, and remove those horrendous things."

I gave him a mock-indignant look as I unlaced my shoes. They were basic and comfortable, but I couldn't defend them. They really were horrendous, and we both knew it.

The door to the shop jingled, and another customer came in. The white-mustached man did a double take as he greeted the new customer. I was curious about who or what had surprised him, but when I turned to look, the customer had already ducked behind a display.

The white-mustached man kneeled before me, lifted one of my feet carefully, and measured it. To my surprise, he didn't use a metal or wood device. He placed my foot against his forearm. Sole to skin. He had small markings up and down his forearm, possibly tattoos. The fitting process was more intimate than I'd expected, but after a few days in Wisteria, I was starting to expect the unexpected.

"Interesting," he said. "You have a foot twin, and she's sitting right behind you."

"Foot twin?" I glanced over my shoulder. The other customer who'd just arrived had taken a seat on the wooden bench behind me. I couldn't see her face, but her long hair was the same shade of red as mine.

The shopkeeper didn't say more about my alleged foot twin. He winked at me and said, "I'll be back in a jiffy with your new favorite boots."

When he returned, he had a long box containing boots. He'd completely ignored my request to try on the saddle shoes. He must have known I wasn't serious about buying them. The boots he'd brought out were buttery soft and fit like they'd been custom made. I hadn't even finished lacing them, and they were already my new favorite boots. I reached for the price tag with some trepidation, but the price was very reasonable.

"Perfect," I said. "I'll take these ones, and I'll even wear them out."

"Of course you will." He wore a wide grin below his bushy white mustache. He flicked his gaze up at something behind me, frowned, and looked into my eyes again. "I hope you don't mind me asking, but how closely are you two gorgeous redheads related?"

I turned around just as the woman on the bench behind me turned. We looked into each other's hazel eyes.

I felt my eyebrows rising with surprise. I saw hers rise in unison. I opened my mouth. She opened hers. The effect was like looking in a mirror.

The stranger and I had the exact same coloring, from our red hair to our hazel eyes, and the same oval-shaped faces. She was a few years older than me, but I could see why the store owner pegged us as being related. To me, the woman with the red hair looked like a computer simulation of an imaginary person, halfway between me and my mother. I tilted my head to the side, wondering who I looked like to her.

Without waiting for an answer, the shopkeeper said, "You must be sisters."

"I don't have a sister," I said, breaking eye contact with the woman to take in her floral blouse and flower-dotted skirt. She had been the person who'd caught my eye from across the street.

The woman smiled. "Such a shame you don't have a sister."

"But I do have a few stray relatives," I said. "Weird ones."

She gave me a knowing look. "Is that so?"

I folded one leg under me so I could face her squarely. She looked exactly like my mother, the way I remembered her. I reached out and touched my finger to her shoulder to make sure she was solid. She was real.

"I know your name," I said. "You're Ms. Riddle."

She smiled. "I am."

"And you know a man named Griebel. He's a short man who looks like a gnome."

Her eyebrows rose higher. "Have you been following me around, Zara?"

I looked down at the flowers on her skirt, and it hit me. My mother had always refused to wear anything floral because it reminded her too much of her weird, bratty little sister.

I snapped my fingers. "Aunt Zinnia!"

My mother's younger sister smiled. "In the flesh."

"Well, this is quite the coincidence," I said.

She narrowed her hazel eyes and pursed her lips. "Don't tell me your mother raised you to believe in coincidences."

CHAPTER 10

I stared at my long-lost relative.

Zinnia didn't think that the two of us bumping into each other in a small-town boot store was a coincidence?

Wow. She was exactly as crazy as my mother had always said.

The eager shopkeeper, who'd been listening quietly the whole time, clapped his hands. "How wonderful! A surprise family reunion happening right here in my shoe store. I knew something was afoot, so to speak, when I noticed you were foot twins."

I couldn't tear my eyes away from my aunt. She looked so much like my mother, who'd been dead for five years. It had been at my mother's funeral where I'd last seen my aunt. Before that, she hadn't been part of our lives.

Since the last time I'd seen Zinnia, she had grown to look even more like my mother. Looking into those familiar hazel eyes was like staring at a ghost.

My whole body was numb. My jaw ached, and my eyes burned.

I didn't know whether to laugh, cry, scream, or put my head between my knees and wait for the nausea to pass. Just when I thought I was going to embarrass myself by exploding into a million sobbing pieces, a cool breeze tickled at the back of my head.

The coolness reached around, pressing on my forehead like a cool hand. My ears and nostrils felt icy, as though the air around me had turned to liquid peppermint and I was breathing it in.

The coolness floated up, through my sinuses.

I sneezed three times.

And then a wave of tranquility washed over me. I was staring into the eyes of my crazy aunt, who I never thought I'd see again, and I knew exactly what to do.

I heard a little voice in the back of my head. *Never pass up the opportunity to be a gracious hostess and make the first move!*

"Zinnia, darling," I said calmly. The words flowed from my mouth like liquid peppermint. "You simply must come for dinner at my house. We shall have rack of lamb, and you can meet my daughter. How about seven o'clock? We'll have cocktails at seven and dinner by eight, like civilized people. How does Friday work for you, darling?"

Zinnia's hazel eyes twitched. Her jaw moved a few times, but no sound came out.

We faced off a full minute before she slowly turned away from me, leaned forward over her knees, and began taking off her shoes.

"Friday works for me," she said without looking up.

The shopkeeper, who had disappeared while I was sneezing, returned with a tissue for me and a pair of boots for Zinnia.

Her boots were a different style from mine, only ankle height, but they appeared to be the same size. We really were foot twins.

Zinnia cleared her throat. "When did you move to Wisteria? Myself, I adore living here, but most of the country has never heard of the place."

I glanced over at the shopkeeper. He was still grinning and staring but had moved himself over to the shop's front counter to give us some privacy.

I answered, "What makes you think I'm not here on holidays?"

"You invited me to dinner at *your* house, which I presume is here in Wisteria."

"Oh, yes. *My house.* How I've always loved the sound of that phrase. My house. Mine. I'm going to be working that phrase into every conversation I have for the next year."

"You're so much like your mother. She did love having things that were all her own." She chuckled softly, still leaning over her knees and tying her laces. "I miss her so much."

I raised my eyebrows. How could you miss someone you never saw in the first place?

I wanted to press her for more, but sitting on a bench in a shoe store was not the place to dig into the intricacies of Riddle family dynamics. Whatever happened between her and the rest of the family, it hardly mattered anymore.

By some strange coincidence—and I did believe it was a coincidence—we were both now living in the same town. And we were family. We'd be seeing a lot more of each other.

I borrowed a pen and paper from the store owner, wrote out my address, and handed the paper to my aunt.

"Beacon Street," she said, frowning at the paper. "This address looks familiar. It's not a red house, is it?"

"As a matter of fact, the house is a gorgeous shade called Wisconsin Barn Red." As soon as I'd named the color, a question echoed in my head. How did I know the house was Wisconsin Barn Red?

"I do know that house," Zinnia said. "I used to visit someone there."

"Was it a woman named Winona Vander Zalm?"

Zinnia's face lit up and then slowly fell as realization dawned on her. "Oh, dear," she said. "Is Winnie okay? I haven't seen her in ages. Now I can't remember if she sent me a Christmas card last year." Her pale face grew even more pale, highlighting the smattering of freckles on the bridge of her nose. She looked up at me with sad eyes that reminded me of my daughter's.

"The former homeowner died peacefully," I said. "Or at least that's what I've been told."

Zinnia coughed into her fist. "How did she die?"

I held both of my hands out, palms up. "Peacefully, in her sleep. Or so I heard. It all happened long before I arrived on the scene. I only got here on Saturday."

"The day before your daughter's sixteenth birthday," Zinnia said.

"For a lady I haven't seen in years, you sure keep close tabs on me." I reached for my wallet, ready to pay for my boots and leave Open Toad Shoes. The quaintness was starting to feel claustrophobic.

Zinnia said plainly, "I have an excellent memory for dates."

"Did you follow me in here?"

She wrinkled her nose and frowned. "Of course not. Don't be a ding-dong."

Don't be a ding-dong? Was she making fun of me through imitation? No. Calling people ding-dongs was something I'd picked up from my mother. It had to be a family trait.

I looked at the piece of paper in her hands and wondered if it wasn't too late to retract my invitation to dinner. Family has a way of rubbing off on each other, bad habits and all. There was something very odd about my aunt, and I didn't want it to rub off on my daughter.

The store owner clicked away at his computer keyboard and announced the total for my boots.

Zinnia piped up, "Put my niece's boots on my tab, please." To me, she said, "I know it doesn't make up for missing out on so much of your life so far, but I hope you'll accept this small gift from me. It's the least I can do, considering your kind invitation to dinner."

"Uh, sure, but you might change your mind after you taste my cooking on Friday." Had I actually promised to cook? And had the phrase *rack of lamb* actually come from my lips?

Zinnia got to her feet and came at me in a twirl of floral fabrics. She grabbed my arm and let out a sound that can only be described as a cackle.

She squeezed my arm. "Zara, darling, I'm sure whatever you whip up, it will be intriguing!"

She cackled again.

Just like a witch.

That was it! That was what my mother used to call her. Zinnia the Witch.

CHAPTER 11

Zoey leaned on her elbows on the kitchen island and watched with equal parts of interest and disgust as I wrestled the meat from its butcher paper packaging.

Four days had passed since I'd seen Zinnia Riddle and invited her to dinner. I'd been so busy learning the ropes at the library and trying to get the household in order that I hadn't given much thought to the cooking of the meal. My aunt, who my mother always referred to as a crazy witch, was coming to dinner.

Zoey had taken the news in stride. Her chief concern was over what to call this new relative. She was Zoey's great-aunt, but the woman was only forty-eight, and great-aunt seemed like a title for a much older person. Zinnia was only sixteen years older than me. Other than that, I didn't know much about the woman.

I finally got the chunk of meat free from its paper wrap. *Now what?*

Zoey wasn't much help. "Mom, what possessed you to promise you'd cook someone rack of lamb?"

"Funny you should mention me being possessed," I said. "When I invited Aunt Zinnia to come for dinner, it felt like I wasn't even the person inviting her. The words came out of my mouth like I was in a play, reciting lines. And before that, my feet pretty much walked themselves into the shoe store. I wasn't in control of myself."

Her light-red eyebrows arched up in amusement. "How's this different from usual?"

"Ha ha," I said. "Two points for the teenager. Good one." I gingerly grabbed the meat and plopped it on a pan. "Seriously, though, it didn't feel like me talking. And when we were talking, I told her the house was painted Wisconsin Barn Red. When I got home, I googled it, and," I lowered my voice to a dramatic whisper, "that's exactly what color this house is painted. Spooky, huh?"

She frowned. "I think you're being paranoid. Dorothy the Realtor must have told you the color. It was buried in your subconscious until you needed a fun fact. That happens to me sometimes. For example," she picked up the squeeze bottle of honey on the kitchen island, "honey bees control the temperature inside the hive to affect the development of their young. The smallest change in environment can change their programming and determine what job duties their young will do once they mature."

"Does it work on young humans? What temperature should I program into the thermostat to make you answer the doorbell without being prodded?"

"Ha ha," she said. "Two points for the mother."

I went back to poking the blob of meat, and she pulled out her phone to look up more fun facts about honey bee colonies. Zoey was a natural student, always hungry for information about the world around her. We could never finish a trivia game because she'd get distracted looking up facts and history related to a question. When we did play a game, it was usually Scrabble. She was the reigning champion. I knew more words, but she was better at spatial relationships and seeing ways to maximize her score.

After a few minutes, Zoey looked up from her phone and asked, "If it wasn't you controlling your body, who was it?"

I'd given it some thought over the week and had a weird theory. "Have you ever heard about how objects might hold on to something from their previous owners? Sort of a vibration, or energy?"

Zoey frowned as she pushed the groceries on the kitchen island aside to make more room for herself. She was sitting on one of the barstools we had bought earlier that week for the kitchen. She reached for her school bag and set her books on the counter. It was Friday night, and my daughter was already doing her homework.

She opened a science textbook to the index page and ran her finger down the list. "I don't see anything in here about vibrations," she teased.

"Well, you're not going to find anything in a *science* book. But there are things scientists can't explain."

She stretched, pulled the elastic band from her hair, and began fluffing out her long red hair. "Like what?"

"Like how I decided to move to the same small town where my long-lost aunt lives."

She narrowed her hazel eyes at me. "Chaos theory," she said with relish. "All complex systems rely on an underlying order. The smallest events can cause very complex behaviors or events that appear to be coincidence but are not." She sat up straight on her kitchen stool. "Someone in your family must have spoken favorably about Wisteria. Or else"— she stuck her finger in the air —"maybe there's something in your genetics that makes you particularly sensitive to the chemicals given off by blossoming wisteria vines. Neurons that fire together wire together. And so when you heard of a town that was named Wisteria, your body responded with a rush of motivating dopamine. All this happened on a subconscious level."

I blinked at her. "You're like a wizard."

She rolled her eyes.

"Speaking of magic," I said, "maybe it's the house itself that's possessing me."

"Hmm." She looked skeptical. "Should I be concerned about you levitating in your sleep, or your head spinning around?"

"Not possession, exactly. Remember the architect who lived in our building? He said that all structures cast spells on people, in a way."

"Do you mean the bald guy who grew orchids? He went to school to be an architect, but he worked in the accounts receivable department at a shopping mall. He did, however, wear very nice suits. And he had over a hundred pairs of shoes."

"Now you're making me miss home." I waved a hand. "Anyway, he said that structures have the power to manipulate people. If you squeeze visitors in through a tight mudroom and then let them pass into an airy, lofted foyer, they'll stand up straight and feel like they can fly, even though they're inside. A building can make people feel things."

Zoey looked around the kitchen. "This place does give me good feelings."

"Exactly. The kitchen is so welcoming that it's bringing us even closer together. We never hung out together in our old kitchen, because it was like the galley of a small boat. When you sat at the table with homework and I was around the corner in the kitchen, there was always a wall in the way. Maybe that's why I never took an interest in cooking before."

Zoey was quiet, probably realizing her mother had a point.

After less than a week, we were already in a new yet comfortable routine. I would get home from work around the same time she got home from school, and we'd been meeting in the kitchen to catch up on each other's days. She would start her homework while I clanged around with pots and pans.

"Maybe this house has cast a spell on us," Zoey said. "But it hasn't literally cast any spells because that's crazy talk. I'm sorry I thought there was a ghost in the attic when we moved in. Trust me, I regret putting that idea into your head. Can we just drop all the mumbo jumbo?" She patted her science textbook.

I looked over the array of fresh herbs and unfamiliar groceries I'd picked up on my way home. "Ghost or no ghost, something has changed. I think the home's former owner, Winona Vander Zalm, has become my muse." I picked up a sprig of rosemary and crushed it between my fingertips to bring out the scent.

My daughter studied me carefully. "Are you saying the dead lady who used to live here is making you get up in the middle of the night and burn toast?"

I dropped my handful of fresh rosemary sprigs. "You know about the sleep-toasting?"

"You're not exactly quiet when you get up in the middle of the night." She opened her textbook, read a few paragraphs from one page, and abruptly looked up at me. "Did you say you've been sleep-toasting? As in sleepwalking and then sleep-toasting? That sounds like a disorder."

"It's not a big deal," I said casually. "The elevation here is different from back home. My sleep cycle has been disrupted, but I'm sure everything will be back to normal soon."

"Not if you're possessed by the ghost of the late Winona Vander Zalm."

I stared down at the pan full of lamb meat, which looked nothing like the photo in the cookbook. "If I really was possessed, I would know what to do with this thing."

She twisted her lips from side to side thoughtfully. "You need little white booties. Whenever I see rack of lamb on a cooking show, it's wearing little booties."

"Aunt Zinnia will be here in three hours. What else do we have in the fridge in case this doesn't work out?"

"We've got vegetarian hot dogs in the freezer. Remember we watched that documentary about the meat industry on Tuesday, and on Wednesday we were vegetarian for almost the whole day."

"And then on Thursday I declared a ban on documentaries."

"And now it's Friday, and you have two hours and fifty-nine minutes to get some little booties onto some part of that meaty monstrosity."

I clapped my hands. "Mix your hard-working mother a cocktail. Make it a *mojito*. That's white rum, sugar, lime juice, soda water, and mint."

She gave me an irritated look. "I've known how to make a mojito since I was twelve."

"Please don't use that phrase when we have people over." I snapped my fingers. "Make it a double."

"I've got homework."

"It's Friday night," I said. "Homework can wait."

"I'm nervous about meeting my great-aunt. Homework makes me feel centered."

I batted my eyelashes at her. "A nice mojito will make your mother feel centered, and she's the one cooking your dinner."

Zoey let out a weary groan but closed her textbook and began gathering the supplies to mix me a drink.

When Zoey was twelve, she'd seen the shiny cocktail shakers and fancy glasses in another family's apartment and had taken an interest in bartending. She didn't drink any of the alcohol, but she loved following the recipe guide and making fancy concoctions straight from a sixties-era book on mixology. I loved tasting her creations, but I drew the line at the drinks that included raw egg whites.

While she filled our cocktail shaker with ice, I raised both hands in the air dramatically. "Oh, ghostly spirit of Winona Vander Zalm, I'm in way over my head with this rack of lamb. Oh, ghostly spirit, I need your help!"

Zoey looked mortified, even though there was no one else in the kitchen except the two of us.

As usual, her mortification only encouraged me. I twitched rhythmically while chanting under my breath. "Winona, I call on you to help me make a rack of lamb. Winona, fill me with your spirit. Oh, wise and ghostly one, close my eyes and open them to another world. Guide me now, you attention-loving, event-hopping, party-throwing, good-looking socialite."

A breeze blew through the kitchen, seemingly from nowhere. The air turned to liquid peppermint, and my sinuses tingled. I sneezed three times, and then the world seemed brighter and more colorful.

My daughter handed me a mojito with crushed green leaves swirling between the ice cubes. "That's fresh mint from our back yard," she said. "Underneath the jungle, there are some good plants."

"This house really is paradise." I took a sip. "Perfect," I said in a snooty voice. "Put this on my tab. It's Vander Zalm, darling."

She ignored me and went back to her homework. "That mint smell is really overwhelming, don't you think?"

"That's the ghost." I raised my arms higher and moaned. "Ghostly one, share with me your wisdom." A shivery feeling snaked up the backs of my legs, like a cool blanket made of silk.

Without looking up from her book, Zoey commented, "You could always try reading the recipe."

"I could, but... I don't need to."

In a flash, the instructions had come to me. I knew exactly how to make a rack of lamb, from the marinade to the final grilling. I knew that the paper frills—the things Zoey had called booties—were used for covering the exposed rib bones, and they were called *manchettes*. I knew it all. All it had taken was a little relaxation, in the form of a tasty fresh mojito, to get things rolling.

As I worked, I hummed a tune I'd never heard before.

I didn't find any of this strange.

That's the thing about being possessed by a ghost. Sometimes you don't even notice until it's too late.

CHAPTER 12

Zinnia arrived at 7:05 p.m. with a bottle of wine in one hand and a large lamp in the other. Seeing her was, once again, like looking at myself in a mirror—if I'd tied my red hair up in a classic librarian bun and gotten dressed in the dark. On her bottom half, she wore a hybrid garment that was neither a skirt nor trousers. It was a *skort*, green and corduroy, ending around her knees. On her upper half, she wore a voluminous blouse, accented with a fitted vest made out of a floral material that would look right at home on a sofa.

I try not to judge a book by its cover, but Zinnia's appearance gave off a seriously kooky vibe. For the first time in my life, I finally understood how my daughter felt when she judged my own fashion choices.

The lamp in her hand had flowers all over the base and even more flowers on the shade. It was so thoroughly ugly that it almost veered toward being cute. Almost.

I invited her in, eyeing the lamp with suspicion. "Are you on your way somewhere else after this?"

"No," she said.

"I guess you walk around with a big lamp for self-defense? Smart. Nobody's going to mess with you when you're packing something that's the perfect size for bludgeoning."

Zoey appeared at my side by the entrance. "Mom and I rate everyday household objects by their bludgeoning capacity. That lamp of yours would score a seven out of ten."

I watched as my two family members laid eyes on each other for the first time.

Zinnia gave my daughter an amused smile. "What would score a ten for bludgeoning?"

Zoey and I answered in unison, "Pewter candlesticks."

"Naturally," Zinnia said, nodding. "Followed by what? A heavy pipe wrench?"

Zoey sniffed in amusement. "Wrenches are no good," she said. "Someone would *notice* if you left a heavy wrench lying around on your fireplace mantel. You'd lose the element of surprise."

Zinnia looked from Zoey to me. "Zara, your daughter is lovely, and so sharp."

I ruffled Zoey's red hair. "Sharpest pencil in the pack," I said proudly. "Time for official introductions. Aunt Zinnia, meet Zolanda Daizy Cazzaundra Riddle, Zoey for short." I looked into my aunt's hazel eyes. "Since you're my mother's sister, that makes you Zoey's great-aunt, and her your great-niece." I put my hand beside my mouth and stage-whispered, "She's very concerned about what she should call you."

Zinnia's hazel eyes seemed to glow as she beamed at Zoey. "Just call me Zinnia. No need to call me *great* until I've done something of greatness to deserve it. Such respect must be earned."

Zoey shuffled from one foot to the other shyly. "How about Auntie Z?"

Zinnia's hazel eyes darted between us. Her nose wrinkled and one of her eyes twitched. "That sounds an awful lot like something familiar. But I can't quite recall."

"Anti-Z," I said. "That's the name of the zombie antivirus they used on *Wicked Wives*."

My aunt made a strangled sound. "That horrible TV show?"

Zoey looked down at the floor. "I'll just call you Zinnia," she said glumly.

Zinnia looked at me for guidance. As far as I knew, she didn't have any children. She was unaccustomed to the teenage roller coaster ride of high hopes and dashed expectations. I gave her a quasi-helpful shrug.

"Zoey, if it's what you want, then you should call me Auntie Z," she said. "I insist."

I gave her a smile and a nod. If this had been a test, she'd have passed with a B+.

She thrust the floral-patterned lamp at us. "Happy housewarming. I'm sorry it only scores seven out of ten for bludgeoning."

Zoey squealed and took the lamp, hugging it to her chest. "Auntie Z, I love this," she gushed. "We went shopping downtown last week, and I tried to find a lamp, but none of the ones we saw had any character."

"It's all yours," Zinnia said. "I bought your mother a pair of boots earlier this week, so you may have the lamp. It's a family heirloom."

I swung my arm in faux-disappointment. "Aw, shucks," I said. "I'll have to make do with visiting the lamp in your room, kiddo."

The three of us exchanged friendly, cautious glances. We were still standing in the entryway. I knew it would be polite to invite her in and offer her a drink, but I was frozen. I hadn't realized how badly I craved familial connection until I'd gotten a taste. I'd never given much thought to my estranged aunt, but now I was nervous that I might screw up dinner so badly she never wanted to see us again.

Zinnia's eyes locked on mine, and I got the strangest sensation she was reading my mind. *I'm nervous as well*, her eyes seemed to say.

She stretched out her arms. "We ought to hug now," Zinnia said. She waved her hands, and a force not unlike gravity sucked Zoey toward one outstretched arm and me into the other. Zoey held out the lamp so it would not be crushed in the fray. We squeezed each other in a friendly three-person hug.

I extricated myself and suggested Zoey take Zinnia on a tour of our new house.

"It looks grander than I remember," Zinnia said, glancing up at the antique hanging light fixtures and ceiling trim.

Zoey said, "Mom told me you knew the former owner."

"I didn't know Winona Vander Zalm as well as I would have liked, I'm afraid. But that's all in the past. I plan to get to know my lovely niece and my equally lovely grand-niece quite well."

Zoey hopped up the stairs, lamp in hand. "Come and help me find the perfect place in my bedroom for the new lamp."

I took the bottle of wine my aunt had brought and told her to go ahead.

Zinnia gave me a worried look. "Do you have a corkscrew?"

"I'm a librarian," I said. "If you ever need a corkscrew, a USB stick, or a new cat, just ask a librarian."

She frowned. "I haven't heard that before." She sniffed the air. "You don't have a cat."

"Allergies," I said. "Go on up and look around while I uncork this and let it breathe."

While they climbed the stairs and toured around the upper floor and the attic, I went to the kitchen to check on the food and final preparations. The lamb had already marinated in rosemary and herbs. It would take almost no time to cook in my preheated oven. Everything had come together as if by magic, and I couldn't wait for our guest of honor to take her first bite.

* * *

We kicked off the party with cocktails—mojitos for the adults and cranberry juice for the minor. Zoey talked about Corvin, the funny little boy next door whom she'd decided to adopt as a little brother.

"His name is Corvin?" Zinnia asked. "That's an unusual name. I believe it means raven."

We were seated in the living room with our drinks and appetizers. I had the wingback recliner, positioned near the doorway so I could run into the kitchen to tend the food periodically.

"Corvin even looks like a raven," Zoey said. "He's got shiny dark hair that's so black, it's practically blue."

"Probably a shapeshifter," Zinnia said with a nod. "He's in the blue house next door? They've got a circle window in the attic. Shapeshifters are drawn to houses with nonrectangular windows." She crunched on a carrot from the tray of crudités.

A shapeshifter? I could see why my mother referred to her baby sister as a kooky witch. The woman had mentioned shapeshifters with such a deadpan tone, I couldn't tell if she was joking or not.

Zoey squealed. "You're so cool, Auntie Z! It's not fair that I'm only meeting you now. If I'd known you my whole life, I'd be so much more interesting by now." She looked right at me. "No offense, Mom."

I held both of my hands up. "Don't blame me, kiddo. Your aunt had some sort of blowup with the rest of the family, and she took off like a leaf in the wind."

Zoey turned back to her great-aunt. "What was the fight about?"

With a sigh, Zinnia said, "It was a long time ago, before you were born."

"You can't remember?"

Zinnia leaned forward on the couch and stroked my daughter's cheek in a gesture that reminded me so much of my mother, my chest ached.

"Let sleeping dogs lie," Zinnia said softly.

"Promise you won't disappear again," Zoey said. "Promise."

Zinnia made a strange series of movements with both hands and intoned, "I promise to stand by you, no matter what."

An icy chill ran up my spine. Something strange was in the air, a pungent spice mixed with the cooking smells emanating from the kitchen. My skin prickled all over.

The timer for the oven beeped, and I jumped to my feet.

From that moment, I lost myself in the flow of preparing a sumptuous feast. The world turned soft, like I was looking at everything through sheer curtains undulating in a summer breeze.

Guided by unseen forces that were much better at entertaining than I'd ever been, I served dinner. The compliments flowed along with the drinks. The wine Zinnia had brought with her went perfectly with the herbs in the dinner.

I lost track of time because time was meaningless. All that mattered was the pleasure of good company and fine food. As soon as my daughter and my aunt finished their plates, I jumped into action, pushing more bites and nibbles their way despite their protests.

Zoey kept digging into history, trying to unearth the reason for Zinnia's absence from our family.

"Just give me a hint," Zoey pleaded. "I need to know what got you upset, so it doesn't happen again."

"I can assure you it won't happen again," Zinnia said to her. To me, she said, "Don't you dare put another rib on my plate or I will forget my manners and stab you with my fork."

Ignoring her threat, I shoved another rosemary-infused chunk onto her plate, along with a scoop of chickpea salad. I skillfully yanked my hands out of stabbing range.

Zoey whined, "But how can I believe you if I don't know what it was?"

"Because you're sixteen," Zinnia said. She hiccuped from the wine and looked mortified for a second.

Zoey quietly stared at her aunt. What did her being sixteen have to do with anything? I didn't know any more than she did, but unlike her, I wasn't terribly concerned. I just wanted everyone to eat all the food I'd made. I tossed another rib of lamb onto both of their plates while they weren't looking.

"How was your birthday party?" Zinnia asked. "Did you receive anything unusual?"

Zoey answered, "I got some new sheets that are made out of bamboo. They're very soft."

"What else? I'm not talking about physical objects." Zinnia narrowed her eyes and watched Zoey intently.

Zoey frowned. "Do you mean a new kind of skill?"

"Yes, yes," Zinnia said excitedly. "How did it manifest?"

"I got *that* when I was thirteen. The cramps were pretty bad at first, but now I take a pill when they start."

Zinnia's face fell. She looked over at me. "No gift?"

"I'm not made of money," I said defensively. "We went shopping, and I let her pick out a bunch of stuff for her room. What else am I supposed to do? Buy her a new car? I'm a working single mother."

Zinnia shook her head. "Never mind. I thought perhaps she'd gotten one of the family gifts."

"Like the lamp?" I asked. "Don't tell me there's a matching one out there." I shuddered.

"Family gifts," Zinnia repeated at a louder volume, which didn't help explain anything. "From the *family*."

"Sometimes I get ringing in my ears," I said. "Tinnitus. Do you mean something like that?"

Zinnia ignored me and turned back to Zoey. "Have you experienced anything unusual since your sixteenth birthday? Any strange sensations?"

"I'm a teenager living in a new town," Zoey said. "My hormones are raging, one of my boobs is growing faster than the other, and I can't seem to study for five hours straight like I used to. One of my legs will fall asleep, or I'll become overwhelmed by an overpowering desire to check my social media accounts. Do you consider any of that strange?"

"Never mind," Zinnia said.

I pushed my chair back and stood, shouting, "Toast!"

My daughter and my aunt stared at me blankly. What was I doing? I shrugged. I had no idea what I was doing, but I did shout, "We need toast!"

Zinnia picked up the empty wine bottle. "The wine's all gone, but we could still make a toast if you'd like. Do we have more cranberry juice for Zoey?"

"Toast!" I couldn't stop myself from saying it. I no longer had control of my body. "Toast!"

I turned and walked jerkily toward the kitchen. My body felt like it was attached to puppet strings. "Toast!"

Zoey and Zinnia followed after me.

"Is she drunk?" Zinnia asked.

"She might be sleep-toasting," Zoey said. "It's her version of sleepwalking. She's been getting up in the middle of the night and making toast. Six nights in a row now. It's very strange."

"Six nights?" Zinnia sounded both puzzled and excited. "I suppose it's possible," she muttered. "Maybe your gift transferred to her."

"What gift?" Zoey sounded frustrated. She tugged on my arm. "Mom! Stop being so weird! What are you doing?"

What was I doing? Just filling the sink with water. Hot, hot water. Nice and full.

Then I was plugging in the toaster. Pushing down the handle. Letting it get nice and hot.

I had to show them something. I was possessed by this urgent desire to show them something, to communicate what had happened to... not me. Someone who was inside me, but not me.

I heard my daughter cry out, "Auntie Z, what's happening to my mother?"

She answered, "Witchcraft."

Witchcraft?

Something happened with the toaster, and suddenly it was leaping through the air, plunging into the sink full of water.

My hands were in the water. The toaster splashed in, and pain jolted through me. Someone screamed.

The blackness rose up, like black velvet waves of calm. In my mind, I saw a wall of darkness, writhing with scorpions, pulsing with a life that could not be. And I saw another wall, concrete. Or was it a ceiling? And yet another ceiling that turned into a sky—a beautiful, cloudy sky. A winged creature flew over. Bigger than a blue jay. A dragon?

I separated from myself. I soared up, away from the pain. I floated up into the night sky, where I admired the beauty of the twinkling lights. Then I caught a rising air current, and soared over the town on wings of pink feathers.

CHAPTER 13

Pleasant dreams of pink feathers and flying through fluffy clouds dissipated.

My body felt heavy and rubbery, like a sack of raw, unbattered calamari.

I was awake. In a bed. In a dimly lit room that was, based on my bleary-eyed first impression, not my bedroom. Probably. I looked again. I'd been having this where-am-I feeling since the move, so I couldn't be sure. I was alone and under the covers but still wearing the clothes I'd been wearing earlier that evening. By the look of the dark window, it was nighttime. The room was softly lit by a bedside lamp with a floral-print shade. The lamp, which was a taller version of the one my aunt had brought as a housewarming gift, cast splotchy shadows all over the walls, which were covered in rose-bouquet wallpaper. *Nope. Not my new bedroom.*

Female voices floated in from the hallway. I tried to move, but my body made a cranky refusal. The rubbery calamari feeling in my bones changed to something brittle. I felt like I'd been taken apart and put together with staples and glue. And there was a smell in the room, or possibly inside my nostrils, like scorched peppermints.

Croakily, I called out, "Nurse? Hello?"

Zoey came running in, her pale cheeks glowing with rosy excitement. Clutched to her chest, she had a giant, leather-bound book—the sort of elaborate thing that looked like a prop from a movie about witchcraft.

Breathlessly, she said, "Mom, is that you?"

I groaned and peeked under the covers. "This body looks like mine, but we can't be too careful. Bring me a mirror."

She flung herself onto the bed next to me. The corner of the ancient-looking book jabbed painfully into my ribs.

"Mom, you had us so worried! You were totally possessed!"

"So you took me to a bed and breakfast?" I looked around at my brightly patterned surroundings. Everything was covered in floral print, from the curtains to the bed linens. "Have I died and gone to heaven? Does heaven look like an overdecorated bed and breakfast? This is the sort of thing I'd expect in hell." My words sank in. "Uh-oh. Am I in hell? Did I drink a bunch of Barberrian wine coolers and do something unbecoming of a lady?"

"Mom, stop talking. I have something important to tell you."

I struggled to sit upright. "Did you find the freight train that ran me over?"

"You're a witch," she said. The book continued to jab into my ribs. She repeated the words slowly for emphasis. "You're. A. Witch."

"Now, now. You may be unhappy with me for drinking too much at dinner and embarrassing myself, but we don't call each other names."

She sat up, shuffled to the edge of the bed, and opened the big book on her lap.

"Look," she said, pointing at an inky page. "This is you."

I finally hoisted myself upright. Stars swam in my head. I leaned over to look at the book. The pages were yellowed and covered in swirling cursive. Zoey pointed to a drawing that looked like something an ancient monk would have created by hand, back in the days before the printing press.

In the center of the page was a long-haired woman with her arms thrown high in the air. Around her floated swirls of text and beautiful, hand-drawn flowers. The look on her face was both serene and powerful. My pulse pounded in my head, but the pain in my body was all but gone.

Zoey poked at the page insistently. "Don't you see? That's you, inviting the spirit of Winona Vander Zalm to enter you."

I looked closer. "Is that a lamb roast in a pan in the foreground? And is that my pink leather purse on a counter in the background? This really is me."

"It sure is," she said.

"Do my eyes look that maniacal in real life? Whoever drew this gave me some serious crazy eyes. Did you do this? How did you get it drawn so quickly?"

"This was drawn hundreds of years ago," Zoey said in a deadpan voice.

"Very funny. Who drew this, really? Was it a new friend at school? Someone with a gift for caricature?" I frowned at the image. "It must have been a hormonal teenaged boy. My boobs are not that big, and I don't wear plunging necklines open to my belly button."

She sighed. "Yes, you do."

"Only at Halloween or other costumed events." I ran my finger across the drawing to see if the fresh ink would smudge. It didn't. "But your friend is really talented. Tell him I'll buy a print of this for our family Christmas cards."

"Mom, this is a very old book. Someone foretold your powers hundreds of years ago."

"Is this payback for me talking about the house being haunted? Okay, you've made your point. Your mother had too much wine and passed out, and you've concocted this elaborate prank to make her think she's crazy." I used my foot to push her off the bed so I could get up. I got to my feet, swayed, and collapsed back onto the bed again.

Zinnia appeared at the doorway, holding a glass of water. "Zara, you should be resting now," she said, her tone motherly and authoritative. "Drink some water and try to relax."

I took the water and sucked it back. Wiping my mouth, I said, "I already relaxed a little too much. Sorry about the dinner party and whatever I did. Was I dancing on tables? My right butt cheek feels tender, and it only gets that way after dancing on tables or bowling, and I'm pretty sure I wasn't bowling last night." I squinted up at my aunt. "Did we go bowling?"

"No," she said.

"Well, I should get out of your house, anyway. This is your house, is it not?"

Zinnia nodded. "This is my house."

"Give me a quick tour as I make my way out, since I don't remember the trip in. Let's talk again during daylight. We'll have a nice, daytime family reunion, and I'll only drink tea."

Zinnia grabbed a wooden chair from the corner of the room and brought it over to the bed. She sat next to me, gently took my hand, and stroked it with her cool fingers. She did something with her other hand, a quick thing that looked like her fingers were dancing, and she made a sound that was halfway between a whistle and a hum.

"Be calm," she said, and a wave of tranquility washed over me. My anxiousness to leave her guest room dissipated. There was nowhere else I needed to be, nowhere else I wanted to be. I could stay there forever. I would live out the rest of my days in that charming room, on that comfortable bed. Zoey stood at the foot of the bed, clutching the book, which was so large it made her look fourteen again.

Zinnia spoke soothingly. "Zara, we brought you to my house because I was afraid of what the ghost in your house would do next. After we left, I had an associate visit your house to do a sweep for spells and devices."

I gave Zoey a dirty look. "You've got your great-aunt in on your ghost prank?"

"It's not a prank," Zoey said. "Our house has a ghost, and you are a witch."

"A ghost and a witch," I mused. "Sounds legit."

Zinnia frowned. "No need to be sarcastic." She did a dancing movement with her hand again, and this time I felt her will being imposed on me. She wanted to suppress my sarcasm.

I steeled myself and fought. "If I'm a witch, what does that make you? A werewolf? No, don't tell me. You're a vampire."

"I'm a witch, like you."

"My mother always said you were a witch. What does that mean, exactly? I always thought it was a comment on your personality. Are you Wiccan or something?"

"No, I'm not Wiccan, though I respect their practices. I'm a witch. Just like you."

I snorted.

Zinnia muttered something under her breath and moved both of her hands in a complicated gesture. The room filled with tiny sparkling lights and the scent of sweet, sugary cotton candy. The smell pleasantly pushed away the lingering burned peppermint in my sinuses.

I reached up for the floating sparks, grinning like a ding-dong. I'd never seen anything like it outside of movies. The dazzling color shifted from purple to blue to teal and back again. I could almost catch the little fireflies of light, but they buzzed out of reach, like the end of the rainbow. In unison, the sparks spiraled up toward the ceiling and began to spin.

"Are you doing this?" I asked with breathless wonder. "What's happening? Am I dreaming all of this?"

She held up one hand and whistled. The lights spun faster. My head couldn't take the sense of motion. I clutched the edge of the bed.

She whistled again, at a lower pitch. The lights dimmed and gradually extinguished. The scent of cotton candy was replaced with the scent of ashes.

Zoey squealed and clapped her hands. "I want to do that! Will you teach me?"

Zinnia beamed at my daughter and explained that she would teach her, all in good time. And then she cast the spell again, this time moving her dancing fingers slower, almost slow enough for me to catch the movements.

And as she cast the light show again for my daughter, something changed inside me.

The little spark of desire that I'd always carried, the desire for there to be more to the world than science and physics, grew hotter and brighter, like a fireplace ember being blown upon.

And then, all at once, the flame caught and burned bright in my heart. I was filled with white light and all that was good. I saw my mother holding out her arms for me, my baby daughter gazing up at me, and countless rainbows and blossoming flowers and moonlit nights and crimson sunrises. I saw the smiles of every patron I'd helped locate the book they needed and the tears of gratitude of others I'd never met, being helped by other kind souls. I saw nothing but the good in humanity, the willingness to forgive, to self-sacrifice, to be open and to love.

Gradually, the room around me came into focus. I rubbed my fingers against the scratchy cotton of the pillowcase to pull myself back into my body.

Having seen and felt the evidence, I became a believer.

Aunt Zinnia was a witch.

I was a witch.

That actually did explain a few things.

CHAPTER 14

"Light magic is harder than it looks," my aunt said to my daughter. "When you both begin your novice training, you'll start with the basics—modulating sounds and shifting air movement. Have you studied musical instruments in school?"

Zoey raised her hand excitedly. "I've played the harp."

"How wonderful," Zinnia cooed. "Learning music is the perfect preparation for spellwork. If you can read sheet music, you'll find reading spells is only about ten times harder."

The two of them continued to chatter about musical scales and sheet music, their words blending into each other as though they were one person. The whole world was blurry and swirling again, even without the magical light show. My head didn't hurt, but it did feel like a theater stage where an avant-garde musical group was banging on garbage cans and stomping their feet to make lousy music.

I glanced over at the empty water glass on the bedside table. *I'd really prefer another mojito*, I thought. Did I? Was that a desire of my own, or of the ghost of socialite Winona Vander Zalm?

Meanwhile, my other redheaded family members were talking about harmonies and triads, and something about threading needles of sound to harness unseen forces.

Was nobody else concerned about my recent possession? My recollection was foggy, but I had a vivid memory of trying to electrocute myself with a toaster. Was I a suicide risk thanks to this wacky ghost?

Even as I worried, I also felt myself letting go of all fears. I was slipping away, separating from the present, sliding across time and space like a silk nightie falling off a hanger.

Somewhere nearby, a machine was whirring to life. I couldn't have known this as a regular human, but now my consciousness was expanding, flooding outward like the contents of an uncorked bottle of smoke. I felt the vibrations of a dark and dangerous machine, one that threatened to erase me. *Erase me?* How could anything erase me? Unless...

Was I, Zara Riddle, nothing more than an inky, large-boobed, doe-eyed drawing of a woman in an old, leather-bound book? I had always thought of myself as a real person, fleshed out in three dimensions, but what if I'd been wrong?

I'm so sorry, said a distant voice. *I can't ask you to forgive me for what I'm going to put you through, but I hope you'll at least understand. Zara, your family is my only hope.*

I needed to ask the voice more, but it was already gone.

My awareness spread further, getting thinner, diluted as it spread.

Now I was a monster who lurked in the water. Cool and dark and deep. Up on the surface, people came and went. They held my hand, they sought my mind, they stole my most precious gifts, but I felt nothing. Deeper and deeper I went, into the dark abyss. *Those who have violated me will pay with their lives!*

The murderous thought, which came with the burning sensation of a white-hot fury, surprised me. From the inky depths, I felt a pull toward my body, my center. The stars streaked by. With a rush of warmth, I was back again.

Flowers everywhere. I was back in Zinnia's room. Back? Had I left? How could I have traveled so far without leaving the bed?

I cleared my throat and said, "I'm feeling a bit strange," which was the understatement of the year.

The other two stopped talking and turned to face me. Zinnia was still sitting on the chair, and Zoey had taken a seat on the bottom corner of the bed. I looked from one to the other and back again. My aunt and my daughter were separated by thirty-two years, but now that both were softly lit by the same golden glow of the bedside lamp, they looked like the same person.

"We're all the same person," I said woozily. "The exact same. Are we clones?"

Zinnia leaned forward and pressed her cool hand against my forehead. "Zara, we're not clones. You've had a very challenging experience tonight, and you're seeing our similarities. Trauma brings us all closer, and with special families such as ours, the women are always quite similar."

Zoey shuffled back on the bed and pulled her knees up to her chest. "Mom, she means in witch families. You're a witch, and I'm a witch, and Auntie Z is a witch. It's a family thing."

My thoughts suddenly shifted into sharp focus around someone I'd had my share of ups and downs with. Someone I'd loved and hated and all the feelings in between.

I turned to my aunt. "Was my mother a witch?"

Her facial muscles twitched before she answered. "No," she said softly. There was pain in her expression. "Sometimes it skips a generation."

I sensed there was a lot more to the story that she wasn't telling me. "Is that why she died?"

She took my hand. "No, Zara. Your mother's passing had nothing to do with our family gift. It wasn't anyone's fault. Sometimes things just happen."

"She knew that you were a witch?"

"Yes, but she didn't know about you. None of us did."

"I'm not going to be a witch," I said with a bit of a snarl. "No, thank you. I decline."

Zinnia gave me a patient smile. I recognized it as the same smile I used at work to kindly let people know it was time to step away from the reference desk. It was the smile reserved for people who, even in the face of indisputable evidence, were clinging to some ignorant belief. It was the smile reserved for ding-dongs.

"You don't have a choice," she said. "Be grateful for your gift."

"Some gift. I feel like goose poop right now, and I feel like I'm having LSD flashbacks, even though I've never actually taken LSD. If this is being a witch, I hate it."

"You only got your gift on Sunday," she said. "When Zoey turned sixteen that day, she got hers, and you got yours at the exact same time. I can only surmise that the channels opened, and the energy transferred from the Divine Bank to both of you." She squeezed my hand. "The only reason you didn't get yours at sixteen was because of Zoey." She glanced at my daughter. "Because of the, uh, accident."

I gave my daughter a loving smile. "Getting pregnant with Zoey was the best *accident* that ever happened to anyone," I said, just as I had hundreds of times before. "Thank you very much."

"I didn't mean to offend you," Zinnia said. "I'm simply explaining what happened. When your gift didn't manifest at sixteen, we assumed you'd been skipped. My sister was so relieved that her daughter would be normal."

Zoey chortled. "Normal? My mother has never been normal."

"I tried to be normal once," I said. "Worst four minutes of my life."

"Your witch gifts have been repressed these last sixteen years," Zinnia said. "This used to happen all the time when girls got married off as teenagers. It's not so common these days, but you had your..." She paused, perhaps considering the least offensive way to state the facts. "You got your *other gift*, Zoey, and now here we all are. Three Riddle witches."

"Here we all are. In my psychedelic nightmare, in a room covered in zinnias, in a town called Wisteria—a town I'd never heard of before I got the idea to apply for a job here." I squinted at my aunt. "You did that to me. You must have done your hocus pocus to bring me here."

Zinnia jerked her head back, looking aghast. "Of course not," she said vehemently, shaking her head so hard her red hair whipped like red snakes. "We witches don't cast spells to influence each other." She bit her lower lip. "Except when safety is at risk," she added quickly.

"What about the shoe store? On Monday, I was *compelled* to buy boots that day, and then I just happened to run into you. That was one of your spells. You all but told me as much when you made fun of me for believing in coincidences." I shook my finger at her. "Witch!"

"No," Zinnia said, still looking upset at the suggestion. "We simply don't do that."

"But it's possible, right?" I pointed to the big book sitting on the bed next to my daughter. "Is there a summoning spell in that book?"

Zoey rested her hand on the book possessively. "Mom, don't be paranoid. This is a whole magical thing that's happening to us. Forces beyond our comprehension."

Magical? Sure. But that didn't mean it was wonderful or even something I wanted. The air in the small room felt burned and stagnant. I wanted to be back home in my house, in my own bed, with my plain, nonflowered duvet cover and my plain, nonflowered walls.

"Enough magic for one night," I said. "Sweet child of mine, help me out of this bed. We're going home."

Zoey extended her lower lip in a pout. Usually, when I saw that lower lip extend half an inch, I'd tell her a bird was going to come along and poop on it, but I wasn't in a teasing mood. I gave her one of my no-nonsense looks.

"You're being such a mom," she whined.

I sounded even more like a mom when I answered. "Whatever this new thing is, it can happen to us in the safety of our own home, during daylight hours." I pushed the blankets out of the way so I could dig my way out of the soft bed. My arms felt as weak as twisty ties, and my head was still full of garbage-can drummers, but I had to get out of there.

"Don't go yet," Zinnia said. "Your powers are fresh, and you don't know how to control them." She gave me a no-nonsense look of her own, and for a moment, my mother, Zirconia Cristata Riddle, was in the room with us.

In an instant, the image of her eyes overlaid a memory of my mother's eyes, glaring at me the same way. Telling me I was too impulsive for my own good, and I'd made a terrible mistake. Telling me I had to give up the baby or lose everything. A terrifying anger billowed up inside me, then and also now. On some level, I knew it wasn't fair to transfer my feelings about someone else onto Zinnia, but she looked so much like her.

"You're not the boss of me," I said, practically growling.

"I am the elder witch, so I am your boss," Zinnia said. She flicked one hand, and the lamp in the room blazed three times brighter. "There are protocols," she said coolly.

I grabbed my daughter's hand and stood on shaking legs. "I don't know how you summoned us to this town, *witch*. And I don't know what you want from us. I will admit that the thing you did with the sparkly lights was really cool, but that's beside the point, and we will be storming out now."

Zinnia's hazel eyes blazed with a fury I knew well. It wasn't just the fury of a redhead. It was the fury of a redhead with the last name of Riddle, and it was a dangerous force.

With my daughter's hand gripped tightly, I stormed out of the room. The house had two stories, like ours. We went down a narrow staircase and stopped by the door for shoes. I couldn't find the boots I'd been wearing earlier that evening, but all the footwear was the exact same size. Zinnia and I were foot twins. I picked a pair of attractive, ankle-high granny boots and started lacing them.

"I'm borrowing some of your boots," I called over my shoulder. "And if you don't like it, you'll have to witchcraft them off my feet!"

CHAPTER 15

I worried that perhaps I'd gone too far in daring my aunt to witchcraft her boots off my feet. But a minute passed and nothing happened.

Zinnia didn't even come downstairs to see us out the front door. I could hear her talking to someone— presumably on the phone with someone. It was a person named Viv, or Finn, or maybe Winnie.

Zoey's eyes were glistening as she stood by the front door. Her pouting lower lip was in danger of getting pooped on by low-flying pigeons.

I listened to the snippets of conversation floating down from my aunt's second floor and then asked my daughter, "Did I just hear Aunt Zinnia call someone Winnie? Do you think she's communicating with the ghost of Winona Vander Zalm?"

"It sounds like she's on the phone," Zoey said.

"Can ghosts talk on the phone?"

"We should wait around and find out."

Wait around? My heart was fluttering in my chest, the way it did when I took a mega dose of vitamins on an empty stomach or when something was really wrong.

"No," I said. "We're leaving now."

I pushed open the front door and looked outside. The sky was red. The sun was coming up. I'd been unconscious most of the night.

I grabbed Zoey's arm and pulled her out of the house and down the sidewalk.

"You're ruining everything," she cried, walking at the slowest speed possible without standing still. "My whole life, I've always wanted to be special. And now that I find out I am, you're wrecking everything."

I yanked her to speed up. "You are special! But more importantly, you're my daughter, and it's my job to look after you. That woman might be family, but we don't know anything about her. There's a reason she hasn't been in our life all these years. Several reasons." Reasons my mother had never explained.

Zoey relented to walking at a normal pace. I glanced around at our surroundings. I didn't know this neighborhood. I barely knew our own street, and yet I was absolutely certain we were heading toward our home. My body felt tuned in to some sort of global positioning system, as though every cell in my body had a compass pointing to my house.

Was that one of the side benefits of being a witch? Direction skills? What a waste of magic. Direction skills could be recreated with modern technology, and there were probably phone apps that didn't even cost a buck.

"You can't stop me from seeing her," Zoey said.

I hadn't said anything about never seeing Zinnia again, but her sass got under my skin. "Sure, I can. We'll move back to the city. You never wanted to come here in the first place."

Zoey expressed her displeasure with a wordless whine. Not my favorite tune.

I kept walking with my lips pressed tightly together.

Before I had a kid, I thought children would be pretty easy, maybe because I was still a child myself. I knew what I wanted, after all. But I underestimated how complicated children's emotions could be and how their unhappiness doesn't always have a quick fix. Some problems can be solved with a nap or a sundae, but those aren't the ones that break you.

No matter how many times I told Zoey she was special, she was always looking for something more. Even as a loving and devoted mother, I was only one person. I couldn't give her everything. I couldn't pluck the stars from the sky and put them in her hands. I couldn't even find a stable male role model other than the various bachelors who lived in our old apartment building. I couldn't make my beautiful, innocent, sensitive daughter happy at all times, and that was painful.

Now she wanted to embrace being a witch. What was I to do? Give her as much guidance as possible and trust that she'd be safe and smart about it the way she was about everything else?

Or did I have to get on board as well?

She'd stopped making the whining sound, but I could still hear it inside my head as a phantom tune of unhappiness.

I broke the silence, speaking gently. "Will you give me some time to think about everything? I don't even know what happened last night. I was having a great time, and the food was perfect, and we were all having a lovely time. My aunt was asking about family gifts, and then something took over me. I was still aware, but I wasn't in control. Like stage fright, but without the fright." I remembered how loose my mouth had felt. "Was I speaking in tongues?"

"You were possessed, Mom. I don't know about tongues, but Auntie Z said something about a Witch Tongue."

"What did I say?"

"You kept saying *toast*. Then you went into the kitchen, filled the sink with water, and tried to electrocute yourself."

The toaster.

"Did you see it happen? Did I throw the toaster into the sink, or did it jump in by itself?"

"What? Toasters don't move around of their own volition, let alone jump into sinks."

"Sure. And witches and ghosts aren't real."

She had no response to that.

That dirty, rotten appliance. It had been in the kitchen when we moved in, quietly pretending to welcome us even while plotting my murder.

The ghost was living inside the toaster. Simple enough.

And I'd been electrocuted. That would explain the soreness I currently had in every muscle, as well as the shakiness in my chest. It also explained my anxiety and agitation, and why I couldn't sit around in my aunt's house and calmly accept this giant bombshell. I'd taken two shocks, one of them physical. I examined my hands. My fingers didn't show any visible burns, but some of my fingertips felt numb.

"That wicked toaster has to go," I said. "We've discovered the source of evil in our house, and it's a small appliance. The minute we get home, I'm throwing it out, and then we can get back to our normal life."

"As normal as life can be for two brand-new witches."

We walked in silence for a block while I digested the information.

Finally, I admitted, "We are going to make excellent witches."

"Do you really believe it? Can I start studying spells at home? Or are you just saying that to keep me from running back to Auntie Z right this minute?"

"Shh," I said.

Zoey went quiet immediately. That was the power of a librarian's professional-quality shushing. Or was it a librarian power after all? I'd always been good at shushing. Even as an entry-level library employee, my shushing had been unmatched. Had this been my witch powers seeping through?

Zoey leaned in and whispered, "*By the pricking of my thumbs, something wicked this way comes*. It's me. And my mom. 'Cause we're both witches."

I snickered and looked around.

It was still dawn, too early for most people to be up yet. I had the creepy sensation we were being watched, but all the houses we walked by had dark windows.

Maybe it was simply the effects of being shocked, but I did sense something different inside myself. A new vitality was coursing through me. It was similar to how I'd felt when I was pregnant—after the morning sickness had passed. I knew I wasn't pregnant, because I hadn't had any wine coolers or other activities in a very long time.

Was this what it felt like to finally have a word for that sense of being weird, of being different from everyone else? Was this what it felt like to know you were a witch?

I put my arm around my daughter's shoulders and whispered, "My name is Zara Riddle, and I'm a witch."

Zoey giggled. "My name is Zoey Riddle, and I'm also a witch." Her voice had risen above a whisper.

"Shh," I repeated, glancing around the sleeping neighborhood. "We don't want the whole town to know, or they'll be beating a path to our door to get love spells and pimple potion and whatever else it is witches make or do. What do you think witches do?"

She shrugged, lifting my arm. "I guess we'll find out."

"We need reference materials. I'll check the library, but they didn't have anything on sleep-toasting, so don't hold your breath. Our occult section is a bit anemic."

"Was my great-grandmother a witch? Gigi's mom?"

I inhaled sharply. "She must have been! Wow, this explains so much about our family. I wish she was alive so I could talk to her about this."

"We could ask her ghost," Zoey said.

A snaky cold feeling shivered up my spine.

"Let's start with the basics before we hold any séances, okay?"

"Sure."

"What are the basics?" I turned to look at her. "You must have been talking to Zinnia for hours while I was unconscious."

Her lips twisted in a funny half smile. "The basics are simple things like finding lost objects and influencing a coin flip."

"That sounds so boring. What about flying?"

"We're not superheroes. You can't go around flying over people's houses on a broomstick. That's how people get burned at the stake. Most of what we talked about was her warning me to keep my powers hidden from the outside world."

"They don't burn people at the stake anymore. I'm no lawyer, but I don't think witchcraft is anywhere in the criminal code."

She stopped walking and faced me, her expression serious. She whispered, "But Auntie Z said there are bad people who will kill others to take their powers."

I groaned. "This is why we can't have nice things."

* * *

My daughter and I turned onto Beacon street just as the lights next door at the Moore residence were coming on.

The faint scent of peppermint was in the air.

"Ms. Vander Zalm?" I sniffed the air and patted myself cautiously.

Zoey narrowed her eyes at me. "Should I be concerned?"

"Only if you see me with a toaster."

She stopped on the sidewalk in front of our house. "It's Saturday, so since I don't have school today, maybe we can go check out the beach?"

"You go inside and get a few hours of sleep," I told her with motherly authority.

"What about you? You're not going to do something embarrassing, are you?"

"Probably." I nodded at the blue house. "I'm going to invite the Moores over for brunch today."

Zoey blinked at me in disbelief. "Brunch?"

"We moved here to Wisteria for a fresh start, remember? We talked about not being such introvert homebodies anymore. We're going to take tap dancing classes and see arty movies with subtitles and watch community theater and have people over for brunch!"

"What about the family gift?" She stared at me like I was crazy, and maybe I was.

"We can handle multiple new things." I shook imaginary pom-poms. "New life in Wisteria. Social activities. Woo hoo!"

Still bug eyed, she said, "But we've only just found out about the W-I-you-know-what thing. Isn't that more than enough for our first week?"

"Today's Saturday, so technically now it's our second week."

She looked skyward. "I don't know why I even try to argue with you."

"It's good practice for one day when you're a lawyer." I shooed her toward our front door. "Go in there and climb into bed. I'll zip over to the store and grab a few things. How about eleven? People have brunch at eleven, right?"

"I'm in high school," she said flatly. "Teenagers don't do brunch."

"I guess if you wait until noon, it's just called lunch, and you can't drink champagne and orange juice at lunch or people think you're a lush."

"Are you possessed again? Look me in the eyes and tell me your name."

With my most snooty voice, I declared, "I'm Winona Vander Zalm, and I throw the most spectacular brunch parties. They're the toast of the town." I snickered. "Get it? The toast of the town."

She shook her head. "That jolt must have fried your circuits."

I raised my arms in the air and twirled around. "I feel great! Sure, the whole world smells like singed Barbie dolls, and I pulled a fiercely charred booger out of my nose when you weren't looking, but I feel spectacular!"

She gave me a sleepy head shake and let herself into our house.

I ran up to the Moores' front door and knocked out a happy rhythm.

The eldest member of the family, Don Moore, opened the door the width of one cagey eyeball.

"Good morning, Grampa Don! I hope you don't mind me calling you that. Your son told me everyone in the neighborhood calls you Grampa Don, and I'm definitely part of the neighborhood now. I'm Zara Riddle. Remember, we met last week when I came over here to chat about your delightful grandson?"

Within the door crack, Grampa Don's eye narrowed. "Witch," he said. "You're the witch."

"What makes you say that?" Was it that obvious?

"You came over here in your black dress, waving a broom." He looked down at the ankle boots I'd liberated from my aunt's house. "And those are witch booties."

I laughed loudly, leaning forward and slapping my knee. "Grampa Don, you're quite the jokester."

He didn't shake my hand or open the door any wider. He turned and yelled, "Chet! Your crazy girlfriend is here!"

"Girlfriend?" I took a step back. "Grampa Don, you shouldn't call people things like *witch* or *crazy*. It's offensive, but not so bad that I won't invite you to brunch."

"Brunch?" He gave me a sideways look. "You mean like a Grownups' Brunch? We haven't had one of those in a long time. Not since..." He frowned. "Almost a year."

"Yes, I suppose you could call it a Grownups' Brunch. It's free, and right next door. Come over at eleven, and bring Chet and Corvin."

He looked over his shoulder again. "Chet must be in the bathroom right now. He's not coming down the stairs. Either he's in the shower, or he doesn't want to see you because he can tell you're—" He cut himself off and muttered, "I shouldn't be rude."

"Will you come over? I'll be offended if you don't."

Gruffly, he said, "Will there be bacon?" He licked his lips.

"Acres of bacon," I promised. "Several kinds."

"See you there." He nodded curtly and closed the door.

I sailed down the steps and nearly knocked over a familiar-looking woman.

"You're up early," she said.

The woman had one hand on her hip and one hand carrying a wicker basket.

"Dorothy Tibbits!" I shook her hand. The real estate agent was dressed, as she'd been the previous times I'd met her, in a blue pinafore and sparkling red shoes similar to the ones Judy Garland wore in *The Wizard of Oz*. She didn't have Toto with her, much to my disappointment. The little dog, a Cairn terrier, was adorable and surprisingly cuddly.

"I didn't expect to see you," Dorothy said.

"Are you selling another house in the neighborhood?" I looked around her for Open House signs. There weren't any to be seen. She was, however, adjusting the tea towel over her wicker basket, seemingly hiding something.

"Not yet," she said, using her free hand to twirl one of her dark-brown pigtails.

I leaned over and snuck a peek into the gap between the towel and the basket. She was carrying binoculars.

"Binoculars? Dorothy Tibbits, you naughty girl, are you stalking someone?"

"I am a naughty girl!" She let out a high-pitched laugh that startled a flock of brown birds to fly out of the nearby bushes.

Something inside me urged me to question the woman. It was the same compulsion I'd felt when I'd decided to invite the Moores for brunch.

Was this the spirit of Winona Vander Zalm pushing me around? Suddenly, I regretted leaving my aunt's house without getting at least a primer on how to deal with possessions.

"Dorothy Tibbits, what are you up to with those binoculars?"

"These silly things?" She batted her eyelashes innocently and smiled. Her overtightened face looked like it might pop something if she smiled any wider. "I use these to inspect roofs without needing to climb a ladder."

"Why not send up your flying monkeys?"

Dorothy blinked at me, her eerily smooth face expressionless. If she was feeling any emotion, the Botox did an admirable job of hiding it.

"Flying monkeys," I explained. "Like in the *Wizard of Oz*." I gestured to her blue pinafore dress and sparkling red shoes. "Because of your whole shtick."

She looked over at my house and then back at me. Skirting the whole issue of flying monkeys and how they might be deployed in a real estate capacity, she said, "I hope you and your daughter are settling in. These old houses can be difficult, the way they're all chopped up into smaller rooms."

"We do get lost sometimes, but we put those map things on our phones."

She blinked again. "You get lost? Inside the house?"

I know when my unique sense of humor is being wasted. I patted her on the shoulder. "It's nice to see you again, Dorothy."

She nodded. "And I am *so* glad that you are *so* pleased with your home purchase. It makes me *so* happy." She looked right through me. "Zara, if you happen to change your mind, for any reason whatsoever, please don't hesitate to call. I'm, uh, running a new special. If you, er, sell within six months of purchase, there's no sales commission. Zero." Her gaze went to my house, and she licked her lips.

Dorothy Tibbits, you are the world's worst real estate agent. When I'd first toured my house, she'd all but told me not to buy it. And then, when I put in my offer, she literally told me not to buy it. She tried to tempt me with a dozen brand new listings. She'd called them Pocket Listings and sworn that the regular public didn't even know they were available.

Why had she been dead-set against me buying my lovely red house? Did she know about the ghost?

"Dorothy, thanks for the offer," I said. "I'll think about it."

"Call me anytime," she said.

I thanked her again and excused myself. Then I stopped and turned around.

"Dorothy, do you know anything about my house being haunted?"

"What?" She brought her free hand up to her face and covered her mouth. "Oh, no. There haven't been any crimes in that house. It would be on the property disclosure."

"Not crimes. Just ghosts. Or one ghost, in particular."

She still had her hand over her mouth, and now the hand was trembling. "I-I-I don't know," she stammered. "I'll have to ask my boss about that."

"Your boss is an expert on ghosts?"

She looked up at the sky just as a giant bird soared overhead. The thing was larger than the biggest eagle I'd ever seen. It had to be the same bird I'd seen on Monday, outside the library.

"Dorothy, do you see that bird? Is that what you're doing with the binoculars? Birdwatching?"

The bird disappeared beyond some tall trees.

I tore my attention away from the sky and turned to look at Dorothy.

She had taken off and was already halfway up the street.

I called after her, "Dorothy, would you like to come to brunch?"

She kept going. She was speed-walking so fast, her red sequined shoes kept slipping off her feet. She picked them up and continued walking barefoot.

CHAPTER 16

After hours of food shopping and preparation, I took a moment to admire my centerpiece. It was a bouquet of flowers carved from fresh fruit. Kebab skewers formed the sturdy stems, which sprang from the top of a colorful teapot. I'd used cookie cutters to make flower petal rounds from various melons and fresh berries for the flower centers. I'd even crushed raspberries to dye the pineapple hearts a lovely pink. The real stars were the blueberry hyacinths.

I had really outdone myself with my first-ever edible arrangement. Best of all, preparing all the brunch food had made me feel calm and centered. There's nothing like working with your hands to let your mind relax, and I really needed it after my whopper of a morning. Not only did my house have a ghost, but the Riddle family tree was —pardon the pun—*riddled* with witchcraft.

On some level, I knew I should be worried that the spirit of Winona Vander Zalm was infecting me with her socialite desires, but I could also see the positive side of her influence. Before moving to Wisteria, I'd sold off most of my book collection. My to-be-read list had been growing faster than I could read them, and that had always been a source of anxiety to me. It wasn't a huge worry, but it was always there, bugging me.

I should build more of a social life, I'd told myself. *Even introverts need some positive interaction to feel balanced.* Besides, I wasn't so sure I was an introvert. My daughter certainly was, and introversion is common among librarians, but I'd never been a typical librarian.

So, with the goal of becoming more social after the move, I'd declared bankruptcy on my to-be-read pile. I put the books up for sale, converted my heavy stack of stress back to cash, and even saved money on the move. *To new, nonfictional adventures*, I'd told myself as I cleared away the last stack.

And then, like the answer to my prayers, a very social and outgoing woman had come into my life. By magic.

Did it matter that Winona Vander Zalm was dead? She could still be a great mentor.

I smiled and hummed a happy tune to myself as I placed the finishing-touch berries on the sweet-smelling centerpiece.

The doorbell rang again.

I tilted my face up to the kitchen ceiling. "Doorbell!" I knew Zoey was out of bed because I'd heard floor squeaks from her movements.

My daughter ever-so-helpfully yelled back, her voice floating down the stairwell, "Mom! Doorbell!"

I yelled again, "Doorbell!" Did she not remember the conversation about how getting the door was her job?

The bell rang again.

She stomped down the stairs and came into the kitchen, rubbing her eyes.

The doorbell rang again.

"Doorbell," she said.

"You think?"

She finished rubbing her eyes and blinked at the operation that was taking place in the kitchen. The edible bouquet was complete, and I was stirring the contents of three pots on the stove plus four bowls on the kitchen island. Spread out around me was more food than I'd cooked in the past year.

The doorbell rang again.

"I'll get the door," she said.

"Great idea."

She rolled her eyes as she left the kitchen.

While she got the door, I grabbed a clean bowl and blended my raspberry sauce with fresh whipped cream. I listened, smiling, as she greeted our brunch guests.

The elder Moore was friendlier to her than he'd been to me. "Call me Grampa Don," he said with a pleasant, grandfatherly tone. "Or even Grampy. I like that. But not Grumpy. I don't like that."

I heard Corvin whine, "No, Grampy! That's my special name for you! She can't say it."

"You heard my grandson," Grampa Don said. "That's his name for me, so you can't call me Grampy when he's around." He chuckled then said in a more serious tone, "I was promised there would be acres of bacon. I don't smell any bacon."

"Absolutely no bacon for my father," Chet said. "He's got to watch his cholesterol."

"What the wing dang doodle!?" The old man made a grumpy face. "I'm leaving if there's no bacon. I'll stay only if I can have five slices."

"Two," Chet said.

"Three slices of bacon," Don said. "Plus all the coffee I want. Final offer."

Chet sighed. "Deal."

My daughter steered them toward the dining room while asking about food allergies. They didn't have any food issues except for Corvin's "extremely horrible" allergy to Brussels sprouts, which were "basically poison," according to him. Zoey assured him there would be no Brussels sprouts at brunch.

Zoey returned to the kitchen. "Need a hand?" She reached for a slice of crispy bacon and started munching it. "Here, I'll fix the bacon. There should be an odd number of slices when you serve it, because odd numbers are more aesthetically pleasing."

"How did you count the bacon so quickly? Is this a sign of your you-know-what powers kicking in?"

"Bacon comes in even numbers from the package, so I just deduced."

"Speaking of *deduce*, you can run *de juice* out to our guests."

She groaned at my pun, which was the main reason I cracked puns.

"Take the coffee pot," I said. "And the young gentleman may have his choice of juice boxes."

She grabbed the coffee and looked over the spread with widening eyes. "Did you leave any food at the store for the rest of Wisteria?"

"You've always wanted me to cook more. Don't look a gift horse in the mouth. Tell our guests the first batch of crepes is on the way!"

She used her free hand to pick up the tray of cream and sugar. "Mom, are you sure you're feeling okay? Most people would want some quiet time to get used to the idea of being a you-know-what."

"Idle hands are the devil's playground," I said. "Or the devil's *workshop*, depending on your choice of translation."

"Talking about the devil is not exactly reassuring."

I shrugged. "I've got the rest of my life to learn how to curdle milk, or talk to beavers, or whatever it is we witches can do. Today, let's have a stylish brunch with our neighbors."

"As you wish." She tossed her wavy red locks over her shoulder and left with the coffee.

Alone again, I silently thanked my house for having an old-fashioned layout with the kitchen in its own private area, walled off. I wouldn't have felt comfortable contorting my body to stir multiple pots of food at once if I were on display for guests.

With one hand on the crepe flipper and one hand swirling the raspberry topping, that left me with zero hands to stir the chocolate sauce in the top of the double boiler.

What to do?

If only there were a way for me to stir the sauce with no hands.

I felt a swirling, trembling feeling inside myself, as though I was about to sneeze, but I didn't sneeze.

The spoon in the chocolate sauce righted itself and began to stir.

Hands free.

By magic.

Hot diggity dog. I've got telekinesis.

Ziggity!

CHAPTER 17

Telekinesis.

Wow.

The floating water glass, I thought, remembering my first night of sleep-toasting. The water glass had appeared to hover over the floor by magic because it *was* hovering by magic.

My magic.

I experimented with my new power and found that telekinesis could be more distracting than it was helpful. While I *could* use my powers to magically stir a spoon through chocolate sauce, it required enough concentration that my hands slowed at their tasks—like trying to pat your head and rub circles on your stomach at the same time. I needed to grow a bigger brain, or at least get some practice. Telekinesis apparently required a special type of focus—a focus I did not yet have.

Zoey returned to the kitchen to help me platter the food.

"Is everyone behaving out there?"

"Yes." She gave me a suspicious look. "Why are you staring at me with googly eyes like that?"

"Me? Googly eyes?" I blinked innocently.

"Yeah. Like you've got a big secret and you want to tell me, but you know you shouldn't, because it would be inappropriate—not that it stops you. Or like you've done something bad and secretly you want to get busted." She looked over at some empty bottles next to the sink. "Are you drunk?"

"That wine bottle is from last night's dinner with Zinnia. And the beer bottles... Actually, I don't know where those came from."

"Those must be from Zinnia's *guy*," Zoey said. "The one who came over to sweep the house for listening bugs or spell bombs. He set up some wards, which are kind of like burglar alarms for magic. Zinnia said the wards wouldn't keep out any ghosts who were already in." She walked over to the bottles and looked at the labels. "These are from a local brewery."

"What kind of professional drinks two bottles of beer on the job? What did she say this guy was?"

Zoey shrugged. "Sort of a cleaner."

"Like in *Pulp Fiction*? I've seen that movie enough times to be concerned. The cleaner goes in and cleans up, all right. And then he kills everyone, Zoey."

She seemed more interested in the label than my dire warning. "This guy's a friend of Auntie Z's. I'm sure he's not a professional *murder* assassin." She stole two more strips of crisp bacon. "Probably."

"Help me get this food to the dining room before you eat it all."

* * *

The three generations of Moores were dressed in crisp dress shirts, all in shades of green, like a multi-generational sports team. Grampa Don had shaved since I'd last seen him. He was handsome for a man his age, even when arguing with his son about how much bacon he could have.

Chet and his father both rose from their chairs when I entered the dining room.

Chet gave me a warm smile. "You look well rested, Zara. You must be settling into the house." He returned to his seat and added, "If you ever have trouble sleeping, I can pop over and tell you another one of my stories."

Grampa Don gave us a dirty look and demanded, "What's going on here?" He looked at his son. "Is it her? Has she already caught the—"

Chet elbowed his father. "Dad, it's just a joke," he said. "Remember how Corvin and I came over here last Saturday for pizza? I was trying to entertain Zara, and she fell asleep on the sofa. That's all." He flashed his eyes at Grampa Don.

"All right, all right," Grampa Don said. He turned to young Corvin, who was watching everything intently with his huge, dark eyes. "Corvin, never pass up an opportunity to shut the hell up."

Chet cleared his throat. "Language," he said.

Corvin grinned mischievously. "Hell, hell, hell," he whispered. "Hell."

Chet shot me a pained look and reached for his coffee. His hands looked even more rugged and manly holding the small porcelain cup, which was meant for tea. His thick finger barely fit through the filigree porcelain handle.

"Let's eat," I said, and we passed around the platters of food.

While I ate, I kept looking over at little Corvin. He was so adorable, with round cheeks that begged to be pinched.

I resisted for at least ten minutes before I gave in to my urges and reached over to give one cheek a pinch. He gave me a funny look but didn't protest. After a second good pinching, I used both of my hands on his plump round cheeks, squeezing his face to give him fish lips while I made popping sounds.

"Who's a little fishie?" I cooed.

Grampa Don said, "*Little fishie*? That's exactly what Winona used to say to the boy." He turned to his son. "Damn! Is it her?"

I yanked my hands away, suddenly embarrassed. The entire Moore family was staring at me with expressions ranging from curious to horrified. Grampa Moore was so surprised, he'd actually stopped cramming bacon in his mouth.

"Hazelnut spread," I announced, jumping to my feet. I dashed off to the kitchen for some privacy.

Alone in the kitchen, I scolded the ghost. "Winona Vander Zalm, control yourself! Don't make me do embarrassing things, or we can't be friends. Keep the entertaining hints coming, but don't take control of my body. You'll leave me with no choice but to get a ghost exterminator to get you out of this house."

"Who are you talking to?" Zoey asked from the doorway. "Is the ghost back? We should call Auntie Z. She gave me her phone number in case of emergencies."

I grabbed the hazelnut spread I'd come in for, along with a tray of deviled eggs.

"I can handle this myself," I said to Zoey. "Of course she's here. It's a beautiful house. You can't blame the woman for sticking around, even after death."

"Mom?" She gave me one of her patient looks—the same expression that made people say she had an old soul.

"Don't give me that look," I said. "Winona is a sweet little old lady, perfectly harmless. Whatever happened last night with the toaster was just an accident, and it won't happen again. It was the toaster, not Winona. I threw that demonic appliance into the garbage can. All's right in the world." I paused and glanced over at the kettle. "Do you suppose anyone wants tea? I just assumed they were all coffee drinkers."

Zoey took the tray of deviled eggs from me. "Let's get through this brunch, and we'll talk more later. I already phoned Auntie Z, right after I got out of bed, but she's not answering her cell phone. She's probably sleeping after we kept her up all night."

I picked up a dish towel and twisted it. "I'm not sure if we can trust my aunt. I know she's family and the ghost *isn't*, but the ghost never tried to hurt me before last night, when Zinnia just happened to be here in the house."

Zoey wrinkled her brow and stared into the distance, the way she did when she was thinking about something she'd just read. After a moment, her expression brightened. "We should ask the Moore family what they know about Winona and the history of the house."

"Duh," I said. "Why do you think I invited them over in the first place? All part of my plan."

She gave me a look that said she wasn't buying it but appreciated my efforts.

We returned to the dining room, where Zoey got to work with the single-mindedness she brought to everything.

She asked the Moores, "How long did Winona Vander Zalm own this house?"

Grampa Don answered, "She was here before I bought the place next door, thirty-six years ago."

"I was born inside this house," Chet said. "On this old wood floor." He pointed at my dining room floor.

Zoey exclaimed, "What? No way!"

Chet's green eyes twinkled as he looked at me. "I should have broken out this story last Saturday. I might not have put you to sleep."

"I'm listening," I said. "Did your mother plan to give birth here?"

"No," Chet said with a chuckle. "There was a terrible electrical storm when my mother went into labor. A couple of fallen trees and power lines—"

Grampa Don made a contrary noise. He scrunched his face and then waved for Chet to continue.

Chet said, "The fallen power lines blocked the way to the hospital, so my mother came over here, because she knew Winona could handle anything. Miss Vander Zalm didn't have kids of her own, but she took charge of the situation like a professional. My mother gave birth here, with a small group of neighbors attending."

Grampa Don snorted. "I wasn't here. I was busy..." He eyed the bacon. "Ooh, bacon. Don't mind if I do!"

Zoey said, "That's quite the story, Mr. Moore. Did Miss Vander Zalm have any medical training?"

Chet smiled. "Winona had all the skills she needed. According to the neighbors, she tended my mother and also served cocktails all through the delivery. Manhattans, I believe. Or was it mojitos? She was an incredible hostess." He looked at Zoey and rubbed his chin. "I think maybe she did serve as a nurse during the war. Some sort of war. I never could nail down exactly which one, but I believed her." He glanced around the room, his eyes glistening.

Grampa Don chimed in. "She was a spectacular woman."

Zoey practically pounced on the elder Moore across the table. "How spectacular? Were you two an item?"

The grandfather's moss-green eyes darkened. "After my dear wife passed on, Winona would seek my company from time to time." He glanced over to his son as though asking for permission to continue.

Chet said, "It's okay, Dad. I've always known there was something between you two. You should go ahead and talk about it. Healthy people talk about their feelings. That's what Dr. Bob says."

Don snorted and reached for another slice of bacon. "If it's so healthy to yammer on like a fool, I deserve this."

Nobody stopped him.

Zoey gave him a moment to chew before asking, "Were you dating up until she passed away? No offense, but she was a lot older than you, wasn't she?"

He talked around the food in his mouth. "Dating? She wasn't *that* old, young lady. The two of us made the beast with two backs whenever the moon was full. Does that count as dating?"

Young Corvin, whom I'd all but forgotten about, piped up, "What's the *beast with two backs*?"

Chet quieted him with a hand clamped over his mouth. "I think that's enough talking about Grampa's private nightsports."

Zoey giggled. "Nightsports," she repeated.

I smiled at the Moore family. "Thank you for sharing your memories about such a remarkable woman." I held my hand over my heart. "She sends you all her love." I winked at Grampa Don, seeing him briefly through Winona's eyes. *My hero*, I thought with a lovesick sigh.

Chet removed his hand from his son's mouth and gave me a puzzled look. "If you're interested in learning more about the history of this house and Winona, I've got access to old town records. We could visit the archives together sometime." His gaze flicked over to Zoey. "With your daughter, of course. Zoey, you seem very interested in history."

"That would be nice," I said. My gaze drifted over to the edible centerpiece. "Help yourself to some flowers, please. Everything except the stem is made of fruit."

My guests admired my handiwork, and each took a flower.

The table was quiet while everyone munched away. Everything was perfect. I felt a warm pressure on my shoulder, as though someone was patting me on the back for a job well done. Winona approved.

Suddenly, a spoon clattered to the floor.

Corvin pointed at the air above my head and said, "You're dead. You're dead!"

His father gave him a stern look. "Corvin! Don't be morbid or I'll give you something to be morbid about."

I leaned forward and looked into the little boy's eyes, which were as dark as night. "Who's dead?"

He answered with a low, growling voice. "You know who."

"How did she die?"

"Someone killed her," Corvin said. "Ding dong! Ding dong, the witch is dead!"

Zoey made a squeaking sound and shot me a look.

Chet got to his feet and pulled his son up as well.

Corvin squeezed his eyes shut and made a keening sound.

"Zara, Zoey," Chet said warmly as he nodded at each of us in turn. "Great brunch." He nodded down at Corvin, who still had his eyes squeezed shut. "This one gets feisty when he eats too much sugar."

Corvin opened his huge eyes and laughed-a cruel, nasty laugh. "Ding dong! Ding dong! Who's there? Pop-Tarts! The Pop-Tarts are done and so are you!"

Zoey circled around the table and shoved Corvin. "Stop it! Shut up, you creepy little monster!"

He reached out and shoved her back. He was much shorter and couldn't reach her shoulders, so he struck her in the chest. "You're the monster! And I don't want a big sister! Not you! You're ugly and stupid and I hate you!"

Chet grabbed his son and pulled him back. I did the same with Zoey, for everyone's protection. She wasn't usually violent, but then again she'd never been called ugly and stupid in her own home while being punched in the chest.

"Zara, I am *so* sorry," Chet said, dragging his son away as quickly as he could.

Grampa Don grabbed a handful of bacon and followed them. He gave me a pat on the arm.

"You're a good neighbor," Don said. "Winona is glad to have you in this house. I can feel it." He glanced at his son, who was wrestling Corvin out the front door. "I'd tell you we Moores are usually better behaved, but you strike me as the type who sees right through bullcrap."

I smiled knowingly. "This is as good as it gets, right?"

He finished his bacon and licked his fingertips. "What you see is what you get. Thanks for the grub! You make this old house proud."

I tilted my head to the side. "I make the house proud? What do you mean?"

He grinned mischievously, which erased about fifty years from his face. *My hero*, I thought again, feeling a rush of Winona's affection.

"You'll find out soon enough," he said ominously.

CHAPTER 18

After the Moores left, I looked over the remaining food. We'd barely made a dent. Except for the dirty plates, the table looked like it had just been set up for entertaining. *That Winona.* It was just like the amazing hostess to have ten times as much food as needed.

As I surveyed the leftovers and thought of all the packing-up work that lay ahead, I remembered why I didn't cook much.

At least the dishes would be an excellent opportunity to practice my new levitation skills.

"Wanna see something cool?" I asked my daughter.

"Not really." Zoey crossed her arms and slumped into a dining room chair. "Corvin is such a brat," she said. "I can't believe I ever wanted a little brother. They're awful and rude, and they smell like goats."

"True. And that particular one can see spirits. You heard what he said. He could see Winona Vander Zalm standing with me. I'm a witch, and I can't even see her."

"No, he can't see anything," she scoffed. "You might not have noticed, because you were drooling over his father and shoving food onto people's plates the whole time, but Corvin was saying a ton of random crap that didn't mean anything."

"Are you back to playing the skeptic? The Scully to my Mulder? I swear, he looked over my shoulder and saw something. Winona Vander Zalm's ghost."

Zoey shifted her gaze to a spot above my shoulder and smiled sweetly. "Hello there, Spirit Lady. What a beautiful frock you're wearing today. What's that? You think I should get a raise in my allowance? I agree. Let's tell Mother."

"Fine," I said, nodding. "I'll raise your allowance, since the Spirit Lady suggested it."

"She's not really there. I was making a point, Mom."

I played dumb. "Really?"

She groaned and went limp, slumping crookedly in her chair. "You're the worst."

"I'll raise your allowance anyway. You've been a good sport about the move, and now you'll be too busy with all the new witch stuff to get a part-time job."

She didn't argue.

Pouting, she said, "The next time I see Corvin, I'm giving him a wedgie."

"Good," I said. "The kid probably needs more social interaction to level him out. His mother must have been the weird one, because Chet seems normal enough."

She snorted. "Normal enough? Don't you mean dreamy? You love him. You have a super-big crush on him. Mom and Mr. Moore, sitting in a tree, K-I-S-S-I-N-G."

I didn't like where this conversation was heading. I'd tried my best to shield my daughter from the highs and lows of my love life. I wasn't always successful, but I did what I could to respect her boundaries.

She carried on with the sing-song teasing. She was six years older than Corvin, yet I could see the childlike resemblance.

Luckily, I knew how to change the topic instantly.

With a flick of my wrist, I levitated an empty coffee cup using my magic. It danced merrily in the air between us—no hands, no strings, no net. Just magic.

Zoey stopped her singing mid-word and held very still, her gaze riveted to the cup.

"Telekinesis," I said. "Or psychokinesis, if you prefer that term." I didn't. It was the *psycho* part at the beginning.

"You really are a witch," she said with a wondrous sigh.

I twirled the cup clockwise and then counterclockwise. "I feel like a kid with a new toy."

"Can you make those pretty light sparkles that Auntie Z did?"

"I could try, but I don't know where to even start. I'm afraid I'll make something explode, which wouldn't be so bad if it was just a scone, but a human head could be really bad. I'm sticking to simple levitation until I know more about these powers." I levitated the cup's saucer and matched them up mid-air.

Zoey clapped her hands, her teen grumpiness completely forgotten. "Do some more tricks, Mom."

"As you wish."

For the next ten minutes, I showed her how I could perform a myriad of small tasks hands free. I shifted plates and poured liquids from cup to cup. For my grand finale, I floated a glob of chocolate-hazelnut spread from the container and smeared it onto a waffle, all without getting a knife dirty.

She clapped her hands, squealing, "Again! Do it again!"

I repeated the smearing and then floated the waffle over to my mouth, where I made the waffle disappear in the usual, not-so-magical manner.

"Now you try," I said.

ANGELA PEPPER

She wrinkled her nose. "You think I can move stuff with my mind? I've been trying for the last ten minutes, and nothing's happening for me."

"Keep trying. You're so smart that you're used to things coming easily to you, and you don't know how to stick with something through failure."

She raised an eyebrow. "Are you talking about me or you?"

"Catch the cup," I said, and I floated an empty cup toward her quickly.

She scrunched her face and clenched her fists. The cup sailed over her shoulder, hit the wall, and crashed to the floor, where it broke.

"Don't!" She glared at me angrily. "Don't."

"Try again," I said, and sent a saucer sailing at her.

This time, she reached out with her hand and tried to catch the dish. It bounced off her fingertips and smashed on the floor with the cup.

Her cheeks flushed red, and she began huffing audibly. "Don't," she said tersely. "You're just making me feel stupid."

In my most encouraging, motherly tone, I said, "Sweetie, you have to keep trying."

With a grumble of displeasure, she narrowed her eyes at the objects on the table, her gaze moving from spoon to cup to waffle. Nothing moved or even wiggled.

"Try something small," I said.

"I am." She flicked her gaze up to meet my eyes. My ears flushed with warmth. The longer she glowered at me, the more my ears heated up.

"Maybe we should take a break," I said. "And by we, I mean you. I'm worried about getting my head exploded."

She sighed and used her hand to pick up a leftover waffle stick, which she rolled up inside a crepe. "My powers need me to carbo load," she said as she took a bite.

"Sounds legit." I used my magic to draw closed the sheer curtains on the dining room's window. The house sat on the corner lot of the block. The dining room had a quaint view over a side hedge and down the cross-street, but any people walking along the sidewalk might be able to peer in at us practicing magic. I thought of wacky ol' Dorothy Tibbits and her binoculars. I twitched the curtains back and looked around for the odd, blue-pinafore-wearing woman but didn't see her.

When I turned back to Zoey, she let out an exasperated sigh. "I can't even budge the smallest crumb." She threw down her partly eaten wrap, crossed her arms, and thrust out her lower lip.

"Don't pout." I took a seat across from her. "You know what happens to little pouty lips." I hadn't teased her like this in years, and it was fun to bring back one of our childhood rituals.

She kept pouting. If anything, she pouted harder.

With a flick of my finger, I pulled up a dollop of custard, floated it across the table, and dropped it straight down on her pouting lower lip.

Her eyes bulged in surprise.

My mouth twisted into a wicked grin. After so many years of me warning her what might happen to little girls who pouted while a bird just happened to be flying by, it had finally happened. Sort of.

Zoey didn't find my new trick quite so magnificent. From the look on her face, you would have thought an actual bird flew into the room and pooped on her.

"Evil!" She rubbed the custard away with a napkin and pointed at me with an accusing finger. "Witch!"

I shrugged. "Tell me something I don't know."

She spluttered, "You're not supposed to do things to other witches!"

"It must have been an invisible bird," I said, craning my neck to search the room's upper corners. "Didn't you see it flying around?"

"Witch." She pointed a finger at my face accusingly.

While she was distracted, I used my magic to fold a napkin into an origami bird. I covered my hand with my mouth and said, "Caw! Caw!" The white napkin bird fluttered up from the table and flew around the room.

"Evil," she said, not even cracking a grin. "And you won't even show me how you're doing all these cool tricks, so that makes you double evil."

"I swear I'm not trying to keep anything from you. I don't know how I'm doing these things. I'm sorry if I'm making it look easy, but it is. I simply look at something, imagine the motions needed, and it starts happening." I shrugged as a miniature scone topped with peach jam sailed through the air toward my mouth. I made it disappear to where the waffles had gone.

Zoey's arms were still crossed. "You're going to gain a million pounds," she said.

"Nope." I shook my head. "This sort of thing burns a ton of calories." I didn't know how I knew that, but I did. "I can *feel* the calories burning away inside me, in my witch furnace."

She narrowed her eyes. "You might be right," she admitted. "It takes energy to move matter, and the energy has to come from somewhere."

"If that's true, then becoming a witch is the greatest thing that has ever happened to anyone, anywhere. Oh, the things we're going to eat!"

Zoey twisted her lips to the side. "I've got homework," she said plainly.

"On Saturday? You always have your homework finished Friday night."

"I just remembered I have more," she lied, unconvincingly.

"But what about this mess? You think these dishes are going to wash themselves?"

She walked over to where I sat and patted me on the shoulder. "Yes, Mom. I think the dishes *are* going to wash themselves." She let out a witchy cackle. "Go to it. Make the dishes wash themselves. It will be good practice."

I clenched my fist and swung my arm theatrically. "Curses!"

"No curses," she said. "Auntie Z said something about a curse at dinner, and she wouldn't explain what she meant, but it didn't sound good."

"I was joking," I said.

"Right." She gave me a somewhat dirty look and then stomped out of the dining room.

I stared after her and let the smile drop off my face.

I'd tried to keep the tone light and breezy so she wouldn't feel too much pressure. One of the reasons Zoey did her homework on Friday night was because she hated leaving things to the last minute. She couldn't take the pressure, especially if any performance was involved. Despite our similar appearances, that was one key difference between the two of us. If we were to attend a karaoke party, I'd be the first to volunteer for a song and she'd be the last. That was, assuming I could even drag her to a karaoke night. She could be fun, but it had to be planned in advance. It caused her immense anxiety to have last-minute plans sprung upon her.

I wondered, was my daughter's dislike of spontaneity the thing keeping her powers from manifesting?

Or was there something more sinister—or disappointing—going on?

CHAPTER 19

While Zoey did her pretend "homework" upstairs, I used my witch powers to clean up from brunch.

Small objects were easy, but I struggled with the coffee pot. I could lift it, but I couldn't pour without making a mess.

I wasn't that surprised heavy things were beyond my skill level. The power had to be like a muscle, needing repeated practice and concentration to get stronger. Unfortunately, my concentration skills were lacking. I did manage to get the dishes "washing themselves," but as soon as my mind wandered, the scrub brush and sponge would stop moving. The regular dishwasher outdid my magic easily.

What I didn't expect was how satisfying it was to use magic. For example, wringing out a kitchen sponge was utterly delightful. I could squeeze it either by replicating the way I'd squeeze it without magic, with one hand squishing the sponge, or I could stretch it from both ends and wring it in a perfect twist. The mid-air twist was both aesthetically pleasing as well as effective. If I wrung the sponge for too long, it became bone-dry and unable to wipe up anything.

I could have spent an hour practicing my sponge-twisting technique, but I was interrupted by a knock at the door.

My heart pounded guiltily as my mind raced with paranoia. It was the witch police! They could tell I was practicing magic without their authorization and without half a clue!

The knocking came again, heavier this time. Urgent. Authoritative.

Why weren't they using the doorbell? I couldn't yell *doorbell* at my daughter if there was no ding-dong.

I untied my spotless apron, left it on the clean kitchen island, and went to open the front door.

Nobody was there. The porch was empty. I leaned out and glanced up and down the street. An older male neighbor was walking his brown Labradoodle across the street. He saw me looking and gave me a friendly wave. People in Wisteria were so friendly.

I waved back and called out, "Was someone at my door just a minute ago?"

He held one hand to his ear and crossed toward me. "What's that?"

"Never mind," I said. "I thought I heard someone knocking on my door, but it must have been my teenage daughter playing a joke on me."

He reached my steps and stopped at the bottom. His Labradoodle, which was one of the taller ones I'd seen, launched itself up the stairs toward me. I stretched out my hand to be sniffed and licked by the happy pooch.

The man said, "Teenage daughter? You're too young to have a teenager." He waggled his white, fluffy eyebrows. "Maybe you're imagining things. The Red Witch House has that effect on people."

My ears began to ring, as if an internal alarm had been triggered inside me. He'd said the word *witch*. Did people say *witch* all the time? Had I just never noticed until now?

The soft-curled brown dog continued to nose my hand, and then tried to sneak past me into my house.

I said to the man, "I'm sorry, but what did you say? Does my house have a name?"

The older man chuckled. "All the kids in the neighborhood call this the Red Witch House."

"Because a Red Witch lives here? Or, um, used to?"

"It's probably because of the Gothic Revival architecture," he said. "It reminds people of Tim Burton movies, I suppose. Most of the other heritage houses around here are in the Craftsman style." He looked up at the facade and the gingerbread trim that I'd loved from the minute I'd seen it. He continued, "Personally, I've always loved this home. I found its previous owner eccentric, but in a good way. Winona was a lovely woman. It's such a shame she killed herself that way."

I was petting the Labradoodle, but suddenly I couldn't feel my hands. The friendly dog could have been eating my thumbs and I wouldn't have noticed.

"The owner killed herself?"

"That didn't come out right," he said. "I meant that she killed herself in the same way people who drive dangerously kill themselves by their own carelessness."

I glanced over at the blue house next door. Chet had told me Winona Vander Zalm went peacefully, but it seemed he'd been lying to me.

"Forgive me for asking," I said. "How did she die?"

The man tugged on the dog's leash. "Doodles, leave the nice lady alone. Let's go home, girl. Or do you want to go monster hunting? What do you say, girl?"

"Monster hunting?" I stopped petting the dog with my numb hands and walked down my steps. I met the man on the sidewalk and extended my hand. "Zara Riddle," I said. "My daughter, who really is a teenager, and I just moved in here."

He shook my hand. "I'm Arden, and that's Doodles." He wrinkled his nose and glanced down at our hands, which were both slick from his dog's tongue. He chuckled as we released our handshake. "Zara, you and I are now dog-spit bonded."

"Oh." I couldn't care less about the dog spittle, but I wiped my hand on my hip to conform to social norms.

With a casual tone, I said, "Arden, I don't mean to be morbid, but nobody will tell me how Ms. Vander Zalm passed away." I batted my eyelashes in a manner I hoped was charming. "Since we're dog-spit buddies now, you'll tell me, right?"

Arden's gray eyes got a faraway look. "That woman loved her Pop-Tarts," he said. "She could whip up a five-course meal fit for a king, but when it came to comfort food, she loved her Pop-Tarts. She told me all about her habits whenever we met up at the dog park down the street." He smiled wistfully, his eyes still unfocused. "She hadn't had a dog in years, but she always brought home-made dog treats for Doodles. That's why my dog's trying to get into your house. Poor girl doesn't know the old lady's gone."

Right on cue, Doodles sat by her master's feet with a sad whimper.

We still weren't any closer to the method of my ghost's demise. I ventured a guess. "Did she stick a fork in the toaster while making Pop-Tarts and electrocute herself in the kitchen?"

He chuckled. "Winona didn't make Pop-Tarts in the kitchen," he said. "She made them in the bathroom while she took long baths in the claw-foot tub."

A cloud of chilly air whooshed up my back and blew right through me. Was that the point of the sleep-toasting? Had the woman's spirit been trying to tell me about her accident? Trying to warn me not to make the same mistake?

"Did she drop the toaster in the bathtub?"

He nodded, his expression turning serious. "That's what folks figure happened. It was very odd."

"But that shouldn't kill a person," I said. "It's just one of those urban legends. I saw the toaster thing demonstrated on that TV show where they try things from movies. Dropping a small appliance into a tub would short out the circuit and blow the electrical breaker long before it delivered enough electricity to kill someone."

Arden blinked and stared at me, forehead wrinkled. "Are you calling me a liar?"

"Of course not," I said quickly. "Just wondering if the toaster thing is a rumor. Maybe something the pesky local children made up." I was thinking of one pesky local child in particular. He had big eyes, blue-black hair, and might be able to see dead people.

Doodles whimpered again. Her owner glanced up at the highest peak of my roof. "We're being watched," he said.

I followed his gaze to my roof, where a blue jay was perched. Was it the friendly visitor who'd greeted me with an ominous warning the day I'd moved in, or yet another bird who didn't belong this far west? The bird ruffled its blue head crest and stared back at us.

I waved at the bird. "Hello, blue jay."

Arden's clothes rustled as he shuffled away from me. "Nice to meet you, Zara. You have a good day, and I'll see you around." He gave the dog's leash a tug, and they were on their way.

"Nice meeting you," I called after them. "And I'll have you know my house is just a regular house. I'm going to paint it a different color, so it won't be red anymore and stupid kids can't call it the Red Witch House!"

Change the paint from Wisconsin Barn Red? I could do that. I could do anything I wanted to. Now that I was an actual witch, I needed to keep a low profile, and living in something called the Red Witch House wasn't ideal.

I put my hands on my hips and looked up at the bird on the peak.

"Hey, blue jay. What do you think? Should I paint the house blue, like you?"

The blue jay let out a squawk.

"I suppose not," I said in agreement. Blue would be copying the Moore house next door.

"How about green? Something to complement the wisteria vines?"

The blue jay squawked again.

"Did you say purple?" I shook my head. "No way. That's the most eccentric color there is." A purple house? I might as well write Witch House on the mailbox.

"Yellow?"

The blue jay stretched out its wings and took to the air.

"I'll take that as a yes," I said. "Sure. Everybody loves a yellow house."

My daughter darkened the open doorway. "What are you doing out there on the sidewalk?"

"Talking to a blue jay. It might have been the same one we saw when we moved in."

"Was it talking back?"

"Sort of. Just squawks, though. We were talking about painting the house."

"Oh. Is that all you were doing out there?" Her tone was dripping in accusation.

"Why are you so suspicious? What did you think I was doing?"

She didn't answer.

"Zoey?"

She huffed. "I thought you were trying to lift this whole house. I felt it creaking and rattling. You were trying to levitate it, weren't you?"

"What?" Even if I could, why would I lift our house?

"Don't be a show-off," she said grouchily. "Don't you dare levitate this whole house, or I'll scream. Plus you'll break all the pipes and stuff."

"Oh, shush!" I ran up the stairs toward the door. Something dark yet winking with bright light zipped across my path. There was a rat-a-tat sound, not unlike a woodpecker banging on a metal shed roof.

The moving object caught me by the toes. I tripped and fell into Zoey's arms. We both tumbled into the house and landed in a tangle of limbs, flying red hair, and mild cursing.

"You've gone off the deep end," Zoey howled, wriggling under me. "I'll be more discreet from now on, but there's no need to tackle me. We're not a tackling family."

"It was an accident," I groaned. "Something tripped me. It scampered across the porch and caught my toe."

"Like a stray cat?"

"Maybe."

We got ourselves untangled. Nothing was damaged except my pride.

Zoey looked both ways cautiously before she stepped out onto the porch. She leaned down and grabbed something.

She asked me, "Didn't you throw this out?"

It was the evil toaster. "I swear I threw that into the trash as soon as we got home this morning."

"Then why's it on the porch?"

I didn't know. I just stared at the evil toaster in her hands. It gleamed maliciously.

CHAPTER 20

Zoey and I sat in the dining room, staring at the toaster.

The evil appliance sat in the middle of the table, trying to look nonchalant with its extra-long cord wrapped casually around itself.

Zoey asked, "Did you actually see the toaster dart across the porch and trip you?"

"Not exactly. But I did see something dark shoot across, plus some flashes of light. And I might have heard the pitter patter of little feet."

She picked up the toaster with a grunt. "How can a toaster go pitter patter? It doesn't have feet." She turned the rectangular appliance over. "Or does it? There seem to be some retractable parts here in the base. Plus the thing weighs a ton. Is it made of iron?"

"In the olden days, before Wal-Mart, appliances were a lot heavier. And they were built to last."

She gingerly poked at the interlocking parts of the toaster's base. "Is this a removable crumb tray, or are these feet?" She got a piece free and pulled it out. Unfolded, the metal-and-spring part did resemble a foot.

"That's disturbing," I said.

She released her hold, and the foot snapped back into place, tucking to be flush with the base. She turned the appliance upright, again grunting at the weight, and poked at a round glassy bulb on the side. "And what's this?"

"An eyeball," I said.

She flinched, pulling her hands back and holding them close to her neck. "Creepy. It *does* look like an eyeball."

"Zoey, we are the proud owners of the world's only walking Cyclops toaster. I name him... Talkie Toaster."

"But he doesn't talk."

"No, but he reminds me of the toaster on *Red Dwarf*. Remember? Dave Lister bought it, or *him*, at a second-hand junk shop on planet-leave, along with a cat that he stowed away."

Zoey nodded. "And the toaster is allegedly smarter than the ship's computer but always tries to steer the conversation toward toast." She smiled and shook her head. "I was raised on way too much PBS."

"What should we do with it? Smash it to three thousand separate pieces with a fourteen-pound hammer?"

Zoey prodded the glass eyeball. "I don't know if we have a hammer, let alone a fourteen-pound hammer."

I nodded at her cell phone. "Want to try calling Aunt Zinnia again?"

She sighed. "It keeps going straight to voicemail. I think she's mad at us for leaving her house the way we did."

"Maybe this is a test," I said. "Didn't she say something about levels?"

"The toaster is a test?" Zoey's hazel eyes brightened. She was good at tests. "Let's put it somewhere safe while I do some research. Auntie Z said there isn't any genuine magic information on the public internet, but you never know."

"Put it somewhere safe," I mused. "How about the freezer? The door sticks anyway, so even if Talkie Toaster sprouted legs, it would have a tough time busting its way out."

"Good idea," she said.

"Promise you'll be careful and not take it out to use," I said. "This toaster may have already taken a life."

She eyed the squat appliance warily. "Did the ghost of Winona Vander Zalm tell you that?"

I bit my lip and debated how much to tell my daughter. I didn't want to worry her unnecessarily, but now that she was sixteen—old enough to drive with a learner's permit —she was old enough for adult-level worries.

I explained to her how I'd met one of our neighbors outside, and he'd told me not only that the neighborhood kids called our home the Red Witch House but that Winona Vander Zalm had apparently electrocuted herself with the toaster while making Pop-Tarts in the tub.

"But that's impossible," she said. "We saw it on that TV show, *MythBusters*. An appliance dropped in the tub would have blown a circuit before it killed her."

"That's what I said." I smiled proudly at my smart daughter. "But the woman was quite old. Even a small shock might have stopped her heart."

We both looked at the toaster.

"It must have sprouted legs and jumped in with her," I said.

Her eyes widened. "That's the strangest thing I've heard all day."

I raised my eyebrows at her. "Stranger than finding out we Riddles are witches? Stranger than Corvin singing *ding-dong the witch is dead*? Stranger than this?" With some effort, I managed to levitate the heavy toaster an inch off the table.

"Hmm. You shouldn't taunt that thing," she said.

* * *

By Monday morning, my levitation skills were strong enough for me to lift and shelve a heavy book. Theoretically, anyway.

The library wasn't a safe place to practice magic since it was a popular public space, never empty during open hours. And if I wasn't within visual range of a browsing patron, I was being watched by Kathy Carmichael, her golden-brown eyes ever alert behind her round glasses. She watched me the way an owl watches a mouse who threw out the owl's weird acorn jelly on her first day at work, completely by accident and with no malice whatsoever!

I got through the morning without using magic or getting into other trouble.

At lunchtime, I went for a walk outside with another coworker who was running some errands.

His name was Frank Wonder, and he was an older man with a dramatic flair for dressing, from his bright-colored trousers to his dyed-pink hair.

He also did a hilarious impression of Kathy.

"Whooo stamped all these books?" Frank demanded in Kathy's voice. "They're crooked!" Frank used his thumbs and forefingers to form the circles of Kathy's glasses frames. "Whooo doesn't know how to hold a rectangular stamp parallel to a rectangular book?"

We were walking down the sidewalk together, three blocks from the library.

I cuffed Frank on the arm, laughing. "Stop! You're hurting my sides. And Kathy really is nice, despite her obsession with stamps being perfectly parallel."

We reached the corner. Frank used his elbow to press the button for the crosswalk light, and turned to face me, his expression thoughtful.

"Kathy is the best, actually," he said. "She's just been down in the *dumperoo* lately. Bit of an empty nest situation for the ol' bird, with her youngest son off doing whatever it is he does." He made a vague flipping gesture with one hand. "Baseball or soccer or something. Or is it football? What season does football run?"

"Beats me. Do all of Kathy's sons play professional sports?"

"Yes, unfortunately for her," he said.

The light changed, so we began crossing the street. Frank gallantly held out his elbow for me to hold onto. I took his elbow and looked around as we entered the main downtown shopping area.

My coworker was fifty-five years old, as fit as an acrobat, had hair the color of a pink flamingo, and wore a wardrobe straight out of the circus. And yet nobody inside the library or outside on the streets batted an eyelash at him. Wisteria was pretty chill for such a small town. I wondered how the local residents felt about witches.

"Kathy has three sons," Frank said. "The oldest are twins, and they've always been very active boys. The poor woman has washed more sweaty, grass-stained laundry than you or I can imagine. But now they've all flown the nest, and the boys' father is always out of town managing them, so Kathy's got their house all to herself, and she's going a bit nutty."

"I don't know what I'll do when my daughter leaves home. Maybe wait a year and then move in with her." I snorted. "She'd *love* that."

We reached the other side of the street, where he stepped over the curb while giving me a dramatic look. "Kathy has taken to *crafting*," he said. "With a *vengeance*. Don't be surprised if you get invited to a magical evening of bedazzling."

"Sounds almost as much fun as a bedazzling evening of magic." I grinned at the joke that only I understood.

"Laugh it up now," Frank said. "It won't be so funny when all your sofa pillows are covered in scratchy rhinestones and you have to buy new ones."

"Now I'm afraid," I said with mock terror. "Very afraid."

"At least she won't get rid of you," he said. "Your job is totally secure, thanks to that glowing letter of recommendation from Zinnia Riddle. How are you two related? Are you sisters? I don't know her well, but even a guy like me takes notice of such a gorgeous redhead." He looked me up and down. "And you look so much like her."

What did he say? My aunt gave me a job recommendation? I skipped to keep up with Frank's quick pace on the sidewalk. The man walked like he had long flamingo legs to match his hot-pink hair.

"Zinnia Riddle is my aunt," I said casually. "And she forgot to mention that she wrote a letter of recommendation on my behalf."

My fists were clenching. *She lied to me. That dirty witch.* She'd pretended to be as shocked as I was that we were both in Wisteria, but apparently there had been a *letter*. Her lie had been recorded on paper evidence.

Was the letter the reason she'd been avoiding me since Saturday morning? Zoey had called her several times over the weekend, but she hadn't returned the calls, except for the briefest of text messages letting us know she'd get back to us after checking on some things.

When I finally did see my long-lost aunt again, she was going to get a piece of my mind.

Frank didn't seem to notice me clenching and unclenching my fists. Nor did he notice the swirls of dust and debris sweeping themselves from the sidewalk shortly in front of us. I wasn't *trying* to levitate anything, but my emotions were having an effect on my environment. *Clear a path*, my magic seemed to say.

"It must have been a very good letter," Frank said. "There were other applicants more qualified, and I do mean *way* more qualified, but Kathy was moved by your aunt's words. Almost like she was under a spell." He chuckled. "Ain't life grand?"

"Grand, indeed. I'll have to thank my dear, sweet aunt," I said. "Thank her properly."

Frank gasped and stopped in his tracks. "I know! Chocolate. Nothing says thank you like chocolate." He nodded at a narrow storefront we'd just walked past. "And these chocolates say *thank you*, and *please*, and *let's have another*, and *oh you shouldn't have*. We simply must pop in." He winked and doubled back, skipping toward the door.

I called after him, "I thought you had to visit the post office and the bank."

Frank waved one hand. "There's no Monday chore in this world that can't wait until Tuesday."

I followed him into the chocolate shop.

As I looked over the assortment in the display case, I couldn't stop fuming over my aunt. If there was a Witch Code that banned us from messing with each other, why had Zinnia manipulated my destiny and then lied to me?

Yes, I would take Frank's suggestion to thank my aunt for her letter by getting her some chocolates. Sharp-cornered, heavy chocolates. And then I would go to her house and throw them at her while I demanded some answers.

CHAPTER 21

I looked at the array of hand-dipped chocolates, deliberating over which ones would make the best projectiles for lobbing at my lying aunt.

Eventually my mouth began to water. I tasted some free samples, then a few more, and pretty soon I didn't feel quite as irate. That's the magic of chocolate for you.

The chocolate shop had a soothing atmosphere, with heavenly harp music playing on the stereo to match the heavenly sweet aroma. My coworker Frank hummed along with the music while he looked over the featured specials and new creations.

Other than us, there were two other people inside the store, an employee and another customer. The employee was a woman with short, golden-blonde hair and an hourglass figure. She was helping a tall, dark-haired man.

She asked him, "How are the guys at work? I haven't seen Rob in a while, or Knox."

"Everyone's fine," the man said.

"I hear the Taubs are expecting. Any word yet on what it'll be?"

The man paused before replying, "What do you mean by that?" He had his back to me, so I couldn't see his face, but his voice was familiar. I found myself eavesdropping as they talked about people I didn't know.

"Boy or girl," the woman said, laughing. "What did you think I meant? Puppies or kittens?"

He didn't say anything.

"Anyhoo," the woman said in a sing-song voice. "What can I do you for today, Chet?"

My ears pricked up. I'd thought the voice was familiar.

Chet said, "I need some chocolates for a new neighbor. It's part welcome, and part apology."

I turned and stole a look at them in time to see the woman's eyebrows rise with keen interest. She fidgeted with her short, golden-blonde hair, attempting to tuck it behind her ears even though it was too short to tuck.

"Chet Moore, you haven't bought chocolates for anyone in ages. You must really like this woman. It is a woman, right?" He nodded. She reached for a gold box shaped like a heart. "Shall I fill this up?"

He crossed his arms and shook his head. "Not the heart. Give me that square box. The plain, gray one."

The blonde looked around, seemingly confused. "Do you mean this box?" She held up a gray rectangle. "This holds our supply of staples."

"Yes. That's the box I want."

She made a tsk-tsk sound. "You can't give a girl chocolates in a container for office supplies."

"Fine," he said with a huff. "Give me that other box. But not the heart one."

As I listened, I could scarcely breathe. Chet was buying me chocolates. The news should have filled me with delight. It would have had he not sounded utterly miserable. He didn't like me the way I liked him. He was only buying me a gift to smooth things over after Corvin's outburst at brunch.

I quietly backed toward the door and subtly signaled to Frank that I was going to wait outside.

Frank said, at full volume, "Zara, don't you want to get some chocolates for your aunt?"

I froze. Chet's head jerked up, and then he turned around in what felt like slow motion.

"Howdy there, neighbor," I said cheerily. "Fancy meeting you here." I looked at the blonde, who was grinning with relish.

"Helloooooo, yourself," the blonde purred. "You're Chet's new neighbor?"

Chet didn't say a word as he glanced from me to Frank and back again.

"Guilty as charged," I said to the blonde. "I've been causing all sorts of trouble on Beacon Street."

Frank interjected, "Beacon Street? Zara, did you buy that lovely Victorian Gothic on the corner? The Red Witch House?"

"Hah!" I chuckled and mimed wiping sweat from my forehead. "Again, guilty as charged," I said. "I guess everyone knows everyone else's business in a small town like this."

The blonde kept staring and grinning. *This is what passes for entertainment around here.*

I took a few steps over to where Chet stood and looked at the box in the blonde's hand. "That box is perfect," I said.

When I turned to look at Chet, he wasn't frowning, exactly, but he did look like he wished he could be absolutely anywhere else.

I gave him a neighborly smile. "Chet, go ahead and get the chocolates anyway. Don't let me ruin everything. You can bring them over tonight, and I'll pretend to be surprised, I swear."

I turned and leaned over the display of fancy chocolates. "I do love a good marzipan," I said. "And mint. Plus anything with nuts is always good. And I don't mind the fondants. Now, some people, my daughter for example, take a bite of fondant and put it back in the box because it's too sweet, but I say there's no such thing as too sweet." I straightened up and turned to face Chet once more.

He still looked like he was plotting an escape route. "No such thing as too sweet," he repeated.

I backed away slowly. I got the sense Chet might startle at sudden movements.

I pointed a thumb at the door. "I'm going to skedaddle now." I looked over at my coworker, who was watching with just as much fascination as the blonde. "Frank, I'll see you back at the library. I just remembered I left my coffee in the microwave. It's probably the perfect drinking temperature right now."

I pushed open the door and left for the library, walking quickly.

* * *

I got back to work, drank my tepid coffee, and then threw myself into my job. I tried hard not to think about my handsome neighbor, chocolates, heart-shaped boxes, or any combination thereof.

At the end of my shift, I punched out my time card with a thunderous KERCLUNK.

I was heading toward the door when Frank caught my eye and beckoned me over to his crafting table. He was cutting shapes from construction paper for a display.

"Those mountains are very pointy," I said, admiring his work.

"They're supposed to be trees, but thanks." He gestured for me to lean down closer. I did, and he whispered, "Tell me more about your *beau*. The one from the chocolate shop."

"My beau? Frank, you're so old-fashioned for a man with pink hair and orange trousers. Do you mean Chet Moore? He's just a neighbor."

"We'll see about that," he said with an eyebrow waggle. He glanced over at the reference desk, where our boss was talking to two teenagers. "How's Kathy doing today?"

"I think she's warming up to me. She invited me to craft night at her house."

He snipped a pointy tree from green paper. "That doesn't necessarily mean anything. The woman's gone craft crazy. She's probably trying to trick those teenagers into coming back to her crafting lair."

"I said I'd get back to her. Would you go with me?"

"Depends on the size of the bribe." He looked over my shoulder. "And here he comes. My devious plan worked."

I got the tingling sensation on the back of my neck that someone was approaching. "Your devious plan? Do tell, Frank Wonder."

Frank grinned. He wasn't Southern, but he enjoyed saying people's first and last names just like a Southerner. "Why, Zara Riddle. If you must know, I stalled you long enough for your beau to work up his courage and approach you." Frank flashed his eyes at me. "You're welcome."

"That pink," I said, eyeing Frank's bright locks. "It's called Apex Predator Pink, isn't it? Only animals at the top of the food chain can risk being so bright and flashy."

His eyes twinkled. "Save some of that sass for your *beau*. Take notes and tell me everything tomorrow."

I gave him a teen-quality eye roll and turned around.

Chet stood there, his green eyes bright as he flashed me a smile. He didn't look quite as uncomfortable as he'd been in the chocolate shop.

This is backwards. Our relationship was moving in reverse. Chet had been his most relaxed on the first day I'd arrived on his street. Each time since then, he'd appeared less comfortable around me. He didn't act at all like someone who'd been an acquaintance on the internet years ago and was becoming a friend now. He was acting more like someone who feared contamination, with each exposure increasing the risk of something terrible happening.

The man was troubled by something, and that something was me. My presence in his life. He'd wanted me there, but he also didn't want me there.

What was his secret? I felt like I'd known all about him once, long ago, but I couldn't remember now. His secrets were hidden in murky depths.

"Hello," I said, because someone had to break the awkward silence.

"Hi." Chet looked down at my pink leather purse, which was slung over my shoulder. "I see you've got your purse," Chet said. "If your shift is over, I can walk you home."

"And I see that *your* hands are empty," I said. "What did you do with my chocolates?"

He glanced around, looking like an animal in a trap. "I got hungry and ate them all," he said.

"I don't believe you."

"Fine. I didn't get any. It was a stupid idea." He looked down at his shoes. "But we can stop at the chocolate shop on the way home. I'll buy you anything you want. I'll buy you the whole store."

Behind us, Frank piped up, "In the heart-shaped box!"

CHAPTER 22

"It feels good to walk," Chet said. "I'm glad I had to get my work vehicle serviced today."

"Me, too. Not the work vehicle part, since I don't have one, but it does feel good to walk."

We were at the entrance to a park I hadn't noticed before. It was only a few blocks away from my usual walking commute, but since I'd only walked to my job a total of six times including that Monday, I hadn't yet explored alternate routes. The woodsy area was called, according to the sign, Pacific Spirit Park. It was a densely treed area with several walking trails, including some designated as off-leash runs for dogs.

We continued walking, entering the park. The air was a few degrees cooler on the trails, and the air felt relatively moist.

"I haven't been entirely honest with you," Chet said.

"You don't like marzipan? That explains why you made that face when I fed you the last chocolate." We had visited the chocolate shop on our way, where Chet had made good on his promise to buy me as many chocolates as I wanted. He hadn't been keen to eat many himself, but I'd insisted he partake.

Chet guffawed. "I only made that face because I've never eaten my weight in chocolates before, and I was going to explode."

"You did your best," I said. "Thank you for picking up the tab for the chocolate, but you didn't need to apologize. I'm not bothered by what Corvin said at brunch. He's a kid, and kids do unpredictable things."

"But he kept carrying on about people being dead. The boy needs to learn how to be civilized and act like a human."

"If you think he's bad now, wait 'til he hits his teens. You might want to subscribe to a Wine of the Week delivery service and start stockpiling."

"Is it really going to be like that? You and Zoey get along so well."

"Oh, well, my daughter is *amazing*. I lucked out and got better than I deserved. People say she has an old soul."

He slowed his walking pace, falling behind by a few feet. "Who says that?"

"Mostly her teachers. What do Corvin's teachers say about him?"

"Not much if they know what's good for them." Chet took big strides and caught up with me. "But I did get an email this morning congratulating Corvin for going a full week without biting anyone."

I wasn't sure if Chet meant to be funny or not. He sounded so serious. And what sort of ten-year-old goes around biting people?

"Your daughter is very important to us," Chet said.

Very important to us? What an odd thing to say. I turned to study his face. His expression was neutral, but the shade of the forest was making his cheeks appear hollow. Hungry. He could use more visits to the chocolate shop.

He caught me looking at him and bared his teeth in a quick smile. "What I mean is, Zoey could be a good influence on Corvin. Other than his outburst on Saturday, the boy's behavior has been much improved. He's happier now to spend time on his own in his room. He likes looking out his window and seeing Zoey in her room."

"It's hard for kids to not have a sibling," I said. "I would know, being an only child. Then again, nobody gets to have it both ways, so we can't really compare."

Chet's grin faded. "There's a connection between some siblings, especially twins and triplets, that nobody understands except for them. It can be powerful. And downright scary if you're dating one of them."

"Chet Moore! Have you dated twins?"

"It's not what you think." He swiveled his head left and right, looking behind us without slowing. He'd been scanning our surroundings that way since before we'd entered the forest. He checked the immediate vicinity, then the middle distance, then the far-off distance. Our visibility was limited here in the dense Pacific Northwest rain forest, but whenever we crossed another branching trail, he took a good look.

"Were you in the military?"

He coughed. "What makes you say that?"

"The way you're looking around us, like you expect Robin Hood and his band of merry thieves to swing down from the fir trees at any moment. It must be your ingrained training, and not that you know this park is a crime hotspot, because it was your idea to go through the park, and you wouldn't have brought me here if you knew it was dangerous. So, were you in the military, or are you in law enforcement, or what?"

He slowed his pace again, looking at me very carefully, as though seeing me in a new light. "I'm an engineer," he said. "I work for the town."

"That's all?"

He shrugged and put his hands in his pockets. "Would you like to see my resume?"

"No," I said. At the mention of a resume, my thoughts went back to my aunt and her letter of recommendation. I had forgotten to buy sharp-edged, heavy chocolates for lobbing at her.

"How's Zoey settling in at school?"

"Great, as far as I know." I grinned. "She hasn't bitten anyone."

"Has she changed since she turned sixteen?"

"She's not eager to learn how to drive, if that's what you mean. It was actually her idea to sell our old car before the move. She said it was to raise funds for the house deposit, but just between us, I think she wanted to avoid learning how to drive for as long as possible." I slowed and hopped over a small puddle in the middle of the trail. "Zoey's funny. In some ways, she's wise and mature beyond her years, and in other ways, she's just a little kid."

"Like how?"

I pressed my lips together to slow myself from oversharing. Zoey wouldn't appreciate me divulging all her deepest feelings to our neighbor.

"Girl stuff," I answered.

Chet, as expected, didn't press further.

"How are *you* doing, Zara? I hope they're treating you right at the library. Your coworker with the pink hair seems interesting."

"Frank? He's hilarious."

Chet kept looking around us and up at the sky.

We talked for a while about my new coworkers and the loud time card punch and even the Grumpy Corner. Chet gave the appearance of listening, but I could tell his mind was elsewhere.

"I heard a rumor about Winona Vander Zalm," I said.

This got his attention.

"Tell me what you know," he said, sounding irritated.

"I talked to another neighbor of ours on Saturday, a man named Arden. Do you know who I mean? He's got a Labradoodle named Doodles. Sweet dog."

"Arden? I believe he goes out on the ocean in a yellow boat."

"I don't know about his boat, but he told me Winona Vander Zalm electrocuted herself in the bathtub." I punched Chet on the arm. "You told me she died peacefully. That doesn't sound very peaceful to me."

He rubbed his upper arm and increased the distance between us while continuing to walk.

"That's what I wanted to talk to you about today," he said. "I'm glad you brought it up, actually. We're opening an investigation. According to the coroner's report, she did die by electrocution."

"You lied to me, Chet Moore."

He flinched as though I'd actually slapped him. "Please forgive us," he said softly.

"It's fine," I said. "I understand. You were only trying to protect me. You didn't want me thinking about getting a bazillion jolts of heart-stopping electricity every time I try to enjoy a relaxing bath."

"Exactly," he said quickly.

I stopped walking and stared at him. "Back it up a sec. What do you mean, *'We're opening an investigation'*? You're a cop? I thought you were an engineer."

"I am an engineer," he said. "But can you keep a secret?"

I bit my lower lip. A secret? Like the fact I was a witch? "Somewhat," I said.

"I work for a department that sometimes acts in conjunction with law enforcement."

"Is this a small-town thing? Like how the mayor is the coroner and also the morning radio DJ?"

"Not like that." He'd stopped along with me and now was twitching as his eyes darted around. If his ears could swivel, they'd be swiveling, scanning for sounds.

There was no one around to overhear, but I leaned in and whispered anyway. "Secret agent? FBI? Private detective?"

He nodded in the direction of a narrower path that branched from the one we stood on. "Let's keep walking."

I followed as he led us into a darker patch of forest.

The temperature here was even cooler.

I'd taken a dozen steps down the side path when I heard a GONG sound inside my head. The muscles at the base of my skull clenched, sending a blast of migraine-like pain through my head. I blinked away the stars. The pain left as quickly as it had manifested. *What was that?* It had felt like a tiny gong being rung by a tiny person living inside my skull.

Was it Winona Vander Zalm, trying to take possession of my body? Or some sort of Witchy Warning System?

Darkness flitted overhead. Did a supernatural danger lie waiting for me along this forest trail? Or was it simply a normal, human response to the overstimulation of Chet's handsome company plus digestion of a dozen rich chocolates?

I rubbed the base of my skull and waited for another blast. Nothing happened. When I looked over at Chet, he had a curious expression.

"Is everything okay?" he asked. "We can talk somewhere else if there's something about this forest that upsets you. Some people say the trees here have eyes and souls."

He had a purposeful tone, like he was trying to provoke a response. What was he up to? I mentally ran my current situation through my Zoey-simulator, where I imagined how I would feel about her doing a thing that I was doing. Would I scold her for walking in the dark forest with a guy she barely knew? Probably. But Chet was our neighbor, not a stranger. Plus Frank knew I was with him, and since Frank was such a gossip, all my coworkers knew as well.

Chet said, "Zara, talk to me. What's going on?"

"Nothing," I said with a smile. "This forest doesn't scare me. Unless you think it should? Any bears in these parts?"

"We're in the middle of a town," he said. "The scariest thing in this forest is a raccoon."

"They can be rabid," I said.

"Duly noted. I'll be on guard for rabid raccoons."

He pressed his hand lightly against the small of my back to get me walking faster. We continued on the dirt pathway, switching to single file where it narrowed further. The lush canopy overhead blocked the sun. The gong in my head hadn't gone off a second time.

After a few minutes, I said, "Tell me more about this secret investigation thing you do."

"I'll tell you what I don't do. I *don't* work for the FBI or the CIA or Homeland Security. I work for an organization that prefers to keep a low profile, and my job is to look into unusual events."

"How unusual?"

"Things that go bump in the night."

I barely restrained myself from jumping up and down. "You mean like *The X-Files*? I knew it. I knew the X-Files were real. Are you a believer, like Fox Mulder, or a skeptic like Dana Scully?"

He didn't even crack a smile. "The X-Files are part of the FBI, and I already told you I'm not with the FBI. And, more importantly, the X-Files aren't real. It's a TV show."

"Like *Wicked Wives*? That's my other favorite show," I gushed.

"Never heard of it," he said.

"Are you kidding? If you were a fan during my Zara the Camgirl days, you must have heard of it. I talked about that show constantly."

He snapped his fingers. "Oh, right! *Wicked Wives*. I remember now. That was the one about..."

"Regular housewives who are secretly witches." I laughed a little too loud. "Totally unbelievable."

Slowly, he answered, "I have an open mind."

"How open? Are you secretly a warlock or something?"

"Not a warlock," he said without hesitation. "I told you. I'm an investigator."

"There's something you're not telling me."

"Zara, I haven't told you everything about this town. There are—" He stopped walking and cupped one hand around his ear. "Did you hear that?"

I froze, putting my hand on a tree trunk for balance.

In the stillness, I heard a branch snap nearby. And then another. It hadn't been branches on the ground, though. The sound was coming from the tree branches overhead.

Chet must have realized the same thing. We both looked up at the dark canopy of lush leaves.

GONG!

The pain at the base of my skull returned with a vengeance. Ouch. I pushed the pain down to a level where it wouldn't cloud my senses. How did I do that? I didn't know and didn't have time to wonder. The canopy shivered as a dark shape flitted from one tree to another. Something was stalking us from above.

"We're not alone," Chet said.

"No kidding."

I crouched down and picked up a staff-sized branch from the side of the path. I turned to face Chet again but found only empty air. He was gone.

I whirled around, searching for him. My head was throbbing. He had to have left the path and gone into the trees.

The murky darkness around me got darker. A black form appeared in the tree canopy and grew like an ink stain.

My fingers tingled. Suddenly, my arms moved with minds of their own. A shockingly bright pulse of blue shot from my fingertips, temporarily blinding me like a camera flash.

The man playing the gong inside my head was the least of my concerns. I'd just shot lightning. From my hands.

The darkness that was descending let out a horrifying squawk. It was coming straight at me.

I repeated the hand movements. I squinted this time. Another blast of blue shot from my hands, brighter than before.

But I was hit. The darkness had struck me, or maybe it was a kickback from my blue flares. The blow knocked me off my feet. Down I went, landing flat on my back hard enough to knock the wind from my lungs. I gasped for oxygen as the darkness expanded, covering me like a cloak.

I made the hand gesture a third time. Go, lightning bolts!

But the spell—assuming it was a spell—felt wrong. Nothing came from my fingers but tiny sparks, no bigger than a struck match.

GONG!

The throbbing in my head was unbearable.

I closed my eyes. I was tired. So tired. I longed for the quiet of the bottom of the sea, the peaceful absence of other minds disturbing my thoughts.

Did I hear wings?

The air around me beat with what felt and sounded like huge wings. The wind swirled around me, sweeping dirt and grime into my nose and mouth.

I heard a voice over the gonging and the wind. *Sleep now, my beauty. Sleep, and wait. You will rise again in the eyes of...*

My fingers tingled. I rolled over and grappled in the darkness for my stick.

Chet had abandoned me to a monster. Or he was the monster.

Either way, I wasn't going down without a fight.

CHAPTER 23

My eyes were watering from the debris flying at my face, but I managed to open my eyelids a crack. I hadn't found my big stick yet, but my fingers were tingling. I pointed my hands straight up and tensed my body. My fingertips sparked once more—barely—with a damp hiss.

The wind was tearing at the trees, knocking down branches all around me.

Something shrieked.

I opened my eyes wider. The wind slowed just as I did, and I could see the darkness taking form. It was a bird. An enormous monster of a bird. It shrieked again, its cry loud enough to make my ears ring. It was descending toward me. Its gold eyes flashed in the midst of its inky mass. They were the largest eyes I'd ever seen outside of a museum. As it neared, its wingspan spread so wide I couldn't see both wingtips at once.

I finally found the stick, gripped it tightly, and thrust the tip into the air. I braced the base of the makeshift spear between my knees and the forest floor.

The creature beat its wings in reverse and hung in the air, its feathered chest inches from the tip of my stick. Gold eyes glared at me. The sharp beak split open to let out another cry, this one a scream. The beast was so close, I could smell its breath, mingling with the sweet pine of the forest and decaying leaves around me.

I raised my free hand and willed my magic to work. Telekinesis, or blue lightning. *Come on, anything!* My fingertips grew hot, but nothing flashed. The energy reservoir for my witch defenses had been drained.

Movement flashed at the edge of my vision.

Not another one, I thought, and began grappling around for a second spear.

This darkness was another beast, but not one of the air. This one was gray and furry, growling. It launched from the ground beside me and flew through the air like an arrow of fury.

A wolf.

The wolf's mouth gaped, big white teeth flashing. It attacked the great bird with open jaws. Their cries mingled, becoming one chorus of rage.

I cautiously crouched down and gripped my stick with both hands. I could try to jab the tumultuous ball of feathers and fur, but the beasts were moving too wildly for me to get a clear shot with the stick. And I wasn't entirely sure which was my foe.

With a staccato squawk, the bird beat its mighty wings. More branches rained down as the darkness headed skyward.

It clutched the snarling wolf in its talons. The two flew crookedly into the canopy, their battle cries receding. Leaves and branches rained down as the beasts fought in the treetops.

And then, with one last angry shriek, the bird appeared in a patch of blue sky overhead. Flying away. Alone.

More branches snapped. Something crashed down to the ground beside me. The wolf. The great furry beast was gasping, standing on shaky legs, but it was alive.

"Chet," I said. "You saved my bacon."

The wolf whimpered and took two steps toward me.

"Chet," I said softly. "We're going to be okay."

The wolf nudged my outstretched hand and licked my palm.

I looked up at the canopy again. How was I so sure the wolf was Chet? He could have been the bird. Or he could have been neither. Humans weren't animals, not unless shapeshifters were real. Just because witches were real didn't mean every monster was. Had I gone completely crazy?

The wolf let out a soft bark.

I knelt down and looked into its dark eyes, which were as black as the bottom of a well. As we stared at each other, I saw a glimmer of green in its dark eyes.

"Wolf, bark once for yes and twice for no. Are you Chet?"

"Woof." *Yes.*

"What was that bird you were fighting?"

The wolf tilted its head and blinked.

"Right. That wasn't a bark-answerable question. Chet, do you know what that bird was?"

"Woof, woof." *No.*

"Are we in danger right now?"

Chet-Wolf didn't answer.

"You should change back so we can have this conversation the human way. Can you change back?"

Chet-Wolf nudged my hand again. I ran my palm over his pelt, stopping when I reached a spot that was wet and sticky with blood. He was hurt.

My mouth watered as a queasiness rose in me. Blood.

I'd seen blood before.

I could easily recall every scrape, cut, and terrifying moment my daughter had put me through—every time there'd been blood. She'd been a cautious child, but she'd still managed to get hurt. The first time it was bad, she'd cut a tooth through her lip when she fell. My vision had grown dark at the edges, and I'd nearly fainted right there on the sidewalk. But I'd managed to quell the panic and shift into medical mode. A mother has this power, the doctor at the emergency room had told me. A mother's love has no bounds.

This was no different. I could tap into that bottomless love and keep my head. I could become Dr. Mom and be calm for Chet-Wolf until we could get him to a doctor. Or a vet. I looked up and down the dim trail. Was no one coming? Hadn't someone heard the animals howling?

I heard a voice in my head. This one was female. *No one's coming*, she said.

It wasn't my own voice. It had to be Winona Vander Zalm, channeling her nurse training into me. She'd helped bring Chet into the world as a newborn, and there was no way he was going out today. *Not today*, she said.

Find the source of the bleeding.

I smoothed Chet-Wolf's fur to find the source of the blood. I gagged. At least my queasiness was of some comfort. It proved I was still conscious.

I found the wound. Jagged. Nasty. I swallowed my fear and leaned in to look. As I pulled at the wolf's shredded hide, my hands pulsed with warmth, tingling and powerful. It was magic again, but different from the blue lightning.

The power flowed through me, along with a rush of something else. Joy. I closed my eyes and saw Chet's mother, panting on the floor. She was scared. "They're coming," she'd said between gasps. I'd taken her hand, looked into her eyes, and told her to drink her damn beverage. The shock had quieted her long enough for me to deliver her baby. The me in this scenario was Winona Vander Zalm, in one of her finer moments.

I opened my eyes to the present, in the forest. I'd barely located the gash in Chet-Wolf's pelt, yet it was already healing, stitching together under the orange glow coming from my hands. He whimpered softly on my lap.

The forest around us blurred as I tended him from head to toe, using my orange-flowing hands and fixing one gash after another. As his breathing settled, he got smaller. He was shrinking, down to the size of a regular wolf, and the wounds were shrinking along with him, but they were still horrific. The flying beast's sharp beak and talons hadn't been for show. *He tried to shred my beloved*, I thought.

My beloved? I hadn't realized Winona's bond with Chet was quite like *that*.

A woman's voice startled me out of my reverie. "Is your doggy okay?"

I turned to find a pleasant-faced woman in a red hat, walking a gray miniature Schnauzer in an equally red vest. The Schnauzer regarded Chet-Wolf with apprehension, one front paw frozen in mid-air.

"Your doggy," the woman repeated. "Is he injured?"

I found my voice deep within my gut and answered. "He got scratched up on some branches, but I think my, uh, doggy's okay."

"He's so big," she said. "Is he a purebred?"

"Definitely," I said with a nod.

"What kind? He almost looks like a wolf."

"It's a European breed," I answered, which seemed to satisfy her.

"See you around," she said breezily, tugging at her dog's leash as she turned away.

I pushed Chet-Wolf off my lap, got to my feet, and waved goodbye. The woman's Schnauzer was so transfixed by Chet-Wolf, it let itself be dragged for several yards on stiff legs before finally getting its paws working.

Once they'd disappeared from sight, I turned again to tend my hero.

He was no longer covered in a thick pelt of fur.

He was standing.

He was human.

He was completely naked.

I let out a surprised shriek.

Chet's eyebrows rose over his bright-green eyes. "*Now* you scream?"

CHAPTER 24

I distracted myself from Chet's nakedness by helping him hunt down his clothes in the nearby brush.

"No peeking," he said. "I can feel you checking me out."

I snorted as I picked up one of his shoes and shook the dirt from it. "You wish," I teased. "If I had been looking —and I'm not admitting to anything—it was only as a professional healer. If you have any more wounds from that nasty bird, let me know, and I'll fix them for you."

"You can look now," he said. "I've got jeans on."

I glanced over and caught an eyeful of his remarkably fit upper body. I inspected his body carefully for scratches. Very carefully. Especially the abs.

"You don't even have any scars," I said. "How is that possible?"

"It's magic," he said. "I don't know how it works. Regular physics don't apply. My weight as a shifted animal is nowhere near the same as my weight as a human. Where does the mass come from, or where does it go?"

"Are you asking me?" I handed him the shoe I'd been shaking free of dirt for at least a minute while staring. "How would I know where the mass goes?"

"You're a witch, Zara. Your kind always has explanations for the physics of magic."

"My kind?" I blinked innocently. "What makes you say I'm a witch?"

"Zara, I saw you shoot a fireball from your fingertips."

"So? That doesn't prove someone's a witch."

"What else could you be?"

I shrugged. "I'm a freakishly good conductor of static electricity. The air is moist here in the forest, but I was working in the library all day. We have multiple dehumidifiers to keep the books from getting musty. Because of my dryness, and the forest's dampness, there was an imbalance. What you saw must have been static discharging."

"Nice try."

I handed over his shirt and waved for him to cover his nakedness. "Regardless, thanks for saving me from becoming bird kibble for Mr. Pointy Beak."

"You're welcome." He continued getting dressed, keeping his eyes down as he dusted dirt and dried leaves from his clothes.

With a gentle tone, he said, "Thank you for healing me, by the way. I could have stitched up on my own eventually, but it's almost impossible to shift with an injury."

"Chet, you owe me more answers. It's no coincidence I moved in next door to you, is it?"

He frowned and looked down as he brushed debris from his jeans. "How would I know? I'm not in charge of the whole world."

"But you know about *me*. You knew I was a witch, maybe before I did. You didn't tune into my webcams and chat with the other Zara-fans on Tuesday nights just because you enjoyed my sparkling wit and my unique take on popular culture, did you?"

He kept looking down. "I can't say I agreed with all your movie reviews. You gave a lot of thumbs-down reviews on perfectly good action movies."

"Chet, don't make me shoot you with a ball of blue lightning."

He met my eyes. "You couldn't hit the side of a barn right now, let alone a moving target. And that's assuming you can even muster one up." He glanced up at the dark canopy and rubbed his arms. "Let's get walking home. We're both depleted. It's a good thing we had all that chocolate, or we'd be staggering like zombies right now."

I stepped over a tree's snaking root and began walking. He caught up with a carefree skip. We continued in the direction we'd been heading before the attack began.

I would have ask him who or what the bird was, but a theory was forming in my head. I didn't dare utter it aloud.

He broke the silence. "You don't fight like a witch with sixteen years of experience. Have you been ignoring your gift?"

"Let's not dig into my history. Enough about me, let's talk about you, Chet Moore. Who do you *really* work for? Is it the MIB? By which I mean *Men in Black*?"

"Don't they deal with aliens?"

"Are you saying your organization *doesn't* deal with aliens?"

He chuckled. "I'm not authorized to tell you about my employer. Just that we're looking into the Vander Zalm case, and I may need your help eventually." He coughed into his fist. "If not on this case, maybe on a different one. Or a cold case."

"Cold case?" I skipped to keep pace with him. I was a speedy walker, but Chet had longer legs and bigger muscles, not to mention the power boost of shifter DNA.

He answered, "I'll tell you more... once you're ready."

We walked for a while in silence before he said, "I'm surprised you're not more skilled with your magic. Your defense was lopsided and weak. It's almost like you're a total newbie witch."

"Thanks," I snorted. I didn't offer more. Sure, Chet had just saved my life, and he looked like a calendar model in the nude, but I didn't trust him. If he didn't know I was a late bloomer, I wasn't going to tell him. Never reveal weakness. The less information people had about my limitations, the better.

"Why were you so shaky?" he asked. "Are you out of practice?"

"Of course I'm out of practice," I said. "For the last sixteen years, I haven't had to deal with horrible creatures flying at me from trees, not unless you count a teenager. And, for your information, my defense skills in that regard are excellent. First, you have to make sure your teenager gets enough sleep. Second, you should always have granola bars in your purse."

"Always?" He lunged for my purse. I reflexively slapped him in the chest with a fizzle of blue light. My flaccid magic slowed him down, but he grabbed for my purse again with remarkable speed. Within seconds, he'd located the granola bars in my purse and gotten most of one into his mouth.

"You might want to take off the wrapper," I said.

"Oh." He swallowed. "Too late. Do you want the other one?"

"Help yourself," I said. "You need it more than I do."

He pulled off the foil wrapper and ate the second granola bar in three seconds flat.

We emerged from the forest. The bright late-afternoon sunshine felt surreal after our ordeal.

We exchanged sheepish looks and continued walking toward home.

"You don't have to tell me the name of your employer," I said. "But does your boss know you're a werewolf?"

He let out a low, disapproving growl. "We prefer the term 'shifter.' We can change at will."

"What's the difference?"

He growled again. "While the moon does affect us, we're not *slaves* to its cycle."

"Are the other investigators all shifters? Or witches?"

"I'm not authorized to provide that information."

"Is the Vander Zalm case a homicide investigation?"

"Yes."

I gasped. "Really?"

"Suspected homicide," he said.

"Who are the suspects?"

"I'm not authorized to provide that information."

I growled back at him, though my growl sounded like a Chihuahua's compared to his. "Am I in danger?"

"We haven't ruled out the possibility it was simply an unfortunate accident. People kill themselves in bizarre, unplanned ways all the time." After a minute, he added, "But accidents don't usually cause ghosts, and you do have a ghost in your house, don't you?"

"Maybe," I answered cagily. This time it was my turn to say, "I'm not authorized to provide that information."

"Touché," he said.

"Am I a suspect?"

He gave me a surprised look. "Of course not."

"Is your son Corvin a shifter?"

He was slow to answer. "Leave Corvin out of this."

"Listen, Chet. I may be a little slow on the uptake sometimes, but your son's name literally means *raven*, and we just got attacked by what appeared to be a mutant radioactive raven on steroids. Don't tell me you're one of those clueless parents who can't believe his sweet little angel could ever do anything bad."

His walking pace slowed. "That wasn't Corvin back there attacking us. Are you always so paranoid?"

"Are you always so quick to label a sharp woman who asks questions as paranoid?"

He let out an audible breath. "Sometimes," he admitted.

"On that note, don't you think it was a strange coincidence that we were attacked by a magic creature at the exact moment you wanted to talk to me about your secret?"

He shot me a wary look. "You're driving at something."

"The whole attack was magnificent. Effective, even. It was a great way for you to win my trust. How convenient that you got to be my big, strong hero."

His upper lip curled up in a wolfish snarl. How had I not noticed how sharp his canines were before now?

He growled, "You think I enjoy getting my hide sliced to ribbons? You think shifters don't feel pain?"

I shrugged. "The end justifies the means. You endure some pain now so you can get what you want down the road."

He stuffed his hands in his pockets and glanced around. "We shouldn't be discussing this in public."

"Plus you're not authorized to tell me anything interesting."

He didn't respond.

We reached a main street, where regular people were out walking their dogs and running errands. How many of them were secretly supernatural? I people-watched in silence for a few minutes.

Chet finally spoke again, his tone gentler. "Zara, you have to be patient."

"Don't tell me what I have to be," I said. "I have my own resources. And if there's one thing a librarian knows about, it's accessing resources."

I sounded so confident, I actually believed my bluff. Maybe Chet did, too, because he shut up.

We walked the rest of the way home to Beacon Street in silence.

CHAPTER 25

Never underestimate a librarian.

Librarians are soldiers in pink cardigans, tirelessly waging war against ignorance.

We get asked more stupid questions than should be legally allowed, and if we could cast a spell to turn people into kittens, half the world would be cats. And yet, we keep showing up day after day, because we know we have the power to save souls. The right book at the right time can save a life, at any age.

A wise man—Neil Gaiman—says, "Google can bring you back 100,000 answers. A librarian can bring you back the right one."

I needed somewhere between one and 100,000 answers, and since my primary source wasn't returning phone calls, I was going to bang on her door.

On Monday night at eight o'clock, I marched toward Zinnia Riddle's house with my daughter in tow. I'd already told Zoey about the attack in the woods and Chet's supernatural abilities. She'd been shocked but had taken the news like a champ. She quickly agreed that we needed to educate ourselves. Her searches on the internet hadn't been fruitful, nor had I found anything promising at the WPL. We wanted information, and we wanted it now.

Zinnia opened the door, took one look at us, and said, "You've been attacked."

I looked down at my clothes. I'd forgotten I was filthy from rolling around on the forest floor. I had Chet's blood spattered all over my favorite charcoal-gray pencil skirt. To a casual observer, it might pass for a patterned fabric. The blood had dried and had a sparkling, metallic sheen.

Zinnia leaned down and picked at the dried blood. "This isn't human," she said.

Zoey said, "You can tell just by looking?"

Zinnia straightened up as she licked the dark flecks from her fingertip. "Shifter," she said.

For some reason—maybe because I was still in shock from the attack—I wasn't at all surprised to see my aunt taste-testing dried shifter blood. She was a witch. A redheaded, forty-eight-year-old witch who wore green corduroy skorts and weird flowered vests. *Of course* she would be sticking horrible things into her mouth.

"We're sorry to show up unexpectedly like this," Zoey said. "I kept calling, but your voicemail is full now." She wrung her hands nervously. As her mom, I knew she was just as upset over showing up at someone's house without an appointment as she was about her mother being attacked in the woods. She really hated to impose on people.

"I'm not sorry," I said.

Zoey elbowed me.

I looked around to make sure nobody was walking by the front of the house. It would be better to conduct our business inside, but Zinnia stood blocking the doorway.

I put my hands on my hips. "We're here because you forgot to tell us about shifters," I said. "Wolf shifters, and scary bird shifters, and heaven knows what else."

"Now you know," she said, putting her hands on her hips as well.

"Also, I can levitate things," I said.

"Good." She scrunched her lips together and looked me up and down. "How heavy?"

"Anything over five pounds is dicey."

She nodded. "You'll improve with practice."

I let out an exasperated sigh. "As our elder, aren't you supposed to be guiding us through these strange new developments?"

Zinnia looked from me to Zoey and then back to me again. Her hazel eyes twitched, like she was planning to cast a spell to shoo us off her porch.

Finally, she said, "Come inside." She stepped in from her doorway. "Don't just stand there on my porch talking about supernatural creatures like a couple of ding-dongs."

I turned to my daughter. "She called us ding-dongs."

Zoey gave me a thoughtful look. "I think that's how normal families are. They can call each other the worst things, but there's always love beneath the surface."

I grumbled as we entered the house, "If she loved us so much, why didn't she return our phone calls or at least warn us about—" I didn't get to finish, because she'd grabbed my arm and tugged me all the way into the house. Her hands hadn't moved off her hips, yet I could feel her fingers on my forearm. It was unsettling, to say the least.

With her hands still on her hips, her fingers tapping impatiently on the green corduroy fabric of her skort, Zinnia used magic to shut her door and lock it.

"I've been busy," she said. "My world doesn't revolve around you two. You know, I had a life long before you two showed up here in Wisteria."

"Busy doing what?" I lifted my chin defiantly. "Writing reference letters and arranging for other long-lost family members to get job offers here in this town?" I paused to let the revelation sink in.

Her expression remained stony. "Pardon me?"

"You heard me," I said. "I know all about your glowing letter—the one that convinced Kathy Carmichael to give me the job at the library despite my being less qualified than the other local applicants."

"You're welcome," she said snippily.

Zoey cut in, "You should have told us, Auntie Z. We wouldn't have been angry if you'd been honest from the start." Zoey turned to me, her brow furrowed. "Why are we angry? I'm confused. What's so bad about Auntie Z writing a reference letter?"

Zinnia simply turned and waved for us to follow her. "Tea," she said, more an announcement than an invitation.

Zoey and I exchanged a look. Zoey's stomach growled loud enough for me to hear. It was past eight o'clock on Monday evening. When I'd gotten home from my walk with Chet, we'd had so much to talk about that we'd actually forgotten to eat. That was a first for the Riddle girls.

I'd have fed her a granola bar from my purse on the walk over to Zinnia's, but Chet had devoured both of them.

"My daughter's stomach is growling," I said as I leaned down to unlace my boots. "If you've got cookies to go with that tea, it would be an offer too good to refuse."

Zoey gave me a playful hip bump, nearly knocking me over. "I can hear your stomach growling, too," she hissed.

"Follow my lead," I said.

"Because you're the all-powerful witch and I'm a big stupid nothing?" She narrowed her eyes at me.

A big stupid nothing? *Uh-oh.* The stomach growl had been a warning. My daughter was now past hungry and veering into *hangry* territory.

I finished unlacing my boots and straightened up as I patted her head. "Don't be sore that you haven't gotten any powers yet," I said softly. "Hang in there. You'll get them eventually. Remember when you were ten or eleven, and you were so worried you'd never get boobs or hips? You would put your Barbie dolls under your pillow as tributes for the Boob Fairy."

Her eyes widened. It was an adorable story, yet for some reason, my teen daughter didn't appreciate me bringing up the Boob Fairy story.

"Mom!"

"Well, it worked, didn't it? Sure, it took a couple of years, but you got your wish eventually."

She squeezed her fists together in front of her chest and gave me a dirty look. Then she stomped off, going in the direction Zinnia had gone.

I finished taking off my boots. They were the new ones my aunt had paid for the day we'd bumped into each other. I loved the long, leather laces, but they did slow me down, thus removing all the dramatic flair from my entrances and exits.

I heard water pouring and dishes clinking. The other Riddle witches were in the kitchen, by the sound of it.

On my way to the kitchen, I stopped to admire the flower wallpaper in the hallway. Well, maybe *admire* is the wrong word.

As I ran my fingertips over the giant rose and zinnia blossoms, I wondered, if Zinnia hadn't been part of a conspiracy to bring me to Wisteria, who was? When she'd told me her only involvement was writing the recommendation that Kathy Carmichael asked for, I'd wanted to believe her. She was family. She was eccentric, but I did like her already. And it wasn't just because her face was a mirror of mine. Or was it?

Stay vigilant, I told myself, and then I felt silly.

I was probably overreacting.

This must be exactly how conspiracy cranks feel. It was a chilling realization to see the similarities between myself and those kooky guys who find an unwilling audience for their talk about the Illuminati and other secret organizations. Every library gets its fair share of this type. They're generally harmless and can even be entertaining. But you wouldn't want to turn into one.

I had a funny thought about turning the tables one day at the library. I imagined myself telling some unsuspecting conspiracy crank all about how witches and wolf shifters are real, and there really *are* secret

191

organizations who investigate homicides and supernatural occurrences. They say two wrongs don't make a right, but three left turns do make a right. What about two crazy conspiracy nuts? Would the conversation suddenly take a turn for the normal?

CHAPTER 26

Zinnia's kitchen layout was similar to mine, right down to the central island surrounded with stools, but her appliances were older. The refrigerator was vintage from the nineteen-fifties—the rounded kind with a moving handle and a full door. Seeing it reminded me of the troublesome toaster we'd put on a time-out inside our freezer. A lot had happened in the three days since we'd seen my aunt, and there was so much to be discussed.

My aunt set out an array of cookies and prepared a pot of tea.

She explained, "You girls ought to know, I've been planning on gradually easing you into the magical world." She gave Zoey a sympathetic look. "But then your mother had her temper tantrum and stormed out of here. Frankly, I was a little taken aback."

"It wasn't a temper tantrum," I said. "It was a perfectly reasonable reaction to an unreasonable situation. Most people would prefer to wake up safe in their own homes after being electrocuted rather than be kidnapped to another location. Especially another location that isn't a hospital." I sniffed twice. "You know, I can't remember the last time the inside of my nose didn't have a funny smell."

Zoey said, "Shooting blue lightning at a shifter bird probably didn't help your nostrils."

Zinnia dropped the tea kettle onto the counter with a clunk. "Shifter bird? Lightning? Tell me everything."

I waved my hand. "It was no big deal. I was walking in the Pacific Spirit Forest, *all by myself*, when a crazy bird started dive bombing me."

"You weren't alone," Zoey said.

I shot her a be-quiet look so she wouldn't divulge Chet's big secret.

"Right," I said. "I wasn't alone, because there was a big dog who came charging onto the scene right when I was running out of blue lightning juice. The dog was big, like a wolf, and it chased away the bird."

Zinnia frowned at me. "How big was this bird?"

"Pterodactyl sized. But you know how fear exaggerates things. It was probably just an owl mistaking me for prey." I glanced over at Zoey to gauge her reaction. When I'd first told her about the attack, I'd downplayed the size of the flying beast.

Zinnia slowly picked up the kettle and resumed making tea. "Interesting," was all she said.

Zoey and I took turns making her plate of cookies disappear.

Zinnia refilled the plate with more cookies, put everything on a tray, and nodded for us to follow her out of the kitchen. She led us into a small yet comfortable living room. There were brocade curtains framing the windows, tapestry rugs covering most of the wood floor, and every piece of furniture was buttoned, tufted, and tasseled like a showroom for buttons, tufts, and tassels.

"Cute room," Zoey cooed. "It's so girly. The decorating gene skipped my mother entirely. Her idea of style is anything that doesn't show grease from pepperoni fingers."

Zinnia's mouth curved down in distaste. She eyed us both with suspicion, like we were about to go full slob in her pretty room.

"My daughter's right," I admitted, glancing around at the dizzying floral surfaces. Even the wallpaper had roses, ivy, and zinnias. "But rest assured, there's nothing in here I'd wipe my pepperoni fingers on." I took a napkin from the tray and spread it across my lap to put her at ease.

Zinnia poured the tea.

She asked me to explain to her again what had happened in the woods, and I did.

"It's a wolf shifter's blood on your skirt," she said. "Was it badly injured?"

"At first, but I put my hands on the wounds, and they glowed with an orange light, and then its hide stitched together by magic. I also got these visions, or memories, I guess. From Winona Vander Zalm. Other times in her life she was helping people in medical emergencies. Was she a witch, too?"

Zinnia nodded. "In a manner, yes. Winona was a healer." She looked down at the dried blood on my skirt and scrunched her lips. "Please be careful of the upholstery."

"Oops." I moved myself over to a wood chair. "We wouldn't want to infect your sofa and have it shift into a zebra," I said.

Zoey giggled at my joke. Zinnia did not.

"It appears Winona Vander Zalm has imbued you with some of her abilities," Zinnia said. "I wonder if it's permanent."

"You mean you don't know?"

Zoey uncrossed and recrossed her legs. "Auntie Z, we hoped you had all the answers." She looked at me. "Mom, tell her about the toaster."

Zinnia gave off the vibe of someone who didn't want to hear about our evil toaster, but I told her anyway.

"Hmm," she said in response. "Where is this walking toaster now?"

"Having a time-out in the freezer. Should we have put it inside a circle, or a pentagram made from chalk?"

"Salt," my aunt said. "We contain dark forces with salt, not chalk."

Salt. I'd have to try that next. "Now what? Wait around to see if Winona's old appliances try to kill me again?" I clutched my chest. "What if it's the dishwasher? I can't live without a dishwasher."

"Give me a minute," she said, getting up.

She left us alone in the overdecorated room.

Zoey turned to me and whispered, "She's probably getting us a potion. She's really into potions."

"The kind that turns people into toads? Or more like love potions?"

Zoey gave me a serious look. "She makes a sandwich spread that tastes exactly like mayonnaise but has zero calories."

"You're pulling my leg."

Zoey wrinkled her nose. "She says that unfortunately, there are side effects. You have to go to the bathroom within five minutes of eating it. She says she'll iron out the wrinkles eventually."

"Good to know. If she offers us any sandwiches, I'll politely refuse."

"You could use your telekinetic magic to scrape all the witch-mayo out of your sandwich." She sighed.

I leaned over and gave her knee a loving squeeze. "Zoey, be patient. Your magic is coming. Mine probably came on fast because it was sixteen years overdue. We'll keep trying together, okay? We're in this together." I squeezed her knee again. "Everyone else comes and goes, but you and I are forever. Family is something you're stuck with."

Right on cue, Zinnia returned to the room. She had a book in her hands.

"Let me explain about the letter," Zinnia said.

"Nobody's stopping you," I said.

She sat in a tapestry-upholstered chair across from me and folded her hands on top of her thick book. I leaned over, trying to get a peek at the spine, but I couldn't see a title. The brown binding appeared to be leather, wrinkled and cracked with age.

"I've known your boss, Kathy Carmichael, for years," Zinnia said.

Zoey interrupted, "Is she a witch, too?"

Zinnia smiled. "Not everyone in this town has supernatural powers." She pursed her lips and tucked a strand of loose red hair behind her ear. "Kathy noticed that one job applicant had an unusual name similar to my own, so she asked if we happened to be related. That was when I seized the opportunity to put in a good word for you."

I gave her a suspicious look. I was still feeling distrustful of my aunt, but not too distrustful to help myself to a few more cookies.

Zinnia smoothed her hands over the book in a bewitching, delicate gesture. "Have I convinced you?" She arched her red eyebrows. "Or do you still want to waste time accusing me of being a liar?"

Her voice betrayed her hurt feelings.

The woman was sixteen years older than me and far more worldly, but she was on her own. She lived alone in a big house. All at once, I sensed her desperation for connection. The flowers and elaborate furnishings filled the rooms in her house to compensate for a lack of family or friends. Zinnia was lonely. She needed us more than we needed her.

I could see it on her face because her face was a mirror of my own. I craved connection as well.

"No more accusations," I said.

Her eyebrows continued to climb. "Are you certain? If you look closely enough at any yard of fabric, you'll find a loose thread. Examine any human heart and you'll discover imperfections." Her lips pursed into a tightly wrinkled heart.

"Auntie Z," my daughter said gently. "Nobody here thinks the Riddle family is perfect. We want to get to know you. The real you."

Zinnia blinked and looked down at her hands. "You're here because you seek knowledge and magic. Let's not beat around the bush." She held up one hand, palm out. "Please, don't embarrass us all by pretending otherwise. I know I haven't yet earned your trust. For tonight, however, please humor your dear old aunt."

Zoey and I exchanged a look. "Sure," we both said.

My aunt's chair creaked as she leaned forward and held the book out toward me. "Take this, Zara, and open it to a random page. Completely random."

I took the tome, which was even heavier than it looked, and flipped it open at the one-third mark.

Before I could even look at the ornate script or drawings on the page, Zinnia snatched the book away again.

"It worked," Zinnia said, leaning over to study the page.

"We're new to this," I said. "You're going to have to explain everything to us like we're a couple of magical ding-dongs, because we are."

She smiled and held up the book to show us an ornate page. Then she flipped the page to show the next one in the book. It was blank. So were the following dozen pages that she flipped through.

Zoey gasped, "It's a magic book! The text only appears when you need it."

"Our youngest novice catches on quickly," Zinnia said proudly.

"What about the page I picked?" I asked. "Did it fill up with a message just for me?"

She flipped back and turned the book around to face me. The swirling words seemed to move, undulating like kelp at the bottom of the ocean.

"This confirms that you are Spirit Charmed," she said. "Zara, you are charmed against harm by ghosts, and you may communicate on their behalf."

"Like *The Ghost Whisperer*?" I turned to Zoey and explained, "That was a TV show. It's not on anymore. Maybe they'll reboot it for your generation and you guys can pretend it's brand new, like you do with everything else."

Zinnia said, "You won't learn anything about your skills by watching that show, but I admit I do enjoy programs about ghosts and witches. Even though they get absolutely everything wrong."

"My favorite was *Wicked Wives*," I said.

Zinnia's face twitched. "Well, you might learn a thing or two from that one. One of our own must have consulted in some fashion."

I slapped both of my knees. "No kidding!"

She nodded down at the book. "A witch who is Spirit Charmed will become a magnet for lost souls caught between worlds. This witch doesn't communicate directly with the spirits, but they can do things through her." She scrunched her face and scratched her head. "Those things don't usually include electrocution by toaster."

"A toaster is how she died," I said. "Apparently, she loved heating up Pop-Tarts while she was in the bathtub."

Zinnia blinked. "I can't tell if you're joking."

"I wish I were," I said. "A guy who lives in the neighborhood told me all about it. Oh, and the neighborhood kids call our place the Red Witch House. How's that for keeping a low profile?"

"We ought to paint the house," Zinnia said. "Yellow?"

I bounced up and down on the wooden chair. "Great minds think alike. That's exactly what I was thinking."

Zoey leaned forward, reaching for the book. "What about me? Will the book say anything about my gifts?"

Zinnia handed her the book. "Let's find out."

We all held our breath as Zoey opened the book.

The pages opened. They were blank, and they stayed blank. She made a tsk of disappointment. I leaned forward and patted her knee.

"Your page is still unwritten," I said. "That means you have unlimited potential."

"You're only saying that because you're my mother."

"That doesn't make it any less true," I said.

"Magic works in circuitous ways," Zinnia said. "Magic has a mind of its own. It's probably why you applied for a job in this town and why you went to the shoe store the same day I did. Some people call these things coincidence, but we witches know it's magic."

Zoey sighed. "Except some of us aren't witches."

Zinnia gave her a kindly look. "Your gift might be delayed to give us all time to adjust to Zara's gift."

"Some gift," I snorted. "I wish Winona's ghost would just tell me what she wants."

"Ghosts aren't people," Zinnia explained. "They're more like recordings, like messages that play on repeat."

"I've heard that before," Zoey said. "I read it on the internet. I thought you said the internet got scrubbed clean of real magic stuff?"

"Mostly," Zinnia said. "Some information is just so old that it's gotten embedded in the collective unconscious."

My stomach growled. The cookies were all gone. "Aunt Zinnia, do you mind if we order some pizza, or move this conversation to somewhere with pizza?"

"I've got plenty of food in my kitchen," she said, leaning forward to stand.

"Stay where you are," I said. "I'll whip something up. Other than your mystical mayonnaise, is there anything else in your refrigerator I should steer clear of?"

"Don't touch the jar of white things that look like eyeballs," she said.

"Is it something gross?"

"It's eyeballs," she said.

* * *

Twenty minutes later, I was serving appetizers to my daughter and my aunt.

"This is incredible," Zinnia said.

My daughter said to her, "It's a new skill she's acquired since moving to Wisteria, and it's the strangest thing. Back home, we joked about her burning ice cubes." She held one hand alongside her mouth and stage-whispered, "Which is a thing she actually did once."

"I heard that," I said as I set the tray of food on the coffee table.

"These new culinary skills are part of being Spirit Charmed," Zinnia explained. "You take on the special life skills of any ghost who gets attached to you."

"Attached?" I looked over my shoulder. "I've got a ghost stuck to me?"

She took a deep, serious breath. "I'm afraid you do. Winona Vander Zalm must have attached herself to you when your powers kicked in. That's how you were able to whip up those fancy appetizers. It's something she would have done."

Zoey asked, "How long will this last?"

Zinnia tilted her head from side to side. "Hard to say. Eventually, she'll go away." Zinnia waved her hands like bird wings.

I hugged my arms around my chest. "Where will she go?"

"Where we all go, once we've found peace." Zinnia picked up a tiny sandwich delicately. "Once she's completed her unfinished business."

"What if her mission is to be alive again, living inside her Red Witch House and throwing elaborate dinner parties?"

Zinnia chewed slowly and then swallowed. "Is that what *you* think she wants?"

I scratched my ear, which had a tickling feeling inside the ear canal. *Dinner party*, something whispered. Was that Winona, whispering her wishes to me? *Dinner party!* The voice sounded enthused. Making appetizers at my aunt's house had gotten Winona Vander Zalm in a mood for entertaining.

Zoey gave me a big-eyed look. If I had to guess what she was thinking, it would be that we should tell our aunt about the investigation Chet was conducting.

I gave her a tiny head shake. No. We couldn't trust Zinnia any further than we could throw her. What if she was the one behind the bird attack in the forest? Or what if I blew Chet's secret-agent cover and ruined his whole life?

Zinnia leaned forward and looked into my eyes. "Are you having a vision right now?"

"Maybe," I said. "What are your plans for Friday?"

"That depends," she answered tentatively. "Will you be throwing any small appliances into water that night?"

I patted my left shoulder, where I imagined a ghostly hand resting. "That's the old, misunderstood Winona Vander Zalm. No more toaster hijinks. She and I are taking our relationship to the next level."

"She's communicating with you?"

I nodded. "She was whispering in my ear just now. She wants to throw another dinner party. A big one."

"The housewarming party," Zoey said. "We can invite everyone we know."

Yes, the voice whispered. *Let's have a party.*

My aunt bobbed her head and pulled her phone from a pocket in her skort. She frowned at the screen then looked at the dried shifter blood on my skirt. She frowned at the phone again, then looked up at me.

"That blood belongs to Chet Moore," she said.

I tried to think of something to say, but I couldn't hear myself think over the ghost in my head, buzzing happily about a dinner menu.

"And you knew," Zinnia said, her eyes narrowing. "You lied to me."

"I guess that makes us even."

"Witches don't keep score with each other," she sniped. "What else haven't you told me?"

I looked over at Zoey, who gave me a shrug.

"Chet's investigating Ms. Vander Zalm's death," I said, and I went on to tell her what little information I'd dragged out of him.

When I was done, she said, "That matches up with my information."

"Who's your contact?"

"You'll find out soon enough," she said.

"Is it your guy?"

She nearly choked on the sandwich she'd been eating. "My guy?"

"The one who checked my house for bugs."

"If you must know, yes. But that's all I can tell you for now. I promise, soon I'll share everything with you. Soon."

"You'd better. Because after you come to our rockin' house party on Friday, Zoey and I will be your new favorite people."

"You already are," she said, so softly I wasn't sure if she'd actually said it or I was reading her mind.

CHAPTER 27

I managed to get through the week without being electrocuted or attacked by pterodactyl-sized birds.

By the time Friday came around, I was skipping around with excitement about the dinner party.

The only thing that wasn't falling into place was a guest for the tenth place setting. I told Zoey to invite a new friend from school, but she insisted she had "too many" new friends and couldn't *possibly* narrow it down to one. I suspected the number of new friends she'd made over the past two weeks was close to zero, but I kept my suspicions to myself. She was already self-conscious about fitting in, what with her obsession with being *normal*. I knew, based on my previous sixteen years of living with the girl, that pushing her for details or nosing my way in would help neither of us.

Besides, perhaps I was expecting too much of her in the socializing department. Making new friends isn't easy. When I'd been a young teenager, I used to tag along with a group of older kids, mostly guys. Our friendship had been based more on proximity than shared interests. My mother had rented part of our property out to a few families over the years, including a single father whose son, Nash, had become something like a big brother to me. We shared a back yard, so he couldn't get rid of me. If I hadn't had Nash and his friends around all the time, would I have been any more social than Zoey? Probably not. Like my daughter, I had always loved the company of a good book.

Making friends is tough, but you have to try, even if it means working your butt off getting ready for a party.

Before the guests arrived, I reconfigured the table to seat nine, magically moving all the chairs and place settings without lifting a finger. I could lift items over five pounds with good control.

Zoey sniffed and said, "Show-off." She leaned over the table and carefully straightened the silverware. "Your accuracy could use some work," she commented. "Have you practiced handwriting on a chalkboard or a dry erase board like Auntie Z suggested?"

"Boring," I answered.

She muttered under her breath, "Magic is totally wasted on some witches."

She stretched to reach across the table, revealing a gap between her jeans and shirt where the top of her underwear was visible. I twitched one finger and gave her a hands-free wedgie. As repayment for her sass. And also just because.

She howled, "You're the worst mother in the world!"

"Second worst," I corrected. "Remember, your grandmother kicked me out of the house because I chose to give birth to you. She gets the crown title."

Zoey put her hands on her hips and glowered at me furiously. She was justifiably upset with me for the wedgie, but when I'd mentioned the sacrifices I'd made to give her life, I'd taken the wind out of her sails. I wasn't proud of my devious motherly manipulations, but I sure was good at it.

The doorbell rang.

"Ding-dong," I said. "That'll be the doorbell."

She continued glaring at me with teen angst. "You're the ding-dong."

"According to Aunt Zinnia, we're both ding-dongs."

The doorbell rang again.

"Doorbell," I said.

She gave me one big huff before turning and going to answer the door. Sometimes it was more trouble than it was worth to get her to answer the door. When she was younger, I'd read a book about parenting, and a couple of tips had stuck with me. One of them was about empowering your offspring to carve out a place in the world by giving them ownership of a specific task. It was also a great way to trick her into doing chores.

On second thought, I probably should have aspired to something grander than doorbell duty.

* * *

Our housewarming party had begun.

The Moores arrived first, and soon the conversation flowed. We would have such a wonderful mix of guys and gals, young and old. You'd have thought an expert entertainer or two had orchestrated everything.

Handsome Chet did not show up in his furry shifter form, but he did wear a dark gray suit and a yellow tie featuring foxes hiding behind trees in the woods. I couldn't take my eyes off the tie, which seemed to be a cheeky reference to our adventure in the forest.

We hadn't interacted much since the attack. He still seemed sore about my suspicions, and I was annoyed that he wouldn't tell me more about his employer. We'd left the supernatural stuff unspoken and only chatted a few times over the fence about the weather and this party.

He caught me staring and said, "You like my foxy tie."

"I like your foxy everything." I smiled at him, feeling unsteady when he locked those handsome green eyes on mine. He'd saved my life, and then I'd saved his. Something like that changes a relationship.

"I'm not half as foxy as you," he said.

I felt my cheeks flush at his flirtation. This playful interaction felt wonderful. Apparently, he had forgiven me for my paranoia earlier in the week. It must have upset him when I suggested his son was behind the attack, but he'd had time to realize I wasn't crazy. Maybe it was the soft lighting or the party ambiance, but I felt our friendship was evolving, deepening with trust.

The eldest of the Moore family, Don, began negotiating for forbidden foods. "Is that ham? I can smell honey-glazed ham. Two slices?" He held up two fingers and looked pleadingly at Chet.

"The slices are quite thin," I said.

Chet smiled again, catching me in the tractor beam of his glittering green eyes. "If Zara wants to give you two thin slices, then it's fine with me." He winked at me.

I winked right back before turning to make sure young Corvin also felt welcome.

"So glad you could make it all the way over here," I said to the boy.

Corvin looked me right in the eyes and said, "We live next door, dummy."

I gave him the plastic smile that I used to let Zoey know she was treading on thin ice. "Aren't you adorable," I said. "How old are you? Five?"

Corvin narrowed his huge, dark eyes at me, glowering under his long, blue-black bangs. "I'm ten! You're a dummy!"

Don nudged his grandson. "Don't call people names."

"Drinks!" Zoey announced. "Who wants a fancy drink that may or may not come from a juice box?"

While Corvin and Don were distracted by Zoey taking bartender orders, I sidled up to Chet and whispered, "How's the investigation going?"

"Not bad," he said. "How are things at the library?"

"I've been researching secret organizations. Blink twice if you're a member of the Illuminati."

He didn't blink.

"Freemasons." No blink. "Skull and Bones? The Rosicrucians? Knights Templar? Golden Cross? Druids? Hermetic Order of the Golden Dawn?"

He kept staring into my eyes, unwavering. "You're quite the librarian."

I continued, "Bilderberg Group? The Ancient Arabic Order of the Nobles of the Mystic Shrine?"

His eyes wrinkled at the corners, but he didn't blink. "I'm not a Shriner, but they do excellent work for charities. I have made a few donations."

"I'll keep looking," I said. "Librarians don't give up easily."

He looked down at the foxes on his yellow tie and chuckled.

"Can you tell me anything about the case?" I asked. "She is *my* ghost, after all."

He glanced around to make sure nobody was paying attention to us. "Since you asked so nicely, I've been looking into Winona Vander Zalm's former lovers, as well as any other society ladies she tangled with over the years. She was a well-liked woman, but she lived a long life. Very long. Long enough to cross a few people."

"Your family must have loved her for helping your mother give birth to you." I glanced down at the floor beneath our feet. "Was it right about here?"

He stepped in closer to me. I could feel, through my elegant black party dress, the warmth radiating from Chet's body.

With a low, gruff tone, he said, "You tell me. Are you feeling anything special about this part of the room?"

I batted my eyelashes, temporarily speechless. I did feel something special, but it was all coming from Chet, not some patch of hardwood. We continued to stare at each other. Was his face moving closer to mine? Was I imagining things, or was he about to kiss me?

The doorbell rang.

"Doorbell," I said.

He grinned. "Doorbell."

I pointed over my shoulder and stepped back. "That's not my job, but I'm going to answer the door anyway."

"Sure," he said, glancing around. "I'll check on Corvin and make sure he's being nice to Zoey."

I excused myself and ran to the door.

It was my boss, Kathy, and my coworker, Frank.

While I greeted them and took their jackets, I heard Chet bark, "Corvin! You've got to be more careful!"

"It's just juice," I heard Zoey say. "I'll take him to the washroom and get him cleaned up."

Corvin whined, "Stop touching me! I don't want a big sister."

Meanwhile, at the doorway, Frank caught my eye and raised his pink eyebrows. "Family drama?"

"Neighbor drama," I said, and I explained how my offspring and Chet's offspring had sort of a like-hate thing.

Kathy shook her head. "Boys are harder than girls," she said. "That's the Moore boy? He's an odd one, with those giant, dark eyes."

"Like a spooky cartoon come to life," Frank agreed.

We all listened as my daughter patiently responded to Corvin, "If I'm not your big sister, how about a friend? A friend who's older than you can be very useful, especially when you want certain things that you can't get yourself."

"Like what?" he asked. I could hear him being charmed. Witch powers or not, my daughter had a knack for logical persuasion. I crossed my fingers and hoped they could get along. Then I quickly uncrossed my fingers and cleared my mind before I accidentally cast a spell I knew nothing about.

Zoey lowered her voice, so we couldn't hear the rest of their conversation.

I clapped my hands and refocused on my librarian friends. "Drinks?"

Frank said, "I simply *must* get a full tour of the house before dinner, or I won't be able to sit still." He wrinkled his nose apologetically. "I'd be trying to see through your walls and visualize the floor plan."

"No problem," I said. "Welcome to my house. Please elbow me if I'm saying *my house* too much. It's my new favorite phrase." I finished hanging up their jackets and then led them up the stairs to the second floor. Both made ooh-aah sounds as they admired the bedrooms and the spacious linen closet.

When we got to the master bathroom, Kathy ran her hands over the rolled edge of the cast iron tub. She hooted, "Whooo doesn't love a claw-foot tub? Who?"

"My daughter," I said. "That's who. She says the tub has weird chicken feet."

Frank turned away from us to admire his flamingo-pink hair in the bathroom's mirror. "My sister has weird chicken feet," he said. "And I don't mean on her antique bathtub. But at least her feet go with her weird chicken legs just fine."

Kathy pushed her round glasses up her small, sharp, owl-like nose. "Zara, I adore what you've done with the place. I'm glad you kept some of Winona's window coverings. She certainly loved her colors, but it all goes beautifully with your furnishings."

I turned to her, surprised. "You've been here before?"

"A time or two," she said.

"You knew Winona?"

"Who didn't know Winona? She had her spectacular hands in everything, including countless fundraisers for the library." She beckoned for us to lean in and whispered, "I was right here, in this house, only a month before she died."

Frank made a strangled noise and side-stepped toward the bathroom door. He caught my eye and asked, "Is it true she died in that tub?" His eyes bulged as he glanced at the claw-foot antique.

Something took hold of me. Winona herself. Without warning, she slipped over me like a silk shawl. I tipped my head back and let out a bold laugh.

The two of them stared at me in silence. Kathy's owl eyes grew rounder. Frank's shock of pink hair looked more shocked than usual.

I simply smiled, my face smooth and relaxed. Winona's voice came from my voice box. "Darlings, let us not speak of sad and dreary things on this beautiful evening," I said. "Back downstairs with us, to make merry and quicken the night!"

They followed my lead without argument.

We arrived back on the main floor to find the real estate agent, Dorothy Tibbits, peering in the front door.

Dorothy called out, "Hello? Is this Zara Riddle's intimate little dinner party, or have I wandered into some groovy, exclusive nightclub?"

I waved Dorothy in and introduced her to the librarians. Dorothy had brought a wicker basket in place of a purse, and she had a sheaf of business cards and real estate brochures sitting on top.

Frank looked her up and down, "Oh, Ms. Tibbits and I know each other," he said coolly.

"So nice to see you again," Kathy said, shaking the Realtor's hand. "How do you know Zara?"

Dorothy turned her head from side to side, shaking her long brown pigtails. Thanks to her Botox, her face was expressionless. She seemed lost for words, so I jumped in.

"Dorothy sold me the house," I explained. "She's a terrible real estate agent! Just terrible!" I tipped my head back and laughed the way I had upstairs.

Kathy, Frank, and Dorothy stared at me with shocked, delighted, and blank expressions respectively.

What had possessed me to insult my Realtor? Simple. A ghost. My three guests waited for an explanation, but I couldn't exactly tell them a ghost was partying in my voice box. Nor could I deny what I'd said. Dorothy

Tibbits *was* a terrible real estate agent. A dented can of Spam could have done a better job selling the Red Witch House.

Dorothy kept giving me her blank look. "I'm terrible? Me?"

I turned to the librarians and made something up. "Dorothy is *terrible* because this house is perfect, so I'll never, ever, ever sell it, and she'll never get another commission from me." I grinned to sell the fib.

Frank nodded slowly. "This house won't be sold again, at least not until you die. Then Ms. Tibbits will swoop in like a vulture." He grinned, revealing teeth so white they were blue. "Won't you, Dorothy?"

Dorothy let out a strange cackle. "Oh, Frank, you're so naughty!" She cackled again and punched him on the arm. Hard. Twice.

"It looks like everyone's here," I said, ushering them toward the dining room.

The doorbell rang. Who could it be? Everyone I knew was already there.

I called over my shoulder, "We don't want any!"

The doorbell let out a double ding-dong.

Zoey nearly knocked me over in her haste. She yanked open the door and squealed, "Auntie Z!"

Oops. I'd forgotten that Zinnia was our ninth guest.

As I took her coat and brought my aunt into the dining room to meet the others, I sensed my spirit friend becoming agitated. Winona Vander Zalm had stopped speaking through my mouth and seemed to be withdrawing into the darkest corners of my head.

If I had to guess what the ghost was up to, I'd say she was sulking. What was she upset about? This whole housewarming party had been her idea. Her menu plan. Her guest list.

She'd wanted to entertain, and I'd gone along with her urging. Now I was in the midst of the largest and most elaborate party I'd ever thrown. She couldn't check out on me now. This was how she showed her gratitude?

Honestly, some ghosts. Worse than teenagers.

* * *

If the point of a housewarming is to make the house warm, my party was a huge success. We had to keep opening windows to let out the combined body heat of myself, Zoey, Aunt Zinnia, Chet, Corvin, Grampa Don, Dorothy Tibbits, Kathy Carmichael, and Frank Wonder. Because the climate of Wisteria is so mild, the house wasn't equipped with central air conditioning, so we got rather toasty.

Before that Friday, the only "stand-up dinner party" I'd thrown was the kind where I stood over the sink, shoveling leftovers into my mouth. It had been Winona's idea to create a finger-food menu that would allow people to mingle. On Wednesday, she'd used my hand to write out the shopping list, and on Thursday I picked up the groceries and did some pre-party prep. Everything was going smoothly Friday night.

The evening's meal kicked off with "stick food," as Zoey called it—skewers of marinated vegetables and fresh mozzarella balls. Next were crab wonton cups, asparagus spears rolled in ham, bruschetta with three kinds of tapenade, miniature stuffed potatoes, and Greek-style lamb souvlaki. For the kids, there were miniature hot dogs and burgers. The mini dogs were such a hit, I had to whip up a second batch, and even so, Corvin pouted when they were all gone.

"Wonderful party," Frank said. "Zara, tell me something. I went to get some ice cubes in your kitchen, and I saw a strange appliance inside your freezer. Are you making fresh ice cream?"

The words *fresh ice cream* were as effective as a klaxon at getting everyone's attention. All eyes turned toward me. We were gathered in the living room, half sitting and half standing. Zoey and I had lugged the dining room table in earlier to hold the buffet at the side of the room. It wasn't until that moment, with all eyes on me, that I realized how many eyes eight people had. Sixteen eyes were on me.

"Inside your freezer," Frank repeated. "Am I crazy, or is there a big metal appliance in there?"

"Oh, that's just the toaster," I said with a hand wave. "Long story."

All eyes stayed on me.

Corvin reached into his pocket and withdrew a squashed miniature hot dog. He ate it without taking his big eyes off me.

Dorothy Tibbits took a seat facing me and smoothed her blue pinafore dress. "Sounds like a good story, Zara. Tell us more."

Kathy Carmichael, who'd been lifting a miniature stuffed potato to her lips, returned the food to her plate. "Who keeps a toaster in the freezer?"

I looked at Chet for help. He gave me a wide-eyed look. He didn't know about the toaster's attempts to electrocute or trip me, because I hadn't told him.

Step in any time, I said to Winona Vander Zalm inside my head. *You could riff on the word "toaster" and propose a toast.*

My ghost said nothing. She'd gone on her break and fallen asleep.

Zoey stood up. "The toaster's having a time-out," she said.

Grampa Don asked, "What did the toaster do?"

Everyone waited expectantly.

"It burned the toast," I said.

Kathy snorted. "That's all?"

"Mom's not much of a cook," Zoey said.

I nodded. "I know it doesn't sound so dramatic, but we were down to our last two slices of cinnamon bread, and the evil toaster charred them."

Frank laughed and slapped his knee. "Wonderful story, Zara! Totally worth the dramatic buildup."

I shot him a dirty look. "Thanks, Frank."

"I don't understand," Dorothy Tibbits said, frowning and shaking her brown pigtails. "Zara, how can your daughter say you're not much of a cook?" She gestured to the buffet on the table. "This is the best food I've had in years, and I dine at all the best places."

"Ms. Vander Zalm helped me," I said.

Once more, sixteen eyes turned to me.

"I knew it," Frank said, wagging a finger at me. "That's your secret."

"You got me," I said with an eye roll. "There's a ghost in my house, and she does all my catering. Ha ha, very funny."

Corvin whispered, "There *is* a ghost."

Nobody laughed.

And then, after the longest silence, I heard the most wonderful sound. Chet, laughing.

"Oh, Zara," he said. "You're exactly the breath of fresh air we needed around here." He lifted his glass. "To our new friends, the Riddles," he said. "May we all enjoy many more good times together."

"Hear, hear," said Dorothy Tibbits.

Everyone met in the center of the room and clinked their glasses. Zoey and Corvin clinked their juice boxes.

The little boy didn't speak to me again that night, but whenever I looked his way, he was staring at me with those big, dark eyes.

What are you? I wondered. *Are you a shifter like your father? You changed into a bird and swooped at me in the forest, didn't you?*

I didn't find any answers in those dark eyes.

CHAPTER 28

THREE HOURS LATER

"Zara Riddle, you are one heck of an entertainer," Chet said as he helped gather empty wine glasses.

I surveyed the wreckage of a successful housewarming party. The previous four hours had passed like a dream, no thanks to my ghost, who'd been sulking in the corners of my mind.

Most of the guests were gone. We had moved the dining table back into the dining room for dessert. The table sat seven with the leaf installed, so we'd dismissed the kids and sat the adults around the table.

The children had gladly taken over the living room, preferring movies over grown-up conversation. Corvin and Zoey weren't interested in library circulation numbers or the price of local real estate. Both children were now asleep on the sofas.

When we checked in on the kids, Chet said of Corvin, "That kid gets heavier each time he falls asleep somewhere other than his bed. I've got my workout planned for tonight. Lugging Corvin out of here should make up for half a session with Knox."

"Knox? Is that your personal trainer?"

Chet grinned. "He wishes." He grabbed another drink glass and brought it into the kitchen. He started filling the sink with water.

"Leave those dishes for the morning," I said. "There's no rule about having to clean up the night of the party."

"There should be a rule," he said with fatherly authority. "Especially if you live in a creaky old house with gaps big enough for mice to squeeze through."

"Are you saying I have mice?" I held my hands up to my cheeks, feigning shock. "A ghost is bad enough."

Chet looked down at his feet. "What am I standing in? Salt? Sugar?"

"Probably both." I grabbed the nearby broom and started sweeping around him. "What's the deal with brooms? Why are they so closely associated with witches? I seriously doubt they're the best objects for flying on. Why not something with a seat wider than an inch? Like a bicycle?"

"A bicycle?" He chuckled.

"It's not that crazy. They flew on a bicycle in the movie *E.T.*"

He took the broom from my hands and swept up the spilled salt and sugar.

"Brooms are better for sweeping than for flying," he said. "Most supernaturals prefer airplanes. There's an in-flight snack, and you arrive at your destination without bugs in your teeth." He got down on one knee and shot me a sexy look as he swept the pieces into the dustpan.

Chet's down on one knee, I heard a voice in my head say. *This is just like that night on the beach.*

I asked, *what night on the beach? Winona Vander Zalm, is there something you're trying to tell me?*

The voice didn't answer.

Chet had finished sweeping up and was now staring at me. "Zara, are you still with us?"

"Barely."

He looked around. "I see one bottle of wine that survived the party. I've got half a mind to open it up." He quirked a dark eyebrow.

"Open the wine," I said.

He washed two glasses, grabbed the bottle, and had the cork out in ten seconds flat.

"How'd you do that?" I asked, incredulous. "I didn't even see the corkscrew."

He waggled both dark eyebrows. "Shifters don't need corkscrews." He held up his right pointer finger. The cork from the bottle appeared to be stuck to the end of his finger. It had been pierced by a thick, whirling claw. Now the claw was retracting, disappearing into his nail bed. The cork fell off with a pop. Chet tossed the cork high in the air and caught it behind his back without taking his eyes off me.

I held both hands to my chest. "Be still my beating heart! He lives right next door, and he's a human bottle opener!" I closed my eyes and tilted up my face, whispering, "Thank you for answering my prayers."

Chet poured the wine into our glasses. With a sigh, he said, "It feels so good to be my true self around someone again."

Again? I took my glass of pink wine and held it aloft for a toast. It was a sweet dessert rosé, the perfect sugary pick-me-up for the end of an evening.

"A toast to being our true selves," I said.

"Our true selves," he murmured in agreement. "Now, tell me what's been going on inside that pretty red head of yours. Have you been getting any messages from beyond?"

"Messages? Not really. Winona gives me ideas."

"How about threats?"

"Nothing's tried to kill me since the bird attack in the woods. I suppose it helps that I haven't gone anywhere near Pacific Spirit Park since our incident Monday."

"About that," he said, ruffling his dark hair with one hand. "I'm having Charl... a *coworker* look into the incident. We think it was a stray agent who got confused on a training mission. It was nothing."

"Chet, you were ripped apart. That thing tried to make a Chet-shaped furry rug out of you."

"I told you it was nothing. Forget about it." He made eye contact and held it intensely. "You need to focus on what you do best. Catching souls."

I sipped my wine. "Catching souls? My aunt calls it being Spirit Charmed."

"Zinnia Riddle," Chet said, nodding. "Is she training you?"

I glugged more wine and cursed myself for spilling Zinnia's secret. It would have been a terrible mistake if he hadn't already known all about her.

I walked over to the kitchen island and took a seat on a bar stool. After standing throughout the party, my feet appreciated the break. Chet took a seat across from me and struck a casual pose with his elbows on the kitchen island. He loosened his yellow tie and unbuttoned the top of his shirt.

"Zara, you don't have to tell me anything you don't want to share," he said. "But you will find I'm a good listener."

We'll see about that, I thought, and I began telling him about some of the funny things that had happened at the library that week. It had to be boring compared to his work as a secret investigator, but he really was a good listener.

I kept stopping myself to get him talking about himself, but he was a conversational ninja, always turning it back to me.

I found myself telling him about everything that had happened over the past two weeks, from throwing out Kathy's acorn jelly on my first day at the library to giving my daughter a magical wedgie before the party.

I tried to stop my chatter, but those green eyes kept shifting between shades of moss and emerald, and I kept sharing. I wanted nothing standing between us. Here was the man I'd been looking for, the man I could be myself with. After sixteen years of nothing substantial, I was ready. Ready to open my heart, to bare my soul, to make terrible mistakes in the name of love.

We ran out of wine, but not conversation. I glanced over at the clock on the stove. It was four o'clock in the morning. The sun would be coming up soon. Despite the late hour, neither of us had yawned once.

"Enough about me," I said for the tenth time. "When did you find out about your powers? Were you a shifter already back during my Zara the Camgirl days? Did you and the other shifters hang out in secret internet forums?"

His green eyes darkened like doors closing. "I'm not authorized to share that information."

I groaned at hearing that hated phrase. Using my levitation magic, I grabbed a crusty bread roll, which had become significantly more crusty over the last eight hours of being out, and lobbed it across the kitchen island at Chet's head.

He reached up, wolfish claws extending from his fingertips to catch the bread roll, but he was too slow. The roll crunched into his forehead with full force and then fell away, leaving flakes of brown above his eyebrow.

I giggled. "Too slow," I teased. "You can't defeat my powers."

"You caught me by surprise," he growled. "It won't happen again."

That sounded like a dare. I fired away with three more rolls, all coming from different directions. Chet swatted away two out of three. The one that got through his claw defenses ricocheted off his ear.

"Two out of three ain't bad," I said.

He growled, "Again."

The deep timbre of his voice, combined with the way he leaned forward, eyes flashing, sent a shiver through my spine.

I selected three more rolls and floated them clumsily through the air, feigning exhaustion. Then I reached my hand out awkwardly for a water tumbler, knocking a spoon to the floor. "Oops," I said as it clattered to the floor. As soon as I sensed Chet's distraction, I fired at his head with all three rolls in sequence.

He lashed the bread rolls away in a frenzy of crumbs. The air smelled of burned toast. But the most surprising part was his face, which had contorted. His features were partway between human and wolf, a terrifying, inhuman look. My breath caught in my throat. I blinked, and the angry-looking lumps and deep wrinkles that distorted his features disappeared. He was human again, but the demonic face had burned into my mind. It was the face of nightmares.

"It's late," he said, getting to his feet. He looked down and brushed the bread crumbs from his dark-gray suit. His hands looked normal again, but they'd never look the same to me.

"Sun's coming up," I said.

"I should have left hours ago," he said, his voice gritty but quiet. "Corvin has a schedule. He should be sleeping in his own bed when the sun comes up."

I jumped up and caught him by the arm. "Wait," I said.

He wouldn't look at me. "I'm sorry I scared you."

"I'm not scared."

He slowly met my eyes.

I repeated myself. "I'm not scared. You took me by surprise, but I'm not afraid." I reached up slowly and touched his cheek with my hand.

He closed his eyes.

It was the first time I'd touched him since healing him in the forest. I felt the orange warmth in my hands once more—faint, but present.

"I mean it," I said. "Chet, you can be your true self around me."

"Zara, you're a nice girl," he said. "You didn't sign up for any of this."

"A nice girl?" I put my hands on my hips. "There's no need to be sarcastic," I joked.

"It's late." He turned and walked toward the living room.

Corvin was sleeping like a kitten. His lower half was curled under a patchwork quilt, and his top half was stretched out, nearly melting off the edge of the sofa. Chet leaned over and picked him up as easily as crumpled paper. His comment about the boy getting heavy had been a cover, part of his act of being normal. The man had supernatural strength even in human form. He cradled the sleeping ten-year-old boy easily with one arm.

"Thank you for inviting us," Chet said formally.

"Thanks for coming. Who wouldn't want a guest who comes with ten corkscrews?"

He gave me a blank look.

I held up my hand and wiggled my fingers. "Your special corkscrews."

He gave me the same look Zoey gave me for making bad puns.

Corvin stirred in his arms and made a sound like a sleeping pigeon.

Chet flicked his gaze over to Zoey, who was stirring on the couch at the sound of our voices.

"Please thank Zoey for being such a good friend to Corvin." His voice was low and thick with emotion. "The kindness of the Riddle family does not go unnoticed."

He moved with supernatural speed toward the door, and then he was gone.

I walked over to Zoey and attempted to rouse her. She flopped one sleepy hand over her eyes and mumbled, "Five more minutes."

I leaned over and brushed her red hair out of her face. She looked like a sleeping angel.

"You made me proud tonight," I whispered.

"Two minutes," she mumbled.

"You're so patient with me," I said. "I know you hate it when things change, but we're making good changes."

Her face relaxed and her breathing slowed. She was fast asleep.

"I just want you to be happy." I shook out the patchwork quilt and tucked it in around her. "Happy and safe."

A male voice behind me said, "Safe? You'll have to try harder."

I whipped around, my hands raised to defend myself.

There was someone in the room with us. Chet's father, Don.

"Grampa Don," I said. "What are you doing here?"

He sat like a coiled rattlesnake in the recliner in the darkened corner of the room.

I could have sworn I'd seen him leave with the other guests. I glanced around the room, making note of the objects that were light enough for me to lift with my magic and still heavy enough to do some damage.

CHAPTER 29

"I've always found this home very comfortable for napping," Don said, shifting the recliner into the upright position.

"What did you mean about me keeping my daughter safe?"

He rubbed his chin and looked over at Zoey, who was sleeping soundly on the sofa, her red hair fanned out on the soft velvet pillow.

"This town has many secrets," he said. "And when you two moved here, it gained a few more."

"Grampa Don, is there something you want to tell me?"

"Little ol' me?" He chuckled.

In the low light of the room, Don Moore's gray hair was the color of the ashes at the end of a burned cigarette. He'd seemed like a sweet, harmless senior citizen when he was bartering for pork products. Now, in the thin light of predawn, his facial features took on knife-edge sharpness.

"Either spit it out or hit the road," I growled.

He leaned the recliner back again, so his face was in the shadows.

I used my powers to click the nearby lamp's brightness up a notch. It wasn't the same as shining an interrogation light in someone's face, but it was better than nothing.

Don gave me the smallest of nods. "If you want to keep your family safe, you need to open your eyes," he said. "Chet can't handle everything on his own. He's blinded by his own emotions and too open to influence by the others. Especially the snaky ones." He shook his head. "Those stone-cold charmers."

I was still standing, but Grampa Don seemed to be in no hurry to leave. We were having this talk, and we were having it now.

I pushed over my daughter's feet and took a seat at the end of the sofa.

"How's Chet blinded?" I asked. "Wait. Are you also a... you-know-what?"

His sharp features didn't budge. "These abilities run in families."

I took that as a yes. "Are you a bird? Can you fly?"

"That's not what I do, and that's all I can say until we know each other better."

"Figures," I said. "Are you also an X-Files investigator?"

The corner of Don's mouth twitched up. "They weren't wrong about your sense of humor. You certainly do have a novel way of looking at things. I suppose having your powers lay dormant for so many years has altered you."

I clenched my jaw. He knew about my late-blooming powers? How? Even Chet didn't seem to know that.

"You don't know what you're talking about," I bluffed coolly. "Let's get to why you're sitting in my dark living room like some cheesy James Bond villain. Do you have a message for me? A mission? A potion request?"

"I want you to help Chet with something," he said. "Help him, but don't give him what he wants. He wants to hang on when he should let go."

"How am I supposed to help? I'm a librarian, not a detective. And yes, I already checked the library for reference materials on all things supernatural. I'm sure it comes as no surprise to you that the Wisteria Public

Library, funded by municipal taxes, doesn't carry a huge selection of leather-bound books of spells and prophecies."

"Zara, you were summoned here for a reason."

"Summoned?" My impatience bubbled up. I wanted to shake Don Moore until the truth came out. The recliner underneath the man began to shift and tremble.

The ashen-haired man shot me an amused eyebrow lift. "That's all you've got?"

The recliner rocked, reclining back creakily and then jerking back upright again. It was my power, but I couldn't control it. What had started wouldn't stop, because deep down, I wanted the chair to shake. I wanted it to snap together like the jaws of a crocodile and squeeze the truth out of Don.

Don reached into his pocket for something. At the same time, he barked, "Enough!"

The recliner obeyed and stopped its wild-bronco bucking. Next to me on the couch, Zoey whimpered and rolled over but didn't wake.

"How did you do that?" I asked Don.

"We all have our own defenses." He leaned forward and groaned as he pulled himself out of the comfortable chair. He was making noise, but his movements were steady, and he wasn't breathing hard. His old-man noises were nothing more than an act, a ruse to make people underestimate the ash-haired senior.

"It's past my bedtime," he said with a yawn.

"Don't go yet. Would you like a cup of coffee? More dessert? You haven't told me how I'm supposed to help Chet."

"You're a woman," he said. "You already know what he needs."

I felt my cheeks flush. Was he implying what I thought he was?

"Listen to the souls," he said. "Catch them and help them move on, out of this realm. It's for the best. The ones that linger become malignant."

"Don, I've tried talking to the spirit of Winona Vander Zalm. I even asked if she was murdered, and if so, by whom, but she's terrible at communicating."

"Fool. You can't tell them they're dead. They're not supposed to hurt you, but if you push them, they will."

"I can't tell ghosts they're dead? That's crazy. How am I supposed to know these things? Is there a handbook or something?"

He sneered. "Jorg Ebola would love that."

"Who?"

"Never mind. What have you gotten from the old gal?"

"Not much. Every time I try to get information, I wind up at the store buying spices and gourmet things I can't pronounce."

"What would a homicide detective do?"

Without hesitation, I answered, "Follow the money. Find out who benefits from her death, and check their alibis."

Don headed toward the front door. "Exactly," he said without looking back. "Her main asset was this home, which was sold to you."

"But I paid for it," I said. With a little help from someone.

I thought about the great deal I got. My blood ran cold. I had gotten a really good deal on the home. A steal. Even my benefactor had agreed it was a sound investment. I'd blamed the real estate agent's incompetence for the great selling price, but what if Dorothy Tibbits wasn't a lousy saleswoman? What if I'd used magic without realization or control, like when I'd made the recliner buck like a wild horse?

As my mind raced with paranoid thoughts, I felt the icy embrace of the home's former owner wrap around my heart.

"You need to get involved in this investigation," Don said. "Tell my son you can help. Don't take no for an answer. He needs you, Zara. More than you'll ever know."

"He doesn't want my help."

"Neither do most people who need help."

I sighed. As a librarian, I knew exactly how right he was. Some people, by the time they sought help, were already so angry about needing it they took it out on the person trying to help them. An endless supply of patience was not wasted on librarians.

I thought about what little I knew about Winona, other than her healing and entertaining abilities.

"She had no kids," I said. "Did she have a will? Who inherited her estate?"

Don reached for the door handle and smiled. "Winona Vander Zalm specified in her will that everything would go to *the nice family next door*. The Moore family."

"You guys? The three of you."

"Yes. The executor of Winona Vander Zalm's will was my son."

"Chet inherited this house? And then sold it to me?"

"Are you unhappy with your purchase? He gave it to you for a very good price."

"No, I'm not unhappy," I said. "Just surprised."

"Do you wish they hadn't talked you into coming here?"

"Who? The library? They didn't talk me into anything."

"Oh. So, you don't know. This should be entertaining." He yanked open the door and stepped out into the early-morning stillness. The motion-sensitive porch light came on with a blast of yellow light, and then immediately shattered with a pop and a hiss. Don Moore was a shadow.

"One more thing," the shadow said. "Don't tell Chet about this conversation."

"But—"

"There's a chance even I won't remember we talked," he said. "My memory isn't what it used to be." He looked down and shook his head. "But if I'd wanted my son to know, I would have joined your conversation in the dining room rather than letting all that jibber-jabber put me to sleep."

I snorted. Me, jibber-jabber? Okay, maybe a little.

"Zara, you're not what anyone expected, but you're exactly what we need."

The tone of his voice was as dark as his shadowed face. I nodded mutely.

He continued, his voice even darker and lower, like a growl. "She's going to open the bottle."

"What?"

"The bottle," he growled. "Unsealed. Revealed. Trouble."

"Can you be more specific?"

He coughed. "It's past my bed time."

And then he was gone.

CHAPTER 30

Grampa Don "Hide in the Dark Like a Cheesy James Bond Villain" Moore didn't say anything about not sharing our conversation with my daughter.

"Zoey," I whispered. "There's breaking news. Beep-beep-boop-boop. Breaking news. Wake up."

She lifted her head just enough to free her pillow and use it to cover her head. My daughter was lying next to me, hogging the center of my bed and squeezing me toward the edge, like the notorious bed-hog she was. She was on top of my covers and still wearing last night's clothes. She looked quite comfortable under the quilt that normally covered the sofa.

The night before, I'd left her asleep in the living room because, unlike Chet, I didn't have the shifter muscles to carry her up. She must have woken and decided my bed was the place to be, which actually was convenient for me.

I craned my neck and checked the time. Noon, right on the dot. I'd gotten maybe five hours of sleep, which would have been a luxury back when I was working full time, raising a preteen, and completing my Master's degree in library and information science.

"Beep-beep-boop-boop," I repeated. "Don't you want to hear the breaking news?"

From under the pillow, Zoey moaned, "You and Corvin's dad were looking friendly last night."

"He has a name," I said. "Are you calling him *Corvin's dad* because it's the least sexy way to describe him and you're secretly trying to sabotage any romance potential? Don't answer that. I don't want to know."

"Less paranoia, more news," she said sleepily.

I yanked the pillow away so I could watch her reactions.

I breathlessly told her about Grampa Don hiding in the living room, listening in on my conversation with Chet, and then giving his ominous warnings about keeping my family safe. Zoey frowned and nodded for me to keep talking. I told her about his request for me to help Chet with the homicide investigation, as well as the big kicker. The money for the house sale had gone to the Moores.

She'd been yawning, and the news of the inheritance made her stop midyawn. "What? She gave everything to her neighbors?"

"I know, right? Kinda makes you wonder about motives and stuff."

She pulled a strand of red hair from the corner of her mouth. "Motives? You think someone broke in over here, and threw the lady's toaster into the tub so they could get their inheritance?" She held up one hand. "Don't even say it."

But I had to say it. "How well do you know Corvin?"

She shook her head. "He's barely ten. He's no evil mastermind."

"When you were ten, you had a thriving business. You weren't evil, but you were a mastermind to some degree. You had to turn away work."

"Mom, I watered plants for a few bucks. It wasn't exactly a thriving business."

"You turned a profit."

"My only supplies were tap water."

"Exactly. You were a mastermind. Who else uses free tap water to create a profit? Those geniuses at the major soft drink manufacturers, that's who."

She rolled onto her back and stared up at the ceiling. "My mother the ghost whisperer is crazy," she muttered.

"Am I? We still don't know how Corvin got in here the day he broke our housewarming presents in the den."

"He probably walked right in the back door, like a regular person."

"Or he flew down the chimney." I paused for drama. "In bird form."

She didn't have an answer for that.

"It explains why he can see Winona's ghost," I said. "He killed her, so she has stayed behind in ghostly form, to haunt him until he dies, then she'll, I don't know, keep haunting him. It explains why she's haunting around here now."

"She's haunting him? By throwing dinner parties and making Corvin his favorite miniature hot dogs? She's a real terror, all right."

My daughter did have a good point. You don't make someone miniature hot dogs if you want them to suffer. I ruminated for a minute, staring up at the ceiling along with her.

After a minute, I said, "Zoey, I can't shake this guilty feeling that I have some connection to her death."

"You were nowhere near her when she died."

"No, but I might have done something by remote."

"You mean like hiring an assassin?"

"It sounds crazy when you say it out loud." I chewed on my thoughts a little longer. "The woman was also a magical person, some kind of healer, and she loved this house, and now I'm living in it. I'm only here because she died. If I hadn't seen this house the day I came for my interview, I don't know if I could have made the leap and taken the job." I took a deep breath and let it out slowly.

"The person with the most motivation to kill Winona Vander Zalm is me."

"Mom, don't be so self-centered," she said. "The world doesn't revolve around you."

"But—"

"No," she said with finality. "If Dorothy hadn't sold the house to you, she would have sold it to someone else. Maybe it would have been a witch, or maybe it would have been a wolf shifter, or a tentacle monster, or a sasquatch, or a... whatever they call regular people around here. If you think about it, maybe Winona *wanted you* to have this place."

"Maybe."

"Her spirit might have pulled you here."

My spine tingled. "I did feel like something was tugging at me."

She pulled herself upright and stretched like a cat. "Everyone at the party last night had a different idea about how old Ms. Vander Zalm was. Frank said he'd known her for thirty years and she hadn't aged more than ten years during that time. And nobody could say for certain which war she served in as a nurse."

"We should check the newspaper obituary for her date of birth," I said.

"Already did. They didn't list it. Mom, she was too old. Like, *way* too old."

I yawned. "Your point being?"

"She was way too old, and it was basically her time to go, no matter how it happened."

"Spoken just like a young person," I said. "You'll understand when you get older yourself. There's no such thing as too old, no good time to go."

"Whatever."

I yawned again. "Maybe I'll go back to sleep and visit her in my dreams. Then she can answer all my questions."

Zoey rolled out of the bed and whipped away all my warm bed covers. "Up and at 'em!"

"Five more minutes." I tried to grab the blankets back.

"Nope," she said. "Get up and think up some excuse to go next door. If Grampa Don wants you to help Chet, and our ghost friend wants her death avenged, and you like making kissy faces at your new boyfriend, then it's like killing three birds with one stone." She grabbed my last bit of comfort—my pillow—and pulled it out of reach. "Now march yourself into the bathroom, and hose off last night's makeup. Then march your butt next door to borrow a cup of avocado juice, which is *totally* a real thing and not nonsense I just made up." She pointed at the door to the bathroom. "Go!"

* * *

"Avocado juice?" Chet stood in the doorway of his blue house, looking perplexed.

"Zoey says it's a real thing," I said. "But if you're not up on the coolest, hippest juice blends, I guess any ol' juice will do. Pineapple. Orange. Pineapple-orange medley. Any type of medley."

Chet stepped back and waved me inside. "We do have juice."

"Perfect."

"It's frozen, so I'll have to mix it with water. And it might actually be pink lemonade."

"Made from pink lemons?"

He glanced back over his shoulder as we walked toward his kitchen. "Are you trying to trick me with logic?"

"Not at all," I said. "In fact, I'm here to help you. The avocado juice was just an excuse to get inside your house."

"No kidding." He opened the freezer compartment of a deluxe stainless steel fridge and surveyed the contents. He had several flavors of frozen juice.

"That one looks good." I used my magic to lift a container of orange concentrate. "You can't go wrong with orange."

He skewered the container mid-air with one quick claw.

"You're fast with those things," I said.

He glanced over at the kitchen window, his expression clouding over. "I should be more careful. My father warned me not to get reckless showing off, but I can't seem to help myself."

My cheeks warmed. When he'd left my house earlier that morning, he'd seemed closed off. Now, though, he was warm again. And darn it if a man alternating between hot and cold wasn't like catnip to me.

They say people with no boundaries enjoy flinging themselves at people with rigid boundaries. As soon as my powers got strong enough for me to lift my own body weight, perhaps I would literally fling myself at him. Oh, how I longed to be caught in those strong, muscular arms of his—provided he kept his claws retracted.

Chet used a handheld blender to whip the juice so it was icy cold with suspended crystals. He handed me a glass, caught my eye, and asked, "What devious things are you thinking about right now?"

"Nothing devious," I said, glancing around his kitchen. "Nice renovation. Sort of a farmhouse chic thing. Very sexy. And your layout is a mirror image of my house."

He rinsed the blender under an enormous faucet. "You can't go wrong with a huge, concrete sink," he said.

"No kidding. You could dismantle a body in there."

His nostrils widened and his upper lip twitched. "What are you implying?"

I tipped back my glass of orange juice and chugged it noisily.

When I was done, I said brightly, "Great juice. You can taste that Florida sunshine." I set the glass on his polished-concrete and wiped my mouth with the back of my hand. "So, what's on the agenda for today? I've got some time on my hands, so I'm here to help with your investigation."

His upper lip twitched wolfishly. "How can you help? Has the spirit been giving you new information?"

"Yes!" I held my finger in the air triumphantly. "Winona Vander Zalm wants me to make sure the money from the sale of the house got to her heirs without any complications. Her heirs, who happen to be..." I closed my eyes and rubbed my temples with two fingers. "The *Moo* family? Winona, do you mean cows? For someone who was such a cow lover, you sure know a lot of recipes for veal."

"Zara, what are you doing?"

I shushed Chet and continued. "What's that, Winona? M-O-O-R-E. That's funny. Do you mean the neighbors in the blue house? The Moore family?"

Chet made a *hmm* noise.

I opened my eyes and gave him a curious look. "Is it true? Did Ms. Vander Zalm leave your family her entire fortune?"

His green eyes darkened as they narrowed. "She knew about my work," he said. His tone was low and cold, guarded.

"I don't understand. Did she give you money to investigate her murder? If she was able to see the future, why didn't she just avoid getting murdered? And furthermore, was she a witch or not? My aunt says she wasn't, but my aunt isn't always forthcoming."

"She wasn't a witch the way you are," Chet said, his face and body as tense as his voice.

"Then what was she?" My senses buzzed. Something was crawling up behind me, crawling up the backs of my legs like a hundred tiny black scorpions. I glanced over my shoulder, expecting to see an army of creepie crawlies, but there was nothing.

"She was *careless*," he said. "But that's for me to worry about. Not you. I have everything under control."

The buzzing of my senses increased. I checked over my shoulder again for the army of tiny black scorpions. Still nothing. But then I smelled mint—freshly crushed mint, like you might muddle in a tumbler for a mojito. A feeling like a cool silk scarf slipped over me. Winona Vander Zalm was here. I relaxed and let her spirit take over my body.

"No, you don't have everything under control," Winona snapped, using my voice. "Chet, you boys need a woman around to calm down the masculine energy."

He blinked and took a step back. "Ms. Vander Zalm?"

"That's why I'm willing you my fortune. I shouldn't care what happens after I'm dead, but I'd rather not see my life's savings go to the government after I worked so hard to keep it from them all these years. Take the cash and go on a vacation. Start an education fund for Corvin. That little boy needs all the help he can get. Such a strange child." A minty-cool chill ran through me. This speech was the most she'd said so far, and she showed no sign of letting up. "Why not start a scholarship fund for young witches and all the other beasties? Use my money for something good, Chet. And then use your *life* for something good as well. Don't pine away over the past. Move on, like Don would. And don't argue, my dear. I have spoken."

The minty-cool chill in my body turned to fizzy bubbles and then dissipated. I trembled. She was gone, her recorded words replayed.

I rubbed my neck. "That was her, Chet. She's gone now. Why didn't you ask her who killed her?"

"She couldn't have told us," he said glumly. "Spirits aren't much more than echoes. You, of all people, should know that."

"Right," I said, nodding. "Ghosts are like the holograms in the old *Star Wars*. Yes, I know all about that. She must have said all those things to you some other time, right? Do you remember when? Maybe it's significant."

He looked up pensively. "I remember it was right here in this kitchen, about a year ago. It was the day she met with her lawyer to change her will. I begged her not to make me her beneficiary, but she didn't listen."

"Does your secret employer know about this? I'm no lawyer, but it sounds like a wee bit of a conflict of interest, investigating a murder when you're the prime suspect."

He gave me a wounded look, his lean cheeks showing deep shadows. "You can't actually think I'm a suspect."

"I'd never suspect you, of course." I swallowed. "Or your family."

"Good."

"But what about your boss at the FBI? The guy with the shiny head. What's his name again? Skinner?"

He shook his head. "I don't work for the imaginary FBI X-Files."

I leaned across the smooth polished concrete and rested my chin on my hands. "So, what did you do with the cash? Did you dump all of the old lady's house money into your renovation?" I glanced around, whistling. "These finishings don't look cheap."

He managed to look both offended and flattered at the same time. "I've renovated this house over several years, mostly using my own two hands."

"What about your father? Does Grampa Don like getting his hands dirty? Would you say he's a hands-on guy? Always getting into your business?"

He straightened up and squared his shoulders. "The men of the Moore family stick together." He puffed out his chest. "And as for the money from the estate, I've put it in a charitable fund to help young people. Not that there was very much money left on the table after the smoke cleared."

"She had debts?"

"Ms. Vander Zalm's love of entertaining would have bankrupted her eventually. She'd taken out several loans against the house over the years."

"Oh." *So much for cash as a motive.*

"If I'd realized the full extent of her debt, I wouldn't have hired Dorothy Tibbits to sell the place. She's a *terrible* real estate agent."

"She really is the worst. Why'd you pick her?"

He swished his lips from side to side. "Honestly, I don't know. It seemed like a good idea at the time. I guess I'm just a sucker for a pretty face." He gave me an impish grin. "And that blue pinafore."

"Her face is pretty, all right. Pretty like Saran Wrap stretched over leftover meatloaf." I looked down at my hands. "Sorry. That was unkind. It's not like me to judge a book by its cover."

"You sounded a lot like Winona just now. The ghost's rubbing off on you more each day. You'd better get rid of her before your whole personality changes."

"What?" I stared at him, open mouthed. Was he kidding, or did he know more about being Spirit Charmed than I did?

"Well, you can't be too upset," he said while tidying up some cereal bowls. "Thanks to Dorothy being so terrible, I took your ridiculous low-ball offer on the Red Witch House. My loss is your gain. You practically stole the place."

I jerked my head up and took a more assertive posture. "Excuse me? Just because I know how to drive a bargain doesn't mean I stole the place. I bought it fair and square on the open market. And clearly my offer was better than all the others."

"There were no other offers," he said. "Dorothy thought I should wait it out. She said spring was too hectic and there were too many other houses on the market. She suggested pulling it and relisting in

November. I think she was either being lazy or distracted by trying to sell her own property. Either she's the World's Worst Realtor, or she was up to something."

"At least it all worked out, plus you got a *great* neighbor."

He poured himself a glass of orange juice and stared at it. "Honestly, just between the two of us, Ms. Vander Zalm had gotten a little kooky toward the end. It wasn't just eating Pop-Tarts in the bathtub. She got confused about other things. She kept saying she was done, ready to move on."

"Do you think she might have killed herself?"

Chet winced. "It's a possibility. When she was found, the doors and windows were all locked from the inside. I had to break down the back door to check on her."

"You're the one who found her? I'm so sorry."

His eyes glistened. He turned away and cleared his throat. "We all have to go sometime. And going to the next place is better than lingering for an eternity in the twilight hours."

Lingering. Twilight hours.

I caught a whiff of another scent. It was similar to the minty-cool smell I associated with a spirit arriving but closer to the ozone freshness of the ocean shore. I sensed a presence, and this one was more powerful than Ms. Vander Zalm. I caught a wave of raw emotion—rage. Was it coming from Chet? Or someone else in the Moore household? Suddenly, I wanted to be back in my own house, where I had some hope of protection thanks to the protective wards installed by Zinnia's friend.

I gripped the edge of the concrete and fought to keep control of my faculties.

Chet still had his back to me and hadn't noticed me struggling to stay present.

He said, "The investigation's at a standstill. My bosses are ready to close the case and rule it an accident."

The presence filled the room with ozone and then rushed into me, filling my senses.

Chet was still talking, but I couldn't understand his words.

The world around me narrowed to a tiny pinhole of light. My mouth watered, my knees weakened, and I felt my body buckle.

As I lost consciousness, all was peace and tranquility, like undulating kelp at the bottom of the sea.

CHAPTER 31

"Zara, you fainted." Chet was gently reviving me.

I fluttered my eyelids and closed them again, taking time to savor the contact. He was sitting cross-legged on his kitchen floor with my head cradled on his lap. His body was warm and soothing.

"You're okay," he said, stroking my hair.

I was more than okay. Sure, the fainting had felt like a dump truck's load of sand being poured over me, but having my head in Chet's lap and his hands stroking my hair made it all worth it. I would pack up my things and move into a new haunted house a thousand times to repeat this moment.

As I returned to consciousness, a little voice in the back of my head started heckling. *Really? You're going all melty-guts for this guy you barely know?*

I tried to ignore the little voice, but it did have a point. I'd fallen pretty hard for Chet Moore, right from the first minute we met. Zoey had accused me of being a Turbo-flirter, and she wasn't wrong. But Chet wasn't like other handsome guys. It was as though we'd known each other intimately before now and were only meeting up again after a separation of nearly a year.

Nearly a year? The voice in my head let out a very witchy cackle. *That seems awfully specific, Zara. Don't you find it strange that your connection with this guy was so instant? And isn't it curious how your new neighbor just happened to recognize you from a few minutes of internet fame that happened over fifteen years ago? It's the sort of thing that should make a person wonder.*

The voice was right again. Now I did wonder.

I had to start paying more attention to coincidences that weren't coincidences after all, such as having a gnome of a man mistake me for my aunt.

Moving next door to a former Zara the Camgirl fan was highly unlikely. I'd been popular, but not *that* popular. But I couldn't be suspicious of Chet, because I was the one who'd moved in next to him. If anyone was the stalker in our equation, it was me. My move to Wisteria and my house purchase had been my own personal choices. Impulsive and foolhardy but still mine.

Really? The little voice wasn't shutting up.

Really, I replied. Buying the house had been my decision. How dare the voice question me. I'd been right there in my body when I signed the purchase offer. I remembered it clearly. I hadn't been in a daze because even though the spirit of Winona Vander Zalm would have been floating around at the time, I hadn't yet become a witch. So, unless there was someone else up inside my noggin—someone other than my pesky doubting voice—it must have been me.

I am the captain of my own destiny.

Unless...

Was there another spirit affecting my choices? Or a magic spell? The crush on Chet Moore was intense. The only other time I'd ever fallen in love at first sight was when I first laid eyes on Zoey, in the back of a taxi, swaddled in the driver's extra sweatshirt.

Remembering the night I gave birth sent me further away from Chet's kitchen and my body. I was drifting back through time to that night, back to the words the driver said to me following the surprisingly quick delivery of my sweet baby girl. The man said...

"Stay with me," Chet said. His voice was calm yet sharp with worry.

He was still cradling my head on his lap, and now he was shaking me by the shoulders.

The voice in the back of my head was quiet. *No more from the peanut gallery?* The memory of my baby swaddled in a sweatshirt floated away.

Gravity returned, and with a squeeze all over my body, I was birthed back into the present.

My throat burned. I tried to speak, but all that came out was a groan.

Chet shook me again. "Can you talk?" He pressed his cool hand against my forehead. I remembered another time—another time when he'd nursed me back to health. I'd had a fever. I'd been delirious, worried about my sisters. Chet had dipped me in an ice bath, and I'd screamed. It was just a fever, a flu that had been going around the office, but it had hit me hard. Once the fever broke, I was fine, but he'd been so worried.

"No ice," I said, mumbling through my haze. "Don't put me in the ice bath."

Chet's hands, which had been gently shaking me awake, stopped moving.

He asked, "What ice bath?" His voice was hoarse, almost a whisper. "Is it... is it you?"

I coughed and forced my eyes to open.

"Me? What?"

He was staring down at me with a helpless expression. "Zara, are you yourself again?"

"Coffee," I croaked. "I won't be myself until I've had some coffee."

* * *

After I'd revived, Chet offered me not just coffee but a full breakfast.

I'd made myself comfortable at his kitchen counter and did my best to make a latte disappear.

I kept blinking and rubbing my eyes. My vision was hazy, like I was underwater, seeing the world through a veil. Was I still asleep?

A handsome wolf-shifter man was making coffee and telling me we could have fresh fruit salad with our croissants. He hadn't shaved yet that morning and had an intriguing dark shadow along his jawline. He looked so scruffy and kissable, and I had the sense we'd just woken up together, even though we hadn't.

I had to be dreaming. I pinched my arm. Nothing changed. This—being made breakfast by Chet Moore—was just a thing that happened now in my new life.

Chet looked over his shoulder at me. "We'll be eating in a minute," he said.

"Don't let me ruin your regular Saturday-morning routine," I said.

"You're not ruining anything. You told me you wanted to help with the investigation, and that's what you're going to do. I've got a ton of notes you can help me look over. Maybe Winona will speak up through you again and give us a hint."

I started to say I no longer sensed her presence near me but stopped myself. Thanks to my librarian training and my natural flair with research materials, I did have plenty to offer. Even without getting possessed, I could be a fresh set of eyes on the case.

"Where's Corvin?" I asked. "Does he sleep in on the weekend?"

"He's off swimming with Grampa Don."

"Cool," I said, nodding. "I've been meaning to check out the recreation center. I hear the pool's gorgeous."

Chet smirked. "They're not at the rec center. The Moores prefer the great outdoors."

"Of course you do."

"You can take your coffee over to the breakfast nook. I'll bring the food in a minute."

"You have a breakfast nook? I don't have a breakfast nook. No fair. I demand a full refund on my house."

His smirk turned into a full grin. "You do have one, sort of. It's the potting shed at your place."

"The place where we keep our extra spiders and spider webs?"

"That's the one. I extended out of the back of this house a few years back and turned mine into a solarium. We use it as a breakfast nook when the weather's not nice enough for eating in the back yard."

"A breakfast nook," I said with wonder.

"You can hire a contractor and catch up."

"I'll have to try hard to keep up with the Moores. You boys are very skilled."

He just smiled.

CHAPTER 32

"Mom, wake up. You told me to drag you out of bed on Monday morning no matter what, and it's Monday morning. Rise and shine!"

"I need a new alarm clock." I reached out, found her face with my hand, and tweaked her nose. "This one is too chipper, and I can't find the snooze button."

She swatted my hand away. "We need to get you an enormously heavy alarm clock that you can't levitate and toss across the room."

"I can't help it," I said. "Magic has a mind of its own. I don't mean to throw my alarm clock across the room, but as soon as it starts beeping, my defensive powers kick in and eliminate the threat." I sat up and looked across the room at the alarm clock, lying forlornly on its side. "Do you think I shot it with blue lightning?"

She picked up the alarm clock, returned it to my bedside table, and plugged it in. The red numbers flashed 12:00.

"The poor thing seems to have survived this morning's attack," Zoey said in a chipper tone. She was definitely the morning person that day. We usually traded back and forth. I'd be the irritating morning person some days, and she'd take the others. It tended to balance out.

I pointed my finger at the clock's LED display. "Until tomorrow, alarm clock. Until tomorrow."

Zoey sighed. "You need to get control over your powers. Auntie Z says you should do drills and exercises."

"Boring."

"Yes. But you have to learn the musical scales before you can jump into improvised jazz."

I rolled out of bed and went to my closet to stare at my clothes. "Improvised jazz?" Something clicked in my head. "Do you mean I can make my own spells? If I could do that, I'd cast a spell on my closet so it always picked the perfect thing for me to wear that day."

Zoey snorted. "Just close your eyes and pick something at random. You know, like you usually do."

I used my magic to levitate a pillow from my bed and smack the back of her head with it. She squealed as she grabbed the pillow and manually lobbed it back at me. I could have stopped the pillow, but I allowed it to smack me in the face. Sometimes you have to let your child win a round.

I returned to rummaging through my closet. I pulled out my black skirt with the pink poodle. It came with a crinoline to complete the vintage look. *Not today*, I thought. *Save the poodle skirt for a special occasion.*

I asked over my shoulder, "What else did Zinnia tell you? Did she teach you any spells?" Zoey had spent all of Sunday at my aunt's house, while I'd been busy with my own business.

After breakfast with Chet on Saturday morning, we'd pored over his paperwork and made phone calls to everyone who'd had contact with Winona Vander Zalm during the weeks before her demise. The busy lady had been in contact with what seemed like half the town of Wisteria. Nobody we talked to volunteered a murder confession or even so much as a clue. Chet hoped that Winona would take hold of me again upon seeing something in the files, but I remained possession free the rest of the weekend. Either she knew nothing, or my fainting had scared her away.

Our only lead was the alleged instrument of death—the toaster. I assured Chet it was imprisoned inside my freezer, but I could bring it over if he wanted to examine it for magic spells. He said he would ask some tech-savvy friend at work—Charlie, or maybe he said Sharlene—about examining the appliance, and he'd get back to me when he was ready to take it in. He still wouldn't break and tell me the name of his organization.

I hoped Zoey's weekend had been more fruitful than mine.

"No spells yet," Zoey said glumly. "She's got me learning about the language of spells, which has its own grammar. You know how English is usually subject-verb-object? *She smashes the alarm clock*, for example."

"I haven't smashed it yet." I closed my eyes and grabbed two items at random from my closet. Both were pencil skirts.

"The gray skirt and the blue shirt," Zoey said. "Anyway, the grammar is really fascinating."

I took the clothes my in-house fashion consultant suggested and nodded for Zoey to walk-and-talk me to the bathroom.

She followed, explaining in her excited voice. "In the Witch Tongue, that phrase would be more like this: *Alarm clock be smashing by tired, angry mother*."

"That's not entirely untrue, but it seems a bit judgmental. Is the Witch Tongue supposed to be subjective?"

"It's certainly not *objective*," she said. "And for good reason. People don't hex, curse, or even bless things they feel neutral about."

"I guess the spell needs specific instructions, so there aren't any mistakes of interpretation. That's how you avoid the monkey-paw irony, like that old story about someone who wishes for money and then gets it, but only because someone they care about was killed and they got the inheritance."

"Exactly," Zoey said. "You're catching on almost as fast as I did. Magic has its own ideas, so you do have to give it your own specific subjectivity."

"Sounds dangerous. If magic has its own ideas, casting a spell is like leaving a small child alone in a room with cans of paint."

Zoey snorted. "I thought you *wanted me* to paint a mural on that wall."

"My daughter, the genius finger painter." I patted her on the head. "Are you sure magic has its own ideas, or was Zinnia trying to scare you?"

"How should I know?" She jumped up on the bathroom counter and bowed her head. "I might not even be a witch."

I turned on the water for the shower and checked the temperature. "All this talk about magic gives me an idea," I said. "Maybe someone was trying to *help* Ms. Vander Zalm, and they accidentally hurt her. Do you see how many electrical outlets are in this room?"

Zoey glanced around. There was only one electrical outlet, and it was in a very strange place. It wasn't next to the bathroom vanity but high on the wall, on the opposite side of the room from the claw-foot tub.

I used my magic to tug the end of the toilet paper roll and then stretched the roll in a floating line through the air, from the outlet to the top of the bathroom counter.

"Ooh," Zoey said with admiration.

"If the ol' gal was enjoying Pop-Tarts in the tub, she might have had the toaster sitting here on the counter, where she could reach it from the tub. It would have been plugged in all the way over there, with the cord stretched across the door."

Zoey rubbed her chin. "That's an accident waiting to happen."

"Exactly." I pointed my finger at the door. "If someone came in the door unexpectedly, they would have snagged the cord and flung the appliance into the water."

I used magic to swing open the door quickly. The toilet paper broke along a perforation and fluttered to the floor, but it was easy to imagine something as strong as an electrical cord staying intact and sending the attached appliance flying.

Zoey crossed her arms over her chest and shivered.

"Mom, I think you've cracked the case."

"It's just a theory," I said. "Go get the toaster from the freezer and we'll test it out."

Her jaw dropped open. The water for my shower was running and steaming up the bathroom.

"Kidding," I said. "I'm having a shower then going to work. I don't have time to electrocute myself this morning if I want to keep my new job."

Zoey shook her head and left me to my shower.

I jumped in and enjoyed the luxury of the rain head faucet. I was in steamy paradise for all of five minutes before my peacefulness was interrupted by the doorbell ringing.

"Doorbell!" I yelled.

The doorbell kept ringing. Who would be ringing our doorbell early on a Monday morning? The chimes sounded again, this time with an urgent edge to their ding-dong. It was almost urgent enough for me to get out of my steamy shower, but not quite.

"Zoey, you have one job!"

I heard the thumping of my teenager going downstairs to answer the door.

A few minutes later, my peace was interrupted by a voice that sounded a lot like mine.

"Zara, get out of the shower. This is important."

"Hello?" I tapped my temple. "That sounds like my voice," I muttered. "Is that me telling myself to get out of the shower? Self, stop being cruel. I only just got the water set to the perfect temperature."

Someone yanked back the shower curtain.

"Holy sweatpants!" I exclaimed.

Zinnia stood there, looking less than amused. She had her red hair pulled back in a bun so tight, her face reminded me of a certain terrible real estate agent.

She frowned at me. "Why aren't you answering your phone?"

"Because it's not waterproof."

We stared at each other, standing off. I was learning so much about my aunt. She didn't have a problem with nudity. Since she wasn't leaving, I reluctantly turned off the water and reached for my towel.

"And good morning to you," I said. "Did you run out of coffee at your house?"

"I did a spell." She pressed her lips together and averted her eyes guiltily.

Now she looks away, I thought. *Now that I'm wearing a towel.*

"That's what witches do," I said. "What kind of spell?"

She continued looking around the bathroom, avoiding eye contact. For a change, she wasn't wearing a skort. Just regular trousers with big pleats. *She's the one who needs a closet spell*, I thought with an inward giggle.

With my towel turned into a stylish wrap, I stepped out of the iron tub.

Zoey, who'd been standing quietly in the doorway, came into the bathroom and stood right next to Zinnia. "The spell we talked about? But Auntie Z, you said you were going to let me help you cast the spell. No fair!" She stomped one foot in a petulant gesture I hadn't seen her use in years. "You promised I could help," she cried. To me, she said in a tattle-tale tone, "It's a two-witch spell. She told me."

"Someone had better start talking specifics," I said. "Let's try the Prisoner's Dilemma. The first one of you to confess won't get grounded."

By the look on Zinnia's face, my joke didn't even register, much less amuse her. This two-witch-spell business was serious.

Zinnia finally met my gaze. The whites of her eyes were red, like she'd been crying.

"I opened something," Zinnia said, her voice barely louder than a whisper.

"The look on your face tells me it wasn't a can of whoop-ass you opened."

Her lower lip trembled. "It was a hole to the other side."

Zoey and I exchanged a look. She silently mouthed the words *that's bad* as she shook her head. I gave her my *figured as much* look.

"I'll help you close the hole," I said. "If you need two witches, I'm your witch."

She lifted her chin bravely. "I was only practicing the gestures and incantations for later, but the magic urged me on." Her bloodshot eyes began shining. "I was weak. I did the spell and poked open a hole. There was something dark, like an army of black beetles crawling out of a crack in the ground."

Zoey and I exchanged another look.

Zinnia quickly added, "I closed the hole right away, but I don't know what came through."

I checked the tuck on my towel and then grabbed my aunt by the shoulders. "What size of a hole are we talking about here? How big and how bad? On a scale from one to ten, with ten being the freakin' apocalypse, how much should we be freaking out?"

Zinnia winced. "Four and a half?"

I let go of her shoulders and grabbed my loosening towel-wrap in the nick of time. "Four and a half? That's all?" I waved one hand dismissively. "We can handle that."

"Mom," Zoey said. "Mom!" Her voice was quivering.

She was pointing at something behind me.

I turned around slowly, ready to face something five and a half points short of the freakin' apocalypse.

On the plus side, it wasn't an army of black beetles.

All that had manifested inside the steamy bathroom were drippy streaks on the foggy mirror. As I looked, the streaks became words. Two words. Something or someone had written on the bathroom mirror two words: KILLER DINNER.

Zinnia whimpered, "We're in big trouble."

CHAPTER 33

"Still hung over from last Friday night?" My pink-haired coworker, Frank Wonder, swooshed his hand in front of my face to get my attention. "Did you carry the party straight through to Sunday?"

"Not exactly," I said distractedly. I couldn't tell Frank about my aunt's visit earlier that morning and her subsequent hissy fit over a couple of streaky words on my bathroom mirror.

Frank asked, "Then what's on your mind, pretty lady?"

"Just a case of the Mondays, I'm afraid. One more coffee and I'll be myself again, unless I become someone else."

Frank waggled his eyebrows, which were tinted pink to match his hair. "You're not just distracted." He gasped. "You're twitterpated! You've been getting neighborly with that big piece of beefcake who lives next door. A certain *Chet Moore*. Forgive me the sin of punning, but I dare say you want *more* of Chet Moore, ha-ha."

"Oh, Frank." I gave him a wry smile. "Please say that pun *every* day. I'm sure it will never, ever get old."

He shrugged one shoulder. "Frank Wonder is not too good for lowbrow humor."

"Or referring to himself in the third person."

He yawned. "I'm sleepy, too. Flying all night takes a lot out of a person."

I raised my eyebrows. "Is there something you want to tell me?" *Perhaps a secret of the shifter variety?*

"I suffer from extremely vivid dreams." He wrinkled his nose. "Well, maybe 'suffer' is too strong a word. Truth is, I enjoy my vivid dreams. But they can be tiring when I'm flying around all night."

"Maybe you're a secret superhero. Have you been fighting crimes?"

"Yes," he answered solemnly. "I visit the home of every person with overdue library books and shame them into returning the books."

"Like a less materialistic Santa Claus."

"That's me." He giggled and reached into the staff kitchen cupboard. "Now, where is that white chocolate syrup?"

We were both in the staff lounge, taking our midmorning break together while the assistants manned the counters. Kathy wouldn't be in until the afternoon, and the WPL had been quiet that morning. Earlier, we'd witnessed one of the young pages slumped over the book cart, sleeping on her feet, like a cow. Frank and I got carried away inventing a new game called Page Tipping. It was really funny. I swear. Even the page agreed once we helped her up.

Now Frank and I were experimenting with the perfect blend of chocolate and coffee to make a superior mocha. Frank felt white chocolate syrup was the key. I had strong feelings about my own blend, which used a smoky Earl Grey tea in place of coffee.

He handed me a new sample to taste, served in a tiny mug that I suspected was actually a Christmas tree ornament.

"This one's a winner," I said. White chocolate syrup plus microwaved coffee. Who knew?

"Speaking of winners, have you kissed him yet?" Frank asked.

I had fainted and woken up on his lap, but I couldn't tell my fellow librarian that. He'd probably insist on taking me to the hospital to get my head checked. Non-magical people did stuff like that.

"We haven't kissed," I swore. "But I helped him look over some paperwork, and on Sunday he did that thing where the guy removes a stray eyelash from your cheek and tells you to blow on it."

Frank burst out laughing. "How romantic."

I gave Frank some squint-eyed, triple-strength side eye. "These things take time, you ding-dong."

He sighed contentedly. "I do love gossip on a Monday morning. It makes working for a living almost bearable."

I took another sip of the mocha. The white chocolate made it taste like liquid marshmallow.

"Frank, you seem like the type of person people confide their secrets in."

He rose up on his toes excitedly. "Yes, I am. And?"

"Nothing happened with Chet, I swear. You'll be the first to know. I'm actually wondering if you ever heard anything about Winona Vander Zalm. Specifically about any enemies she made."

Frank rubbed his chin and looked up. "She could be catty," he said. "One time, we were at the big Save the Voles and Holes Event, and—"

I interrupted, "Sorry, did you say Save the Voles and Holes? Remind me, what are voles?"

"Voles are small rodents, related to mice. They're cute."

"People need to save them?"

"Well, the voles were the only living things interested in the Wisteria Golf Course for a few years. Have you seen the golf course?"

"I'm not sure. Is there a mermaid?"

"You're thinking of the Atlantis Mini Putt and Water Adventure Park. No, I mean the actual golf course. It was badly infested with voles. The new owners eventually found a way to humanely relocate them. Relax, Zara, it all worked out for the best. Totally humane." He waved one hand in a circle. "Anyway, Winona was in a real witchy mood that night because two other people showed up wearing the same outfit as hers, with one of those people being yours truly." He patted his chest.

"That sucks when someone shows up in the same outfit," I said. "You wore a dress?"

He made a bird-like squawk. "It was a two-piece pantsuit. Unisex."

"Okay." I held my hands up in a truce-like gesture.

"The other pantsuit lady was a good sport about it. She even posed for a picture with me, in front of the voles. Winona was too snobby, though. She kept shooting dagger eyes at me and the other gal." He held his hand to mouth and stage-whispered, "I *wore it best*, by the way, in case you were wondering."

"Of course you did," I said. "Do you have a copy of that picture? I'd love to see it."

"I'll check when I get home," he said.

"How about long-standing feuds? Did she have any major rivals on the socialite scene?"

Frank narrowed his eyes and looked me up and down. "What's got you so curious?"

I shrugged. "I'm living in her old house now. Humor me, will you? I promise to get a real hobby soon." I glanced over at Kathy's coffee mug, which had been bejeweled during one of her at-work crafting sessions. "Maybe something crafty."

"Long-standing feuds," Frank mused. He glanced up at a poster we had, depicting famous literary feuds. "Hmm," he said. "Let me check the ol' database."

He tilted his head and looked up as he scratched his chin. I'd seen him do this gesture while helping patrons at the library's reference desk. He claimed to have a database of book titles in his brain. After a minute, he'd frown and say, "Let me just double-check something." Then he'd do a keyword search on the computer and say something like, "Just as I suspected. We have two books on that subject." People seemed to enjoy his playfulness.

"Hmm," Frank said as he walked me over to the computer we kept in the staff lounge. He tapped away on the keyboard. "Yes, there it is," he said.

"You're amazing," I cooed.

"That poster about literary feuds reminded me. Winona wrote a book with someone, once upon a time." He turned the screen to face me. A search on Winona's name had brought up a book about Halloween-themed party foods for children. The book was listed in our database as being cowritten by two authors, W. Vander Zalm and Z. Riddle.

"Very funny," I said. "You set this up and put my name in here as a prank, didn't you?"

He pointed to the call number, made a tsk sound, and took off at a speed-walk pace. He returned forty seconds later with a colorful book in hand, breathing heavily.

"It's her," he said. "And the cowriter is none other than your aunt." He made a self-satisfied sound. "Speaking of which, she was absolutely delightful at your party on Friday. I can see that good looks and great taste in clothing run in the family."

"You monster," I chuckled.

"Do they still sell trousers with pleats, or do you suppose she has them custom made?"

"Shush."

I opened the book and flipped to the author photos on the inner flaps. The pictures were at least twenty years old, but there was Zinnia staring back at me, looking like my twin. The picture of Winona Vander Zalm was one I'd seen before, accompanying articles about her fundraising work.

"Zinnia never told me about this," I said. "In all our discussions, you'd think their old partnership would have come up."

Frank tapped at the keyboard some more and then nodded.

"Your aunt might have been embarrassed," Frank said. "This was supposed to be book one of a whole series. The publisher named a bunch of upcoming titles, but none of them were ever published. Sales of the first print run must have been disappointing." He looked over at the cookbook and patted the closed cover. "This copy has only been borrowed a dozen times in the last twenty years. It should have been deaccessioned by now."

I looked over the checkout dates on the screen. "It only misses the biennial purges because someone checks it out during the culling period."

"Someone," he said, tapping the keys again. "Someone named Winona Vander Zalm. Now that she's gone, it'll be the end for her book. It will be tossed out, along with *Be Bold with Bananas* and a few other gems."

I grabbed the book and clutched it to my chest. "No!"

Frank chuckled. "Zara, you can't save them all. Culling day will come, as sure as rain will fall as soon as you've washed your car, and as sure as that page is sleeping on her feet again." He tiptoed toward the open door. "Come on. You push her and I'll catch her."

I held up my hand. "Five more minutes. Let me have a gander at this book, and I'll be right out."

"Gander away." He paused in the doorway. "Hey, speaking of geese, here's a fun fact. Did you know, they're only a *gaggle* when they're on the ground? When they're flying, a group of geese in a V formation is a *skein*, and when they're in a close-knit group, they're a *plump*." He bounced his pink eyebrows.

I actually did know that, but I pretended I didn't and made a surprised face for Frank's benefit.

He disappeared, leaving me with the cookbook.

It was, sadly, not a book of spells. It wasn't magical at all. The recipes were the sort you'd find in magazines at the checkout line.

- Fill a latex glove with red juice to make a bloody hand to float in the punch bowl.

- Stick toothpicks into coconut balls to make spooky spiders.

- Got zombies? Make a gelatin-based salad with elbow macaroni in a bowl, then flip it upside down. Ziggity! You've got a jiggly brain.

Okay, that last one was pretty cool.

I continued flipping through the book, stopping when I encountered a page titled KILLER DINNER.

I froze, my breath caught in my throat. Those were the words I'd seen on my bathroom mirror.

The two words that had put Zinnia into such a tizzy.

KILLER DINNER.

CHAPTER 34

Before I'd left the house for work that morning, Zoey and I calmed down Zinnia and coaxed out a few details about her spell.

My zany, skort-wearing aunt had been attempting to open a portal to communicate with Winona Vander Zalm. It was supposed to give us real-time communication, not just the old recorded greetings I'd been channeling so far.

It did seem to have worked.

Zoey swore on her favorite jeans that she hadn't written the message on the mirror, so it had to be a message from the spirit. But what did it mean?

It couldn't possibly be a coincidence that I was currently staring at a recipe labeled KILLER DINNER, in a book co-authored by the spirit and my aunt.

Was this page in front of me a big, honking clue or what? And if it was a clue, how could Winona have known I would find her book today of all days? My brain churned through possibilities and probabilities. Was that smoke in my nostrils? Yes, my brain was definitely smoking, and I was thinking way too hard for a Monday morning.

I gave my head a shake and read the recipe. Killer Dinner was basically a pot roast with sprigs of herbs jabbed in to make it resemble a porcupine. The accompanying photograph looked an awful lot like roadkill. I grimaced. No wonder the book had sold poorly. The audience of cookbook buyers wanting to recreate the look of roadkill is a very small niche market.

One chunk of text near the bottom of the page did catch my eye.

The caption under the roadkill photo read: *A gentleman doesn't kiss and tell, but your beau will be telling all the fellas at work about the fabulous killer dinner you made for him!*

Was this the clue? Was Winona telling me her former beau was the one who murdered her? The only boyfriend I knew of—who was still alive—lived next door. Don Moore. The gray-haired man had claimed to have made the beast with two backs with her, and on top of that, he'd also threatened me. Or helped me in a threatening manner. Either way, he'd been creepy.

On a hunch, I checked the book's index. Nope. It contained no recipe for a Beast With Two Backs, but there was a Beast With Orange Sauce.

Weren't a significant number of homicides crimes of passion? I'd seen a number of true-crime shows over the years. How often did the killer live right next door? Not often, but it happened.

I licked my lips and said his name out loud. "Don Moore."

I didn't feel, smell, or sense anything out of the ordinary.

"Ms. Vander Zalm? Can you hear me? Show me a sign. Let me know if Don Moore was the one who killed you."

Nothing happened.

And then something did.

My stomach flip-flopped.

They say you should trust your gut. Your gut instincts.

As I doubled over, I realized that either the ghost had just named her killer, or I'd overdone it with the mochas.

* * *

At around two o'clock, Kathy came to check on me in the staff lounge. I'd used a blanket to build myself a fort in the Grumpy Corner. I was shoeless and curled up in the fetal position.

Kathy pushed up her round owl-eye glasses and hooted, "Whooo did this to you?"

"Frank," I said. "But it's not his fault. I should know my mocha limit. He didn't overserve me, I swear."

She reached into the blanket fort and pressed a cool hand on my forehead. The gesture was incredibly motherly and soothing. I liked Kathy. I still felt bad about throwing away her acorn jelly, but at least my diabolical intestinal adventures were finally bringing us together.

"Zara, you're feverish," she said. "You should go home early. You don't need to finish your shift."

"I already punched out my time card," I said. "I'm waiting to get up the strength to walk home."

She took me by the hand and tugged. "Get up. I'll drive you home. I've got to run some errands anyway. Frank and the others can hold down the fort a bit longer. I think the pages wanted to get him alone anyway. They were giggling about tipping people over. Do you know anything about that?"

"Hijinks during work hours? In the library?" I shook my head and made tsk-tsk sounds as I extracted myself from the blanket fort.

"Don't let Frank be a bad influence on you, Zara. He's a wonderful children's librarian, and the families adore him, but sometimes his pranks go too far."

"Good to know," I said solemnly.

Slowly, I did an awkward dance to get my shoes on the corresponding feet without leaning forward. When I was finally ready to leave, I looked up and saw Kathy leafing through the book penned by my ghost and my aunt, *Spooky Gatherings for Ghouls Cookbook*.

"This old thing," she said with a chuckle. "That crazy woman always checked it out during our circulation review. What a kook she was." She held it up. "Are you checking this out?"

I told her I'd intended to, and she disappeared to run it through the checkout system officially.

Five minutes later, I was strapped into Kathy Carmichael's car, which was slightly more luxurious than a broomstick. The Honda's brown vinyl seats had been repaired with duct tape, and by the sound the engine made when Kathy started it up, those weren't the only makeshift repairs.

Kathy gave me an apologetic look. "I can afford a better car, honestly. The library pays me enough. I just like this old thing. It's sort of a nest on wheels." She waved to a pile of stuff behind us. The back seat was packed tight with crafting supplies in stacking plastic containers, as well as loose baskets of twine, fuzzy pipe cleaners, scissors, and what most people would generally refer to as crap.

"A nest on wheels," I said. "I can see that."

Kathy shifted into gear, and the nest emitted interesting sounds and smells as we began our journey toward my home.

"Thanks again for inviting me to your wonderful dinner party," Kathy said.

"And thank you for coming. I don't know how much longer I'll be in the entertaining mood, but it was great to have everyone I know in Wisteria all in one place at the same time."

"You seem to be making new friends easily. By this time next year, you'll need a bigger house," she said.

"You're too kind. If I'm still here in a year, I'll worry about it then."

She made a whistling sound through her tiny, sharp nose. "Of course you'll be here. Why would you ever leave? Nobody leaves Wisteria. The only way out is to die." She turned and shot me a knowing look. "But you don't have to worry about that, now that you have the house. You're living in the Fountain of Youth."

"Kathy, this might be my recent dehydration causing auditory hallucinations, but did you just say my house is the Fountain of Youth?"

"That's what I said. I'm joking, of course. I might be a nutty ol' bird obsessed with crafting, but I'm not crazy. Not like old Winona Vander Zalm, with her wild claims about witchcraft and that old house."

"What did she say, exactly?"

We stopped for a red light. The cloud of stench the old Honda was emitting caught up with us.

Kathy gave me an owlish look, blinking seriously behind her round glasses. "Ms. Vander Zalm told me once, in confidence, that she was *never* going to die. Not ever. She said the Red Witch House had magical energy that protected her and kept her young. She claimed she was a lot older than she looked."

"That's so strange," I said. "Why would she tell you?"

Kathy shifted gears, and we sailed into fresh air again.

"She was lonely, I suppose. Or maybe she wanted to boast about it. What's the point in being a hundred and something if you can't tell anyone?"

"You believed her? You think my house has magic?"

Kathy snorted again, whistling through her nose. "Who would believe such nonsense? Not me. I believe in research and knowledge. Facts. Science."

"But there are countless references to Fountains of Youth in literature throughout time. What if it's real? What if there's far more to this world than meets the eye? What if fiction is closer to reality than you think?"

"But magical fountains are just an *idea*, Zara. Like the plucky underdog heroine in a young adult novel who battles a mighty monster and singlehandedly wins freedom for her people. Or the handsome man in a romance novel who doesn't notice a woman's stretch marks."

I tried to laugh, but the dry sounds coming from my parched throat were less than convincing.

Kathy elaborated some more about her favorite book themes and how she wished they were real. She'd been an adult already when the Harry Potter books broke out as huge literary hits, yet she'd still yearned for her own letter from Hogwarts. She yearned to be a Chosen One. A Secret Princess. A girl who didn't know she was already something else.

"Don't we all," I said, thinking sadly of Zoey, still patiently waiting for her powers.

* * *

We reached my house, where Kathy asked, "Would you like me to help you inside? Whip up some chicken soup?"

"Thanks, but you've already done more than enough."

"How's that?" She tilted her head back and pushed up her round glasses. "Zara, you don't look well at all. If I have to carry you in there and tuck you into bed, so help me, I will."

"No need." I fumbled blindly for the door handle and cracked the door open. "You've helped more than enough by letting me go home early and giving me a ride." I jumped out of the car, my legs wobbly and weak but still holding me up. "See you around!"

"Tomorrow?" Her gaze flitted between me and the house—the Red Witch House.

I snapped my fingers. "Good idea! I'll see you tomorrow, in the big building with all the books."

She shook her head. "You're not right in the head. I'm coming in with you."

"No need!" I flung the car door shut and thumped the roof twice, the way people thump on taxis in movies to send them away.

To my surprise, it worked. The car immediately sped away. Was that magic? Had I cast a spell on the brown Honda without meaning to?

I thought I heard Kathy screaming inside the retreating car. I told myself it was just worn brake pads or old fan belts.

I stumbled up the stairs to the porch, let myself in, and locked the door behind me. I imagined many people in Wisteria left their front doors unlocked during the day, but I still had my habits from living in a big city. Also, even though Zinnia's friend had put protective wards on the house, they worked better if the homeowner took basic precautions.

I listened to make sure I was alone in the house. I was. Zoey wasn't home from school yet.

I went to my refrigerator and yanked open the door to the freezer. I'd been hoping for some Popsicles to soothe my stomach, but the freezer was empty.

Empty?

The possessed toaster was supposed to be in there. It had been there at the dinner party, when Frank had gone looking for ice cubes and commented about it to everyone in attendance. Now the evil toaster was gone. Had it grown legs and walked away?

Or had someone from my dinner party taken it?

The realization hit me like a wallop in the belly with a wet trout.

"Ms. Vander Zalm, is this what you were trying to tell us with the words on the bathroom mirror?" *KILLER DINNER.* "Is your killer someone who was at my dinner party?"

She didn't answer, either because she couldn't communicate directly without Zinnia's two-witch spell, or because she wasn't sure.

Solving this mystery was up to me. Just me. I reviewed the list of people who'd been at the dinner party.

There was Chet Moore, who'd inherited the woman's estate. Grampa Don, her sometimes lover. Young Corvin, who was just plain weird, even for a ten-year-old boy. Frank Wonder, who was way too interested in the house and especially the tub where she'd died. Dorothy Tibbits, the World's Worst Realtor. Kathy Carmichael, whose owlish ways were an uncomfortable reminder of the winged beast who'd attacked us in the woods. And then there was Zinnia, my estranged aunt, who was the most secretive, uptight person I'd ever met.

My stomach gurgled, still roiling with an excess of mochas. I used my magic to grab a can of ginger ale from the top of the pantry, and a glass. Levitation was getting easier. I pulled a barstool up to the kitchen island while I poured the ginger ale hands-free. I got most of it into the glass. Zinnia would have been proud.

I sipped the warm, fizzy drink, and reviewed all the details of the suspected homicide.

Time passed.

I heard my daughter's footfalls on the front porch. She was home from school.

I grabbed my phone and made a call.

"It's me," I said, breathing heavily. "I know why Winona Vander Zalm got murdered. I've also got some ideas about how. If we're going to catch the killer, I need your help."

CHAPTER 35

SATURDAY

One month had passed since my daughter and I had moved to Wisteria. In that time, we'd learned we were witches, gotten to know my wacky aunt, thrown two dinner parties, and survived our first ghost. We had not yet fully unpacked all our moving boxes. But hey, what's a month?

Five days had passed since I'd made two important discoveries: the identity of Winona Vander Zalm's killer and my personal limit for number of mochas consumed in one hour. The answers are A.) to be revealed shortly, and B.) three.

As for the killer, today was the day my theory would be put to the test.

Chet and I stood on the sidewalk in front of the nondescript office building.

He turned to me, his green eyes bedazzling. I'd never imagined that anything other than rhinestones could bedazzle, but Chet's green eyes did exactly that.

"Zara Riddle, are you ready for this?"

I gushed, "Chet Moore, I'm ready for more things than I can even imagine, and I have quite the imagination."

He smiled. "I'll take that as a yes." He took my hand in his. "We should hold hands."

"Good idea," I said. "Schmoopsie Bear."

He recoiled visibly. I made a mental note that Schmoopsie Bear was too far. It was good to know the man had some limits.

We walked inside the boxy municipal building, swinging our arms like a couple of lovebirds, and gave our names to the receptionist. She led us down the hall to a meeting room with glass walls. Chet held my hand the whole way. We only let go to slide into our seats at the metal-and-glass table. He quickly caught my hand again once we were seated.

In a warning tone, he said, "You might have to hold my hand forever."

"Forever?" I let out a laugh that sounded like a cackle. Was that a witch thing? Would I be cackling all the time now that I was a witch? Was cackling inevitable, like the pudge you get over the waistline of your jeans on the day of your thirtieth birthday? Life was full of so many inevitabilities.

My terrible real estate agent, Dorothy Tibbits, came into the room with her brown pigtails bouncing and a huge grin on her inflated lips. She wore her usual blue pinafore dress.

"You two lovebirds," she exclaimed breathlessly. "Married already? As of yesterday? I should have known something was up at your dinner party last week." She looked right at Chet. "You couldn't take your eyes off Zara all night."

I leaned to the side and rested my head on his shoulder. "The man knows what he likes. I told him he could have the milk and eggs and bacon for free, but he insisted on buying the whole farm!"

Chet squeezed my hand. Hard. "Sweetie-pie, I did not *buy the farm*. That's what you say when someone dies."

I laughed, deliberately snorting to keep myself from cackling. "We can't have that," I wheezed. "Not until I've taken out a big insurance policy on you."

He squeezed my hand again. "One thing at a time," he said tersely.

"Right," I said, nodding. "Let's not waste Dorothy's time."

Dorothy Tibbits took a seat across from us and crossed her legs primly. "What is it I can help you two lovebirds with?" Her posture was one of excitement, with her upper body leaning forward. Her breathing was rapid and shallow. "Our receptionist said something about amalgamating your real estate holdings? Selling off one house and moving in with each other?"

"Yes," Chet said. "But we can't decide which house we should sell," he leaned his head from left to right theatrically, "and which one we should keep."

Dorothy practically vibrated with excitement. Her fingers twitched in sequence, making her hands resemble large, wrinkly, pink spiders.

"Let's take this one step at a time," she said with deliberate slowness. "You can let this be an emotional decision, or you can go by the numbers. There are many factors, such as lot size, age of renovations, plus let's not forget about the memories. All the wonderful memories of young Corvin, getting his height measured with those adorable little pen markings on the door frame." She batted her thick row of false eyelashes at Chet. "You do mark his height on the door frame, don't you?"

"Of course I do," Chet said, his voice deep and low, bordering on a growl. "I'm a single parent, but I'm not an animal."

Dorothy let loose frothy giggles. "Exactly! Which is why I crunched some numbers and gave it careful consideration. Are you ready for my decision? I mean, my recommendation?"

Chet and I exchanged a look. "Yes," we said in unison. "We're ready."

Dorothy's grin was maniacal. "I think you'll be much, much, much better off selling the red house." In spite of her Botox, she wrinkled her nose with what seemed like considerable effort. "That house is getting so old now, and I know you're coming up on a huge repair bill for a new roof, and probably re-piping, and heaven knows what condition the foundation is in." She waved one weathered hand. "Why not let the new owner worry about those things?"

I beamed at her. For such a terrible real estate agent, she was surprisingly convincing today. Could it be a spell?

I looked over at Chet. He'd taken a pen from his pocket, which he clicked twice. I heard something pop, but faintly, as though it was just my ears adjusting to a change in air pressure.

Dorothy raised her eyebrows at us expectantly. "Ready to sign the papers?"

I gave her a broad smile. "Dorothy, you and I are on the exact same page," I said. "But my wacky ol' aunt could use some convincing. She's been spouting some mumbo jumbo about the house having magical properties. Have you ever heard such nonsense?"

Dorothy's face was frozen. More frozen than usual.

I tilted my head up, caught Zinnia's eye through the glass walls of the meeting room, and waved for her to come join us. "Here she is now," I said to Dorothy. "You'll talk to her for us, won't you?"

Dorothy stammered, "Uh, y-y-es, I'll certainly, uh, try."

Zinnia rushed in and took a seat, facing me and keeping the back of her shoulder facing the real estate agent. She'd dressed up for the occasion, in a daring blend of two floral patterns: roses on her skirt and daffodils on her blouse.

"Zara, I've done it," my aunt said breathlessly, setting a mirrored jewelry box on the glass table. "It's all inside this box, but we have to release it within the next few minutes before everything expires. I've done the calculations, and we won't have another chance again for seven years."

I clapped my free hand to my cheek and gasped, "Seven years? And we only have a few minutes?" I looked right at the real estate agent. "Dorothy, I must apologize. This will come as a shock to you, but I've come to think of you as a member of our strange little family. Zinnia and I are witches, and we need to cast an important, time-sensitive spell at once."

Chet released my hand and pushed his chair back so hard it toppled over as he got to his feet. He stood, towering over me, and demanded, "Cast a spell? Don't tell me you're a witch."

I shrugged meekly. "Sweetheart, it's not what you think."

"Not what I think? You mean I didn't marry a witch?"

"Okay," I said. "It's exactly what you think."

Chet shook his head and clenched his fists. "Wisteria! It's this whole damned town! Full of witches!"

Dorothy pushed her chair back and got to her feet. She was looking back and forth between the two of us so quickly, she looked like a cat watching a game of ping pong.

I rolled my eyes at Chet. "Don't be so dramatic, Sweetie-pie. Deep down, you knew I was a witch. A regular woman can't do half the things I did to you last night. Not even a redhead." I nodded at his chair. "Now be a good boy and sit."

Shaking his head slowly, he did as he was told and took a seat.

"Zara, we don't have much time," Zinnia said.

I clapped my hands. "All right. Time for the two-witch spell to bring back Winona Vander Zalm." I looked right into Dorothy's eyes. "We just need to check in with the home's former owner about any magical qualities the Red Witch House has. Just to be thorough, and to make sure it doesn't fall into the wrong hands."

Her voice shaking, Dorothy said, "Bring her back?"

I snapped my fingers impatiently. "Just in spirit form, but yes. She'll be here. But time's running out. There were some delays getting her out of this realm and into the next, but I understand matters are moving along smoothly now, and we just have a few minutes."

Breathlessly, Zinnia said, "We may already be too late."

I reached for the mirrored jewelry box. "It's show time!"

Dorothy lunged forward and snatched the jewelry box away from me. She glared into my eyes and hissed, "Zara Riddle, whatever voodoo nonsense you're thinking about doing, you'd better not, or you'll be very sorry."

Zinnia turned her head very slowly and gave the brown-pigtailed, tight-faced real estate agent a bored look. "Or what, Dorothy? You'll tell the whole town I'm a witch? Honestly, it might be nice to stop having to hide what I am." She leaned forward and flicked up the latch on the jewelry box. "Let's get this party started." She winked at me.

Dorothy screamed and tried to throw herself on top of the mirrored jewelry box, but she was too slow. The box was open. A puff of purple smoke wafted out, along with a flash of light and a loud crackle.

I clung to Chet, wrapping myself around his strong shoulder. "It's her," I cried, just as we'd rehearsed the night before.

He played his role perfectly, acting awestruck. "Winona?"

"It's really her," I gasped. "And she's coming right for me. She wants to control me. Oh, Chet, I don't know if I'm strong enough for—" I didn't finish. I was falling to the floor. Once down, I shook and spasmed for a full ten seconds before going limp.

Out of the corner of my eye, I saw Dorothy Tibbits edging around the table toward the exit. Zinnia used her magic to slam the door shut and then lock it. Dorothy let out a strangled cry.

Slowly, I gathered myself and got to my feet. With a calm face and an otherworldly tone to my voice, I began to speak.

"Darling, don't leave our meeting yet," I said to Dorothy. "My witch friends have opened a portal to allow me access to the mortal plane one last time. I have some very important business to attend to. I wish to face the person who killed me, to look her in the eyes, and demand an explanation."

I looked right into Dorothy's eyes.

From beside me, Chet said, "Zara, stop this. Enough of your shenanigans. No wife of mine is going to run around casting spells and acting like—" He stopped speaking at the flick of my wrist. With another flick, he was flying back, both arms windmilling. He struck the wall of the boardroom and slid down, his head lolling to one side limply.

"Husbands," I said with disgust. "That's why I, the fabulously single Winona Vander Zalm, refused to get married. I've had plenty of suitors over the past hundred and fifty years, but I knew the price to be paid was too high."

"Winona?" Zinnia took my hand and stroked it. "How wonderful to see you again. What were you saying before that big beefcake interrupted you so rudely?"

I turned again to Dorothy, who was trying to hide under the table despite it being made of glass and rather transparent. I leaned over the table, stared down into her eyes through the glass, and growled, "Why'd you do it? I command you to answer me."

"Do what?" Dorothy scrambled backward, putting more space between us but staying under the table. "I don't know what you're talking about," she mewled.

I banged my fist on the table. "Dorothy, stop your mewling!"

She switched from mewling to keening.

I leaned forward and growled, "I didn't cross over from the spirit plane to hear your nonsense. You'll answer my question and you'll answer it honestly, or else!"

A hint of emotion twitched across her face. "Or what? You can't hurt me. You can't hurt someone unless they're attacking you. I may not be a witch, but I know about the rules." She straightened up and gave me a defiant look.

"But I'm *not* a witch," I said coldly. "I'm the undead. I do whatever I want. Watch this." I pointed at slumped-over Chet and yelled, "Shaazaba!"

His body jerked in apparent pain. Five seconds later, he went still again, with his head tilted up. Bright red blood ran from his mouth, dripping down his neck in gory rivers.

I turned to Dorothy and bent all the way down to the table, so my hot breath fogged the glass between us.

"Dorothy, you're not in Kansas anymore," I said. "It's time for answers. Why did you murder me? Answer now, or I'll turn your insides to blood pudding and your face into a handbag."

She screwed up her face and finally burst out, "It wasn't fair how you had that house all to yourself for all those years! You should have shared it with other people. You were best friends with my mother for all those years and you could have stopped her from dying, but you didn't. Because you were selfish."

"Are you saying I should have had roommates? Is that why you killed me?"

She cried, "It was time for someone else to live in that house. You had your days and you did nothing but throw frivolous parties. You cared more about whatever fancy dress you were going to wear next than you did about other human beings."

"Enough!" I whacked the table with my fist. "I didn't come here to be insulted by the likes of you, murderess. I have questions that need to be answered. The electricity made me lose some of my precious memories. Answer one more question and I'll let you walk out of this room alive."

"Okay," Dorothy said. "I'll tell you anything you want to know. Is it about the gadget?" Her face contorted into a hideous grin.

I made a fist. "Yes. Tell me about the gadget."

"My friend Griebel made it in his shop, but it was all my design." She let out a high-pitched laugh. "You're too stupid to understand, but I'll put it in simple terms. When you brought in your toaster for cord lengthening, we increased the voltage by adding a second power source, built right into the toaster. The technology available these days is truly remarkable. We added a tiny spy-grade camera, and we also added cheap parts from some dollar-store mousetraps. Using the camera, I was able to spy on you, and when the moment was right, when you were flaunting your immortality by making those wretched Pop-Tarts right next to your tub, I pushed my little red button and sent the toaster sailing into the water."

I hissed, "I remember. It grew legs and sprang up on its own."

"Not on its own," Dorothy spat back. "I did it. Me." She thumped her chest. "Stupid little Dorothy Tibbits who had to take the real estate exam three times. I did it. I killed the unkillable."

Beside me, Chet said, "I think we can wrap things up now." He was sitting upright now.

Zinnia patted me on the shoulder. "Good job, Zara."

I glared at her, eyes wide. "There is no Zara. There is only Zuul. Zuuuuuuuuul."

She kept patting my shoulder. "I see somebody's a big *Ghostbusters* fan. Good. A sense of humor is an excellent quality in a witch."

Beneath the table, Dorothy was making spluttering sounds. "Zuul? What? What's going on?" She pointed at Chet. "You're dead. She killed you!"

Chet wiped his mouth with the back of his hand. "These movie props taste terrible," he said.

Dorothy gave him a bewildered look and whimpered, "Movie props?"

"Silly Dorothy," I said. "How could I cast a spell on Chet when there's no such thing as witchcraft, or ghosts?" I glanced up at the black camera lenses positioned along the ceiling before turning to Zinnia. "Please tell me all the cameras in this room were recording."

She gave me two thumbs up. "All systems are go," she said. "The police should have an easy job once they get this footage, along with the modified toaster. I have a feeling it will turn up inside Dorothy's house. Confessions are great, but juries love to see physical evidence."

Dorothy made more spluttering sounds, these ones almost joyful. "I threw it out! Ha-hah!"

"Don't be so sure you got rid of it," I said. "You gave the thing legs, and extra power, and somewhere along the way it also got a mind of its own."

Zinnia and I exchanged happy smiles.

I turned toward Chet, ready to kiss him in spite of the fake blood on his face.

He was ready, too.

Ready to shake my hand.

"Excellent work, Ms. Riddle," he said, shaking my hand in a businesslike manner. "If it means catching a killer, I'll get fake-married to you any time you want."

CHAPTER 36

I had a tough time coming down from the high of confronting the murderous Dorothy Tibbits.

Zinnia drove me home and walked me into the house, where Zoey was doing her Friday-night homework all over again to calm herself.

We sat in my living room, which was bright with afternoon sunshine.

Zinnia did most of the talking while we caught my daughter up on that afternoon's events.

We'd left Dorothy in Chet's custody, and his contacts with the town's law enforcement would be arresting and charging her.

Over the next few days, more details would emerge. The toaster would turn up at her house, under some newspapers in her hall closet—almost as though it had scurried its way into the house when she wasn't looking and hidden away until the detective on the case came with a search warrant.

The police would find that the man who'd modified the toaster was Griebel Gorman, an odd little man who'd been running an appliance repair shop in Wisteria for as long as anyone could remember. He would claim to be innocent, to not know what Dorothy had planned to do with the appliance, and he would participate in the investigation.

But I didn't know any of that yet, as of that Saturday afternoon. All I knew was that we'd solved the mystery of Winona's death and that her spirit could now move on to a peaceful place. Or so I hoped.

Chet had warned me that the longer Ms. Vander Zalm stuck around, the more I would pick up on her traits. I'd made some flip comments about learning how to cook properly, but the jokes were to cover my fear of changing. I wasn't perfect, but I wanted to keep being me, Zara Riddle.

"Zara," my aunt said. "Are you feeling normal?"

"No, but I've never felt normal," I said, smiling. "I'm okay." I rubbed my sternum and cleared my throat. "Just a little distracted, plus I guess I inhaled a bunch of that pink cloud you made during our big magic show. What was that stuff?"

She wrinkled her nose. "You aren't supposed to inhale pinkwyrm dust."

"Pinkwyrm dust? Is that a monster who causes pink eye?"

She glanced at Zoey and then back at me. "On the contrary. The skin cells they shed can be used to cure conjunctivitis. If you inhaled that cloud, you now have a lifetime immunity from pink eye."

"Wow." I looked over at Zoey, who hunched her shoulders guiltily. "I could have used that back when Zoey was younger. I swear she was attracted to little red-eyed, crusty-faced kids. The teachers could always tell who was about to get sick because Zoey would offer to share her nap pillow with them."

She grumbled, "You're making me sound weird, Mom."

"That's not weird at all," Zinnia said. "Witches are attuned to the needs of others. We are happiest when helping." She looked at me pointedly. "That's probably what drove you to become a librarian."

I nodded slowly. She was probably right. Librarians are driven by a passion for books as well as helping others. You can tell a lot about a society by how many libraries it has. The great author Ray Bradbury knew. He wrote about dark futures without knowledge, and he was quoted as saying, "Without libraries what have we? We have no past and no future."

Zoey made a thoughtful sound and then asked, "Was Ms. Vander Zalm a witch or not? And does this house really have a fountain of youth? It sounds great, but I don't know if I want to be sixteen forever."

"This house will keep you young," Zinnia said. "Any house with stairs will keep you running up and down, working your muscles and cardiovascular system." Her eyes twinkled. "But it's not magic. Dorothy Tibbits was mistaken. She thought the house gave Winona her long life, but she was wrong."

"So, she was a witch," Zoey said.

"Not exactly." Zinnia uncrossed her legs and smoothed her rose-patterned skirt. "She came from a bloodline of healers, people who've worked alongside witches since the beginning of time. She had an ability to intuitively understand the human body. Her kind were the early doctors, the kind who could fix inner workings without barbaric scalpels and bloodshed." She looked up at us and quickly added, "Not that I'm some kook who's opposed to modern medicine. I go in for my regular checkups, and I would get treated if I fell ill and wasn't able to cure myself using ancient treatments."

"Like pinkwyrm dust," I said.

She smiled warmly. "To ancient people, the antibiotics that are in common use today would have seemed like magic." She glanced around the living room, stopping on the television. "And our technology would make their heads explode."

Zoey asked, "How old was she, anyway?"

Zinnia's hazel eyes twinkled. "I wouldn't know. It's impolite to ask a lady her age, so I never did. Not even when we worked together on that silly cookbook."

"Do you think I'm a healer? Is that why my magic isn't working?" Zoey's expression was both hopeful and hopeless at the same time. It tore at my heart so much, I had to look away. I grabbed the WPL's copy of *Spooky Gatherings for Ghouls Cookbook* and leafed through it.

Zinnia and my daughter chatted for a while about powers and how they could be dormant at times.

After a few minutes, I found my mind drifting.

I pulled myself out of the reclining chair with a groan. "Would you two mind if I went upstairs to have a bath? I thought it might be a nice way to say goodbye to Ms. Vander Zalm."

Zinnia blinked at me. "But she's already gone, dear. Her business is finished."

I pulled my shirt away from my chest. "Then I'll just wash my sweaty body," I said.

She blinked again. "Of course," she said crisply. "You should go have a bath. It would be a nice way to have closure."

"You can stay," I said. "I'm not kicking you out. You're family, so my house is your house. This is a Riddle house."

Her eyes suddenly filled with tears. She blinked them away almost as quickly as they'd started.

"We can work on my Witch Tongue lessons," Zoey said with enthusiasm. "If that's okay with you, Auntie Z?" She looked down shyly. "Unless you have other plans."

"My day is yours," Zinnia said. "I'd love a cup of tea."

My daughter ran to the kitchen to put on the kettle.

Zinnia gave me a hug. "I'm so proud of you," she said softly, and as I breathed in the scent of her hair, a memory surfaced.

This memory wasn't one of Winona Vander Zalm's or any other entity's. It was my own. Time folded in on

286

itself, and for a moment, I was hugging another red-haired woman the same height as my aunt. My mother. If I just held on really tightly to my aunt, I could pretend she wasn't gone, hadn't been gone these last five years.

They say our loved ones never truly leave us and that they live on in our hearts. That's not entirely true. They live on in more than just our hearts. I could smell my mother in my aunt's hair. I could see her in the twinkle of my daughter's eyes. I caught a glimpse of her when I walked by store windows. I still came across handwritten notes that seemed to have been written by my mother's hand.

When I stood on my tiptoes at the kitchen sink to look out the window, I felt myself becoming her, like an echo of an entire life. Like a song that finishes playing but you continue to hear it anyway, the notes patterned within the crashing waves of the ocean or the white noise of a kitchen fan. My mother was gone, and yet she remained, resonating within me and speaking in small ways. She'd been at my side when I saw the house, and I'd felt her approval as I looked around the rooms with my eyes, which were so much like hers. I hadn't needed validation from my friends because I already had all the support I needed. My mother would have approved of the house, as well as the move, and that was how I knew it was right.

The Red Witch House on the corner was now a Riddle house, and sure, it had messy closets and some cardboard boxes that might never get unpacked, and it didn't contain a secret fountain of youth, but it was a *home*, and it was ours, and it was filled with love.

CHAPTER 37

ONE WEEK LATER

"Zara Riddle, if you're not a witch, how did you know the killer was Dorothy Tibbits? She had a solid alibi. She wasn't even in town at the time of the murder."

I gave the detective my most innocent look. His name was Bentley, like the luxury car company. Detective Bentley. And he was cute, in a silver-fox way. He appeared to be in his forties, which was why I'd been trying, unsuccessfully, to set him up with Zinnia.

"First of all, Detective Bentley, witches aren't real," I said.

He nodded slowly, watching me carefully with keen eyes that were the same steely gray as the hair at his temples.

"Witches aren't real," he agreed.

"And neither are ghosts, or zombies, or va—" The word caught in my throat.

"I'm glad we're on the same page," he said.

"Yes, we're both quite sane. Just two sane people, trying to keep this town safe from homicidal lunatics."

He thinned his lips. *No comment*, his expression said.

I continued. "Dorothy Tibbits was a believer, though. She believed in all sorts of things."

"Yes," he said. "That should explain why your theatrical performance with Mr. Moore and the other Ms. Riddle had such a... *profound* effect on her."

"Tibbits had some wacky ideas," I said. "But are you really surprised, considering the woman walked around town dressed in a blue pinafore and pigtails, conducting business from a wicker basket?"

"It is odd." He stared at me across the interview room's table without blinking. "But I've come to expect odd things in this town."

"Oh, really? Like what?"

He scratched his cheek and looked down at his laptop's screen. "What was that purple fog that came out of the mirrored jewelry box? It's quite clear from the video footage that something smoky did come out of the box. I've been asking around at the local magic shops, all two of them, and nobody can identify that particular prop."

"You should ask my aunt," I said. "You could take her for a drink sometime. She's a lot more fun after a glass of wine, or seven."

"Most people are," he said flatly. "Never mind about the purple smoke then." He glanced around the Wisteria Police Department's interview room, narrowing his eyes at the ceiling-mounted camera. "Walk me through how you knew it was Dorothy."

"At first, I thought she was just a terrible real estate agent. When I first came to look at the house, she had the Open House signs pointing the wrong way, all the lights off, and boxes of debris blocking the doorway."

Detective Bentley nodded. "Not everyone strives for excellence in their job." He stopped talking, and I heard his silent addition of *the way I do*. Bentley was a striver, and he was, from what I'd observed over the past week, very thorough. If we did cross paths again, I'd have to be careful to keep my powers hidden.

"I toured the house anyway, and I fell in love, but the more eager I got, the stranger Dorothy acted. She insisted

I have a look at her own house, which was also for sale, before I made an offer. She all but begged me to buy any other house instead, but I downloaded a standard offer-to-purchase and registered it with her office. She had no choice but to present it to the estate executor, who was Chet Moore. He accepted my low-ball offer, and—"

Bentley held up a hand to interrupt. "And why was that, exactly?"

He'd stumped me. I still didn't know why Chet had taken the low-ball offer. In my wildest fantasies, I'd imagined it was because he'd seen me, or looked me up on the internet and remembered me from my camgirl days, and wanted me living next door to him.

"Long story," I said with a hand wave. "The important part is, the very next week, Tibbits took her own house off the market. I didn't realize that until I started investigating."

"You mean snooping," Bentley said. "You're not a licensed investigator. You were snooping." He gave the room's camera a victorious I-got-her look. "But how did you come to suspect her?"

"I'm glad you asked! It was my gut, actually. Did you know that people really do feel and think with their guts? The microbial balance in our digestive system affects many of our thoughts and behaviors."

"Your gut told you?"

"Yes," I said, leaving out the part where a ghostly finger wrote the words KILLER DINNER on my foggy bathroom mirror. I also couldn't tell him how the ghost had angrily knocked Dorothy's housewarming gifts off the fireplace mantel.

So I told him the truth, minus the magic. "Detective Bentley, my amazing guts told me."

"Your guts. As in, your stomach?"

"I had too many mochas at work and made myself sick to my stomach, then on the drive home, I had an interesting conversation with the head librarian."

"I'm sure you did," Bentley said flatly.

"Kathy said something that I connected with the fact that someone who'd been present at my dinner party must have removed the killer toaster from my house."

He nodded and typed something on his laptop. "And did anyone witness Dorothy Tibbits taking the toaster?"

"No," I said. "At first, I suspected my coworker, Frank Wonder, because he'd been overly interested in the bathtub on the night of my dinner party. Plus he and Winona had history with a who-wore-it-best thing over a certain sequined pantsuit."

Bentley waved impatiently for me to continue.

"Then I suspected my aunt, who's actually a real gem of a woman once you get to know her." I winked. "She cowrote a cookbook with the deceased, years ago. She's got so many talents. Like I said, Zinnia Riddle is a real catch."

He waved his hand again.

"But it was my boss, Kathy Carmichael, who tipped me off. When she told me about the rumors. Have you heard the one where my silly old house is a fountain of youth? Can you believe such a thing?"

"I'm a man of science," he said.

"Me, too. A woman of science who believes in the collected wisdom of carefully researched and annotated knowledge. I am a librarian."

"Yes. We've covered that, Ms. Riddle. Several times."

"But Dorothy Tibbits is not a woman of science. She's superstitious, and she believed the house would prolong her life. She killed the homeowner to get the property on the market, but she couldn't raise the funds right away, because the market's been so flat lately. She planned to let the listing get stale, and then put in a low-ball offer once she'd gotten her money freed up from the sale of her own house."

"That appears to be corroborated by the hard evidence," he said.

"Indeed." I rested my elbows on the cheap plastic surface of the folding table and tented my fingers, supervillain style. "But what Dorothy didn't account for was the resourcefulness of a broke single mother looking to start fresh in a wonderful new town. I saw through the dust and clutter, spotting a diamond in the rough." I nodded like a bobblehead. "A woman in search of her dream home is a powerful thing."

"So I've heard," he said. "Whose idea was it to put on the theatrical display?"

"Chet Moore came up with some of it."

"He asked to marry you?" Bentley raised one eyebrow. Was he teasing me?

"Detective Bentley, he did ask. But I had to break his heart and only get fake married. Mr. Moore and I aren't legally wed."

Bentley smirked. "His loss."

I stared into his gray eyes, which glowed silver now. Was he flirting with me? He was cute when he wasn't frowning. He even looked younger. If he was in his forties, it was only his early forties. Zinnia was in for a treat if I ever did get the two of them together for a date.

Detective Bentley sat up straight and closed the laptop he'd been using to take notes.

"That will be enough for today," he said.

I gave him my warmest smile. "Come see me at the library if you ever need my help again."

"Oh, I doubt that," he said. "But perhaps I'll see you around."

"I could buy you a donut."

He frowned.

"Two donuts," I said with a smile as I got up to leave.

He reached out to shake my hand. When we touched palms, I got a flash of something, like a memory of an event, except one that hadn't happened yet. He and I were in a convertible, chasing after someone we both loved.

Was it one of Winona Vander Zalm's memories? She had moved on from my world, but traces of her remained. It could have been hers, yet it had a different feeling—a *me* feeling. I'd seen my own red hair whipping around my eyes in the vision.

Bentley tried to pull his hand away, but I gripped it tighter, trying to hold onto the vision, but it was already gone. In its place was... a craving for blueberry muffins. Odd, but fair enough. We had been talking about pastries.

Finally, he pried his hand out of mine, leaving me only with the lingering sense that the man might be a lot more fun than he appeared to be.

Bentley looked down at his hand, then up at me.

"Stay out of trouble," he said.

I tossed my hair back over my shoulder. "I never make promises I have no intention of keeping."

CHAPTER 38

On the way out the police station, I held open the door for someone coming in. I did it automatically, out of politeness, and didn't even look at the person's face until they stopped abruptly, leaving me holding open the door. The person was a very short man, over seventy, with a bulbous nose and tiny dark eyes behind his wire-rimmed glasses. Griebel Gorman. The owner of the appliance repair shop. The devious craftsman who'd modified a toaster under Dorothy Tibbits' orders, turning it into a spy device and murder weapon. A number of emotions hit me at once, including the desire to grab the little guy by the ankles and shake him upside down until all his secrets came tumbling out.

"Mr. Gorman," I said, careful to keep my tone polite. "You must be here to see Detective Bentley."

The man's mouth opened and closed without sound. He continued to chew the air while the color drained out of his face. Then he turned on his heel and started walking away as quickly as his short legs could take him.

What was I supposed to do? Just let him go? I had so many questions, plus the desire to shake him upside down.

I chased after him. It wasn't much of a chase, really. I speed-walked, arms pumping, and started closing the distance between us.

He kept glancing back over his shoulder at me, while picking up speed. The faster he went, the more I wanted to catch him.

After a few blocks, he feigned turning right, but then doubled back shielded by a solid, rhinoceros-looking woman in a gray suit. She stared at me with wide eyes as I shot past her.

Griebel dodged into an alley. I followed, jogging now, no pretense of acting casual.

The alley was blocked at the mid-point by construction scaffolding. *Gotcha! You're trapped and you're all mine!*

Except I hadn't caught him after all. The alley was empty, except for some garbage dumpsters. He'd vanished.

One of the dumpsters let out a rattling sound.

Was he so desperate to evade me that he'd jumped into a dirty old dumpster? I approached the metal bin cautiously and slowly lifted the lid. A blur of dirty white fur flashed out, escaping over my shoulder. It was just a cat. Had Griebel shifted into cat form?

"Change back," I said to the feline. "I just want to talk to you."

The cat gave me a confused look, or maybe it just gave me a regular look. I wasn't that familiar with cats.

I walked toward the cat, arms outstretched. "Here, kitty, kitty."

The cat was having none of it. He or she jumped up a ledge on the construction scaffolding, jumped up again, and disappeared.

I took one last look inside the dumpster and around the alley, then turned to leave.

A heavy steel back door opened, releasing a delicious scent into the alley. The small sign on the back door read The Gingerbread House of Baking. So this was where that bakery was, conveniently near the police station as well as near my route to work at the library. I'd been meaning to visit the place, on the recommendation of my boss plus a few other people.

They wouldn't appreciate my business if I came in through the back door, though, so I continued my way out of the alley. But then I stumbled over a rat-shaped rock and had to stop to tie my bootlaces. While I was leaning over, I heard two people, a man and a woman, talking inside the bakery.

"We need to prepare ourselves," the man said in a worried tone. "You don't know what kind of monster you're giving birth to."

"Oh, Jordan," the woman said. "You're such a worry wart. We're going to have a healthy baby boy."

"But... *my family*," he said. "Not to mention *your* family. We don't know what effects your womb is having on it."

She groaned.

Sounding even more anxious, he asked, "Is that another contraction?" There was the sound of someone breathing heavily, and then a chair moving. "Chloe, sit down. I'll call for transport."

"Don't be ridiculous," she said between gasping breaths. "You can drive me in the van."

"Okay. Let's go."

"Wait." More panting, and some groaning. Finally, she continued. "Before I give birth to this child, you need to promise me something."

"Anything."

"You need to love this child, no matter what."

He didn't respond right away. I held my breath, waiting for his answer.

"Promise," she said. "No matter what happens next, you need to believe we made the right decision, and you need to love this child."

"Of course I will," he said softly. "How can you even ask such a thing? This is our baby."

"Promise," she repeated.

He sighed. "I promise." There was a kissing sound. "I promise to love you, and to love our baby, no matter what." More kissing.

She giggled. "Now help me get up from this chair, and get us out of here before I'm forced to give birth to our baby into the big pan we use for the cinnamon buns!"

I heard more groaning and heavy breathing. Then the door leading to the alley slammed shut.

I'd finished tying my laces, plus the eavesdropping show was over, so I walked out of the alley. I reached the sidewalk just in time to see a pregnant woman with wavy blond hair hop up into the passenger seat of a white van.

I walked up the sidewalk, toward the van. There was nobody in the driver's seat yet. When I reached the window on the passenger side, I couldn't help but peek in at the woman. Her husband's words echoed in my head. *You don't know what kind of monster you're giving birth to.* After hearing something like that, who could resist sneaking a peek

The woman inside the van was looking down at her phone on her lap, so she didn't see me approach.

I found myself staring at her hair, which was not normal hair. It seemed to be alive, writhing around. How could that be?

There was a tinkling of bells as the bakery door opened. A muscular man with dark hair trotted out, keys in hand, yelling back into the bakery what sounded like store-closing instructions. "You've got to jiggle the key in the lock," he said.

A young woman inside the bakery called out, "I'll be fine on my own. Just go already!"

The man let the door swing shut, turned toward the van, saw me, and stopped in his tracks.

We stared at each other. There was something like recognition in his eyes. Did he know I'd overheard their conversation from the alley? Did he know I'd been staring at his partner's hair, which seemed to be alive?

298

"You must be the new Riddle," he said.

"Ah. My reputation precedes me."

There was a whirring sound—the passenger-side window rolling down. "Jordan!"

He whipped his head toward the writhing-haired woman, who was now just a regular woman with a bit of flour dust in her otherwise regular blond hair.

"Coming," he said, trotting around to the driver's side.

As the window whirred up, I caught an earful of her threatening to give birth in the van if he didn't step on the gas.

They drove away, and I stood there like a ding-dong, staring at their tail lights. At the end of the street, they turned left. I found that odd, since turning right would have taken them to the town's hospital. Perhaps they were going somewhere else, somewhere secret, where people gave birth to monsters.

I walked into the bakery, barely noticing the elaborate decorations at the front, and took a business card from the counter. The owners of the bakery were listed as Jordan and Chloe Taub.

Taub. The last name was familiar. I did see a lot of names at the library, but it hadn't been at work. It was the day I ran into Chet at the chocolate shop. The nosy woman working there asked Chet a question. She asked him what the Taubs were having. Now I was also wondering what they were having. Was it a shifter? They didn't come out in animal form, did they? I shuddered at the thought.

"Can I help you?" The young woman behind the bakery counter stared at me expectantly.

"Sure," I said. "Give me one more minute to look first." I tucked the business card into my pocket and looked over the pastries behind the glass. I was planning to meet my aunt and daughter shortly for ice cream, so I didn't want to ruin my appetite, but then again, I didn't want to rouse the bakery employee's suspicion. People don't walk into bakeries just to window shop.

Then I spotted the most beautiful donut I'd ever seen.

"I'll take this one, with the rainbow sprinkles," I said.

"Lucky you," she said. "We're usually sold out of the rainbow donuts by this time of day. Looks like you'll get the last one until tomorrow."

"Lucky me," I said.

"For here, or to go?"

"To go. I'm going straight from here to meet up with my family for ice cream."

She chuckled.

"I have a fast metabolism," I said.

She put the donut in a crinkly white bag and rang up my purchase. "No judgment here," she said, laughing merrily. "This is a bakery. Whatever happens within these walls is protected by baker-customer confidentiality."

"Good to know." I glanced over my shoulder at the empty parking spot where the van had been. "Was that the owners I saw leaving just now?"

"Yes," she gushed. "They're having a baby. It's their first one. We're all so excited."

The phone on the wall started ringing. She apologized to me, excused herself, and ran off to answer the call. I'd already paid for my donut, so I waved goodbye and left the bakery. I tried to push the overheard conversation from my mind. Whatever kind of offspring the Taubs were giving birth to, it was their business, not mine.

And if Griebel Gorman was able to disappear into thin air, that was his business, not mine.

Wisteria was home to plenty of secrets, and I would almost certainly discover more of them the longer I lived in the beautiful town. I didn't need to go looking for trouble. Being a Spirit Charmed witch meant that all kinds of trouble, especially the ghostly kind, would have no problem finding me on its own.

CHAPTER 39

Munching away happily on my rainbow-sprinkle donut, I walked to my aunt's house. Inside, I found both Zinnia and my daughter in the living room with the curtains drawn. Zinnia was playing teacher, showing Zoey how to hold her hands and whisper the spell to make a puff of purple smoke. I could see by the looks on their faces that it wasn't going well.

I took a seat on the tasseled sofa next to a frustrated Zoey, who whined, "There's no point! I'll never be able to do magic."

"Patience," Zinnia said. "You must have faith, and you must have patience."

"Hang in there," I said, wrapping my arm around Zoey's shoulders and squeezing her to my side.

Zinnia's purple smoke reached my nostrils and made my mouth water. It smelled exactly like caramel corn, except twice as delicious.

"Zara, how are you doing?" Zinnia asked.

"Great, except..." I considered telling her about seeing her old pal Griebel Gorman, who ran away from me before disappearing. But she already felt bad enough about a friend of hers being involved in the homicide, and I didn't want to make her feel worse.

And then I thought of telling her about the Taubs' conversation, but the part where I'd been eavesdropping didn't exactly paint me in the best light. And besides, what new parent isn't worried they'll be raising a monster? Jordan Taub could very well have meant *monster* in the metaphorical sense.

Zinnia's eyebrows rose higher. "Except what?"

I smiled and waved a hand. "Except I miss my ghost pal," I said, which was true. "Winona's completely gone now, which is bad news for my culinary future."

Zoey nodded vehemently. "Auntie Z, we had peanut butter sandwiches for dinner last night, and she forgot the peanut butter."

I struck one finger in the air. "But we did have a scary red hand floating in the punch bowl."

"Mom, pouring a bottle of wine into a bowl doesn't make it punch."

I snorted. "Smarty-pants teenagers and their fixation on details like ingredients."

Zinnia said solemnly, "Because of your gift with wandering spirits, you will attract another one soon, Zara."

"I hope it's a chef," Zoey said. "Or maybe a mime. Those are the clowns who don't talk at all, right?"

"Ouch," I said, pulling my arm away from my daughter's shoulders. "Someone's in need of a snack, or a nap, or something."

"You smell like vanilla," Zoey said. She sniffed in front of my mouth. "Did they serve you donuts at the police station?"

"I wish! They didn't even offer me coffee."

Zoey eyed me suspiciously as she got to her feet. "Excuse me for a minute while I go splash some water on my face." She left for the washroom.

Once Zinnia and I were alone, she said softly, "You and I must also keep the faith."

I whispered, "Is it possible Zoey's not a witch after all? You said it skips generations sometimes, and as far as we know, my mother didn't have it."

Zinnia didn't speak, but her expression told me what I needed to know. Nothing was certain. The future held only blank pages.

I unwound my silk scarf and folded it across my lap. Zoey was still in the washroom with the door closed.

I nodded at the small crystals that served as the sparking point for the smoke plumes. "Do you mind if I try?"

She scoffed, "Knock yourself out. Though I shouldn't say that, because you haven't been doing your assigned readings or drills. You'll probably cast the spell wrong and actually knock yourself out. Back when I was a novice witch, I also thought I was too good for drills and —"

She stopped talking. I couldn't see her face through the thick, sweet purple fog hanging in the air, but I imagined her jaw had dropped open.

The truth was, I *had* been doing my drills. I'd been practicing, and I was determined to do everything that was prescribed for a novice witch. I should have told my aunt as much, but it was so fun to see her splutter in frustration over what a "natural" I was with magic.

When the purple fog finally dissipated, Zoey was standing behind her aunt's chair with an irritated look on her face.

"Show-off," Zoey said.

* * *

We packed away the spell books and casting supplies, opened the curtains to let the sunshine into the room, and left the house in search of ice cream sundaes.

"I know the perfect place," my aunt said.

"Don't let me eat more than one," I told the other Riddles. "I've got a date tonight with Chet, and I need to impress him with how much food I can put away in one sitting."

Zoey groaned. "And you wonder why you don't have a boyfriend."

"I'm sure there's more to Chet than meets the eye," Zinnia said. "In addition to the fur and the claws."

We reached the end of the street and turned left at Zinnia's guidance. We passed other people out for strolls with their kids and dogs.

Once we were out of hearing distance of regular people, Zinnia asked, "Did Chet ever find out more about the scary bird that attacked you?"

"Not yet," I said. "And since Dorothy Tibbits didn't turn into anything furry or feathery to get away from the cops, we can assume it wasn't her."

"It might have simply been a large bird," Zoey said. "I researched Pacific Spirit Park, and it's a nesting zone for some large eagles."

"Good point," Zinnia said. "We must only look to magic for answers when there are no other alternatives."

"Sure," I said lightly. If she'd been there, she wouldn't have thought it was an eagle, but there was no point in arguing.

"We're not far from the ice cream place," Zinnia said, and she started listing off the flavors they usually served.

There was a rumbling sound as a large black vehicle, followed by another one, drove past.

My aunt slowed down until she was standing still at the sidewalk, looking dazed. I followed her gaze to the vehicle that was passing by slowly. A long, black hearse.

Zoey asked, "Did you forget the way?"

Zinnia blinked rapidly and licked her lips. "The way to where?"

Zoey shot me a concerned look. "Auntie Z, are you okay?"

Zinnia turned to me. "Zara, dear, I've been meaning to talk to you about this in private, but I suppose now is as good a time as any. Do you have a last will and testament?"

"Everyone should have a will," I answered.

"So, I'll take it by your sassy answer that you *don't* have one." She gave me the same disgusted look she'd made when she saw the inside of our microwave, with the food exploded all over. "Who's going to be Zoey's legal guardian if something were to happen to you?"

"Nothing's going to happen to me," I replied. "I'm in perfect health, except for the fact that my baby toes don't bend at all, but the last doctor I saw assured me it was somewhat normal."

Zoey interjected, "Your baby toes don't bend?"

I shrugged. "It's better than having funky-monkey-finger-toes."

Zinnia waved her hand. "Forget I brought it up." She sighed. "It's just that... last night, I had a prophetic dream that I'm going to kill you."

I held up my hands. "Please don't. I promise I'll stop making such a terrible mess inside the microwave."

"Never mind," she said. "Let's talk about something else."

"No. Let's talk about you killing me. What's your motivation? Are you trying to get my house? Is it true the house has magical powers? I swear it had three bedrooms, then it had only two plus a linen closet. If you want the house so bad, I'll sell it to you. Please don't murder me."

Zoey punched me in the arm. "Mom!"

Zinnia glanced around. We were on the sidewalk in front of a very plain house with a gravel driveway in the front yard. Despite the gravity of our conversation, I couldn't help but notice that the house looked, well, *sad*. It seemed to cast a longer shadow than the others, and the windows in its attic were awfully dark for such a sunny day.

"Zara?" My aunt twisted her hands and gave me an apologetic look. "I shouldn't have brought it up. My dreams are rarely literal. More often than not, they're metaphorical. Do you know what that means?"

Yes, I knew what a metaphor was.

"Oh!" Zoey exclaimed. "Like how the death card in a Tarot reading doesn't mean death. It might mean the end of a way of being or doing."

Zinnia gave Zoey a proud smile. "Very good," she said. "My dream could mean that I will cause your mother to quit doing something."

Zoey grinned. "Mom's going to stop nuking food in the microwave without a cover."

"Sure," Zinnia said, though she didn't sound convinced. "Death to that particular bad habit. Now, let's go get that ice cream."

I paused to take one last look at the sad-looking house. In the window of the attic, the gaunt face of an older man appeared, and then just as quickly disappeared. My spine tingled. Today's list of strange occurrences was really stacking up. I shrugged off the creepy-crawly feelings, and skipped to catch up with the other Riddles.

Zinnia asked Zoey about school, and my daughter gushed about how modern and spacious her new high school was compared to her old one. My daughter was happy, so I was happy.

Happy, happy, happy.

Now, if you're looking for a perfectly tidy, perfectly happy ending, and nothing but giggles and hugs and ice cream sundaes forever, stop here.

From this point on, things take a turn for the, well, *wicked*.

My aunt's dream was going to come true, and not just metaphorically.

But I didn't know that yet, so I kept walking along, smiling like a ding-dong. After all, the person in the story doesn't get the pleasure of hearing the narrator's heavy-handed foreshadowing. So, I kept on walking and smiling, until I reached into my pocket and pulled out the business card I'd taken from the bakery. The card was blank. Both sides. Completely blank.

Well, I thought, turning the card over and over. *This can't be good.*

No, it wouldn't be good.

In five days, Zinnia would kill me.

That wicked witch.

For a full list of books in this
series and other titles by
Angela Pepper, visit

www.angelapepper.com

Lightning Source UK Ltd.
Milton Keynes UK
UKHW020639080621
385138UK00011B/834